CEASE AND DESIST

CALLAHAN SECURITY BOOK 6

LORI MATTHEWS

ABOUT THE BOOK

**One retired SEAL, one former librarian, and one big
mystery combine to make one amazing adventure!**

Thane "*Hawk*" Hawkins is feeling lost. His corporate job no
longer excites him and he's missing his SEAL days. His
friends at Callahan Security dangle an interesting job in front
of him, but require a small favor in return. "Think of it as a
trial run," they said. Their idea of a small favor will send him
on his most dangerous and mysterious adventure yet.

Remington "*Remy*" Tanger is putting the pieces back
together after losing her last family member. Running her
grandfather's bookstore is her way of honoring him. But
Gramps had a secret life that brings trouble stumbling into
her shop and almost gets her killed.

She's determined to navigate on her own; He's determined to keep her alive. They're both determined not to fall
in love. Sometimes fate has other ideas.

For Heidi.
Your keen eye and brilliant ideas make everything better.

ACKNOWLEDGMENTS

Thank you doesn't cover it when it comes to my rock star editors, Corinne DeMaadg and Heidi Senesac. They are truly the most patient people. Thanks also goes out to my virtual assistant, Sara Mallion and my FaceBook guru, Amanda Robinson as well as my beta reader, Jenn Herman. My personal cheer squad which I could not survive without: Janna MacGregor, Suzanne Burke, Stacey Wilk, Kimberley Ash, and Tiara Inserto. My husband and my children who make me laugh every day. And to you, the reader. Your emails and posts mean the world to me. The fact that you read my stories is the greatest gift ever. Thank you.

PROLOGUE

He reached for his favorite leather-bound book on the top shelf, craving the comfort it always brought him.

"I'm talking to you, old man. Pay attention!" snarled the voice behind him.

Remington Tanger Jr. sighed and turned slowly on the ladder. "I'm through listening. I've told you I will not be part of this. This is not why the Society was started. This is not what the original board agreed to."

"It's what this board agreed to," the other man said as he moved forward. "The rest of them are all in on this, old man, so you need to get with the program." He stared up at Tanger, his dark eyes snapping.

The bookshop lighting shone off the dome of his bald head and made him look like some sort of comic book villain. His face was pockmarked, and a long thin white line ran down his right cheek, the scar a memento from days gone by.

"I don't care what they agreed to. None of them were part of the original founder's circle. Not one. They are a world away from what the founders had in mind. They don't get to change things just because they want to. There are rules. My father was one of the founding members, and our family has the least amount of turnover. I'm still alive, so I get the final say. The answer is no."

"That's not the right answer." The man moved forward again and wrenched Tanger's arm.

Tanger immediately grabbed onto the ladder with his other hand and tried to fight the villain off, but at ninety-seven, he didn't have the strength he once had. The other man pulled harder and then reached up and smashed the fingers of Tanger's hand holding the ladder.

Tanger instinctively let go, immediately losing his balance and falling backwards off the tall ladder. He crashed into the bookcase behind him, smacking his head on the shelf, and then landed in a heap at the bottom of the ladder with a whole shelf of books coming down on top of him.

His head felt like it might explode. He opened his eyes slowly to find the bald man leaning over him. "It was your choice, old man. You chose this."

Tanger closed his eyes again. He supposed that was true. It was the right choice. There was no way he would have been able to live with himself otherwise. If only he'd had a chance to explain it all to Remy. But he'd left it too late. He expelled one last breath as death claimed him.

Too late.

CHAPTER ONE

Thane Hawkins leaned against the bar and took a sip of his scotch. He'd never been to the top floor of Callahan Security before, and he was impressed.

The Callahan brothers had made it into a home of sorts, complete with bedrooms in the back, a chef's dream kitchen and even a dining room. But the centerpiece of the place was where they were all gathered at the moment—a great room with large comfy sofas and chairs, a big screen TV above the fireplace, and the top shelf bar area Hawk leaned against. It was the epitome of luxurious comfort in the middle of New York City. No wonder their employees loved them. The Callahan brothers had thought of everything. Made him wonder what the gym one floor down was like. Five floors to do what they wanted with. Must be nice.

He took another sip of his drink and enjoyed the warmth spreading through his gut. It was a dark February night out there, and New York was in the clutches of a cold snap. The roaring fire on the far side of the room cheered the whole space up, and he once again felt truly grateful for the invite.

"Can I refresh your drink?" Logan Callahan asked.

Always the consummate host, he reached for Hawk's glass as he pushed over a large charcuterie tray loaded with meats, cheeses, crackers, olives, fruits, and veggies.

"Sure." Hawk smiled. "Thanks for inviting me. This is an amazing space."

Logan smiled. "Thanks. It's a great place for all of us to relax and spend a bit of down time when going home isn't an option."

"Jameson Drake is going to have to up his game. We don't have anything like this in our offices."

Gage Callahan grinned. "Drake hasn't been here, or I'm sure he'd have done something similar."

Hawk shook his head. "Yeah, no. If he saw this, he'd tell you not to let any of his people know. He wouldn't want to build this type of thing all over the world. If he did it for one, he'd end up having to do something for all of them."

"Hey, Hawk," Alex Buchanan said as she approached the bar. She studied the charcuterie board, snagged a piece of cheese, and tossed it into her mouth.

Mitch Callahan came right up behind her and did the same thing while resting his other hand on her hip. "Hawk, good to see you. Thanks for coming."

"Thanks for the invite. Is there an occasion I don't know about?"

Lacy Carmichael piped up from across the room, "No. Logan and I thought it was just time to get all of us together so we can catch up and relax a little."

"It's been crazy around here." Mitch grabbed a small plate off the bar top and loaded it with a variety of appetizers.

Hawk nodded. "I spoke with Jake Boxer the other day. He said you all are inundated with work and struggling to keep up."

"I can't believe this!" came from across the room, followed by a string of curses.

"Dani, what's wrong?" Gage asked as he walked over to his girlfriend.

"Some asshat thought he could break into *our* system. I caught it, but you need to remind people again. No cat videos on work computers. These hackers are bored and have nothing better to do. I don't want to spend my time cleaning up their shit."

Gage grinned. "I'll send out another email." He closed her laptop and set it on the coffee table in front of her.

She scowled at him. "Hey, I was work—"

He popped a cracker with cheese into her mouth. "You're hangry. You need to set work aside and eat. It will be much better once you get your blood sugar up. Besides, as your boss in Cyber Security I'm telling you… Stop working."

The scowl went away as she continued chewing. She swallowed. "Is there more?" Gage pulled her to her feet and escorted her across the room.

"Hey, Hawk," she greeted him as she ate an olive.

He nodded to her. "Dani. How are you?"

"Good," she mumbled through a cracker.

"Got room for one more?" Dragan Maric called out as he exited the elevator. He joined them at the bar.

"You're back!" Mitch smiled. "How did the job go?"

Dragan shrugged. "It's done. I think it should be fine, but we're going to need two more people on that team. The client likes to change his mind a lot. He's always on the go. His team needs to be flexible."

Mitch grunted. "Yeah, he reminds me of another client like that." He shot a look at Hawk. "Your boss was a huge pain in the ass in the beginning, too."

It was Hawk's turn to smile. "He's still a pain in the ass."

Dragan offered a hand, which Hawk grasped firmly in his own, and they bumped shoulders. "Good to see you, Hawk."

"You too, Dragan."

To Hawk, Dragan looked tired but, apparently, he didn't look too shabby to the women in the room. Every one of them got a dreamy look in their eyes when they stared at Dragan. Apparently, he was universally appealing. *Must be nice.*

"How's Jake?" Dragan asked. "Have you talked to him lately?" He directed his question to Hawk as he took a beer from Logan.

"Yeah, I was just saying he mentioned how busy you guys are. He's swamped over in Europe as well. He's loving it, though. Monty, too. I spoke with her as well. She's very happy with the new job and loves living in the UK." He nodded at Mitch. "You boys might want to be careful. Drake is still not happy about losing her."

Logan smiled. "It was the right move for her in her career. He can't blame us for facilitating that."

Hawk shook his head. "Drake can blame anyone for anything."

They all chuckled. "True that," Mitch agreed.

Hawk sipped his second scotch. He shouldn't really make fun of his boss. Drake was actually a good guy. He was, in fact, a great boss, and Hawk had no complaints. As head of the legal department for the entire Drake Industries conglomerate, Hawk had to deal with a ton of shit, but Drake made sure Hawk got whatever he needed to make everything happen the way it should. He couldn't ask for more. If only it all made him...happy.

He glanced around the room. This. This was what he missed. The camaraderie of being part of a team. The family atmosphere. The team at his current job was solid but it wasn't warm and fuzzy. He was always having to put out fires that his subordinates couldn't deal with or fighting off those ladder-climbing dipshits who had their eye on his job. And he was at the top. The only thing above him was Drake. He could switch and become the Chief Information Officer maybe, or something else on the C level, but the promotion would be hard to get and come with a lot more headaches for not much more pay. Didn't seem worth it.

Someone in the crowd had grabbed the charcuterie tray and Dani grabbed the two dishes that Logan had produced, and the crowd moved over to sit in front of the fireplace. Hawk was about to head over to them when Logan stepped up next to him.

He laid a hand on Hawk's arm. "I hear rumblings that maybe you aren't as happy as you once were. I mean, working for Drake."

He blinked. He had no idea anyone knew about his dissatisfaction. He'd thought he covered it well.

"Don't worry. It's not common knowledge." Logan took a sip of his own drink, an amber liquid in a cut crystal tumbler, most likely a high-quality scotch. All the booze at Callahan Security was top shelf.

Hawk narrowed his eyes at Logan. "Drake told you?"

Logan just smiled.

Fuck. Hawk should have known Drake would pick up on his lack of enthusiasm. "I'm fine."

Logan held up a hand. "Drake said you'd say that. According to him, you're not fine. He says you're bored. No matter what he throws at you, you get it done in an excellent and efficient manner, but you never seem to *enjoy* doing any of it the way you used to."

"I— That's no— It's not that… Why are you smiling?"

Logan grinned. "He said you'd make all kinds of excuses."

"Fuck." Hawk shook his head and took a long slug of his drink. He swallowed and asked, "Why isn't he asking me about this himself then?"

"Because he says you won't tell him the truth. He's hoping you'll be candid with me."

Hawk snorted. "Is that why you invited me?" The warmth that he'd felt at being included was fading fast.

Logan frowned. "No. Not at all. I extended the invite before talking to Drake about something else. He mentioned on that call he would like me to speak with you. You helped us in Hawaii and saved our asses in Florence. We owe you for that, but it also makes you part of the family. You're welcome here anytime."

Hawk searched the other man's face, but all he saw was sincerity. "Thanks. I appreciate that." And he did. Very much.

"Look, you know we're swamped here. If you're interested, there's a job here for you. You can be our head of legal, which would alleviate my workload greatly, but I don't think that's what you want. You can also go back into the field." He smiled, "You can take the boy out of special teams, but you can't take the special teams out of the boy. You want to run a team? Say the word. You can have your pick of assignments. I know both Gage and Mitch value your skills and would have no hesitation about giving you whatever you want in terms of the personal security aspect of things. Jake sings your praises too and that's saying something because he rarely says much about anyone's skill."

Stunned, Hawk just stood there. He was being offered a chance to go back and do what he loved doing the most. He'd loved being a SEAL. Planning ops and keeping the world safe had made his heart sing until it didn't. Burnout was real. He'd needed to get away from it. He had thought permanently, but now he was being offered *carte blanche* to do it again. Did he want to?

He glanced across the room. Gage and Mitch were both watching him. They both gave him a little nod. They were confirming what their brother was telling him.

He focused on Logan again. "I'm… Thanks. It means a

lot that you guys have that kind of faith in me. I… I'm not sure what I'm looking for at the moment. Just that…I'm looking? Does that make sense?"

Logan nodded. "Take your time. Drake would hate to lose you, but he would hate it more if you were unhappy. If you figure out what you want and he can give it to you, talk to him. If it's something we can give you, reach out. We'd love to have you with us on a day-to-day basis."

Hawk nodded. "Thanks. I appreciate that. More than you know."

Logan smiled. "Now, if you'll excuse me, they're running out of food. I have to check on dinner. You're staying, yes?"

Hawk nodded. "Wouldn't miss it. You're an excellent chef."

"Thank you." Logan beamed as he turned and made his way into the kitchen.

———

Two hours later, Hawk helped clear the table. The meal had been tasty as he'd known it would be. The meat was so tender he could have cut it with a spoon, and the potatoes were amazing. Someday, he was going to have to get Logan's recipe.

"I'll take that," Mitch said, reaching for the plates in Hawk's hand.

"I don't mind."

"Yeah, but I do. You're too slow. I want dessert." Mitch grinned as he took the plates and made a beeline for the kitchen.

"You should just sit down again," Lacy said. "They've got it under control and trying to help will just slow them down."

"Fair enough," he said and sat back down at the table.

Dragan came over and offered him coffee, which smelled great as a cup was poured. It was hot and perfectly brewed. He could totally get used to this if working here meant access to food and drink of this caliber. That thought shook him. Was he? Was he going to chuck in his law career and go back into security?

Lacy groaned. Rubbed her temples.

"You okay?" Alex asked as she sat back down.

Lacy grimaced. "I've got a headache coming on.

Concern flicked across Alex's face. "Maybe go lie down for a bit."

"I can't. I promised Remy I'd go read over her paperwork before she files her lawsuit tomorrow, I assured her I would drop by her shop tonight." She let out a long sigh.

"Who is Remy? If you don't mind me asking and what's her lawsuit about?" Hawk asked.

"Remy is a close friend from my law school days. She graduated with me but decided law wasn't for her, so she went back and got her library science degree. She was working as a librarian up until about six months ago when her grandfather died and left her his book shop. She's fighting with another store around the block from her. I am fuzzy on the details, but she wants me to read over her paperwork before she files it. She says she's a bit rusty."

"Where is her shop?" Hawk asked. Lacy looked tired and there was definite pain in her eyes. It was obvious she really didn't want to go out again tonight.

"Upper west side."

"Don't you and Logan live in Chelsea?"

She nodded. "Yeah. It's a bit of a hike."

"If you want, I can drop by for you. I'm not you, but I can certainly read over her suit and see if it needs any adjustments. That is, if she wouldn't mind me helping out."

"Would you?" Lacy asked, hope lighting her face. "I'm sure Remy won't mind."

"Absolutely." He glanced at his watch. It was already after eight. "I'll go now."

"Oh, no. You need to finish your coffee and have dessert. Logan made some amazing cookies."

He waved her off. "If you can give me another coffee to go, then I'm all good. The last thing I need is to taste one of Logan's cookies. It will no doubt be delicious, and then I'll be forced to eat half a dozen more, which I don't need."

Lacy smiled at him. "Coffee to go, I can do. Thanks, Hawk. I really appreciate it. I'll tell Remy you're coming."

"It's not a problem." Or so he thought at the time.

CHAPTER TWO

Remington Tanger the Fourth gritted her teeth in frustration. "Yes, I see that you are here, but as you don't seem to want to buy a book, I can't help you." It had been a long day in an even longer week, and she just didn't have the energy to deal with this strange customer.

The tall man with a buzz cut and cold, dark eyes glared at her. "I have shoe."

His accent was thick, and it had taken Remy a few tries to figure out what he was saying, but even though she now understood the words, she still had no idea what he meant. She glanced down at his feet. "Yes, you have shoes." Did he mean that he was complying with the rule about wearing shoes and a shirt in order to get served? Wasn't that only in restaurants?

She let out a long sigh and tried again. "Is there a book" —she gestured to the over-packed shelves around the cozy little shop— "you wanted to see?" Maybe that was the title of the book he wanted. *I Have Shoes.* It didn't ring any bells for her, but there was always the possibility that it was a new arrival in children's books. Emily, her assistant, had unpacked the new stuff last week. Remy didn't remember ordering anything about shoes, but that didn't mean much. Her brain was fried these days, so she could have easily done so without remembering.

"Is that the title of the book?" she asked as she turned and started behind the counter.

The big man reached out and grabbed her arm. He pulled her back and squeezed. "I have shoe," he repeated, his voice hard and full of menace.

"Let go of me!" She jerked her arm, but his grip tightened. He was hurting her. Panic rose in her chest. Earlier in the week someone had grabbed her from behind and pushed her into her door as she was locking up for the night. He'd told her to stop writing letters if she knew what was good for her. By the time she'd recovered from her shock, he was gone. She didn't want a repeat of that occurrence.

She took a deep breath. "Listen, I can't help you if you don't tell me what you want. If that's the book title, then you need to let me check and see if we have it." She tried to remain calm and patient, but her knees had changed into limp noodles. She'd taken Taekwondo when she was a kid and had her black belt, but that had been a lot of years ago, and she didn't think her moves would work on a grown-ass man who was easily twice her size. He had to have at least a hundred pounds and twelve inches on her.

He shook her. "I have shoe," he said between clenched teeth. "You help me." When he shook her again, her teeth clicked together.

"Let me go!" she yelled and pushed him. Her heart slammed against her rib cage.

He let out a grunt and dropped her arm. She immediately backed away from him and went for her phone behind the counter. When she looked up again, he was still bent over. He straightened slowly, and that's when she saw the blood. His sweater was covered in it, but she hadn't noticed because it was navy, and he wore a long black trench coat over it.

"Oh, my god, you're hurt!" She keyed 911 into her phone. "You need help. You need a hospital." She didn't know if he was going to hurt her or pass out, but she wasn't taking any chances. She reached under the counter and pulled out the only weapon she could find. A heavy flashlight.

"No!" He lunged at her, but she backed up raising the flashlight. He stopped and took a shallow breath. "No hospital. I have shoe. You help!" He leaned against the counter and tried to regain his breath. He was sweating profusely now, and he'd gone pale.

The operator came on. "I need an ambulance and the police," she said and supplied the address.

The man glared at her and then lurched away from the counter. He stumbled up the steps and fled through the door.

She called after him, but he had gone down the block. She canceled the call and told the operator the man had left her shop. She gave all the details she could and then hung up the phone. Letting out a long breath, she bent and pressed her forehead on the counter for a minute. She fought her queasiness over what had been one of the scariest moments of her life. That made two this week. What the hell was wrong with people?

She breathed slowly to calm her racing heart. It had never occurred to her when she'd taken over the shop from her grandfather that she'd have to deal with shit like this. Some of the book distributors were bad because they were obviously trying to cheat her, but having members of the public come in, yell at her, and physically attack her was something she'd never anticipated. Maybe she wasn't cut out to run the bookshop.

Remy straightened and turned a circle in the space, checking for anything out of place or any drips of blood on the floor. Everything seemed to be fine. Books lined every shelf, all neatly in rows with their colorful spines cheering her up. A window seat beside the door had bright red, yellow, and green pillows that attracted any children entering. The front right section of the store was devoted to children's books. Random stuffed animals were placed on the shelves among the books. Her youthful regulars each had their favorite one they liked to visit.

The store extended farther off to the left. Bookshelves ran along the walls surrounding a seating area that had a comfy sofa and some chairs. A couple of small tables with lamps on them book-ended the sofa as well to make the place feel more like someone's living room than a store.

Taking inventory of the space helped calm her. Antique New York cityscape pictures covered the faded rose wallpaper on the bit of wall space that was available between the shelves. Two tapestries hung on opposite sides of the shop, one with a horse that covered the doorway to her grandfather's apartment and the other with trees and flowers. It all came together to create a homey atmosphere, one that she dearly loved.

At the back of the shop, there was a small doorway that led to the kitchenette area. She walked through on wobbly knees and went straight to the kettle. Her hand shook as she filled it with water and then plugged it in. She needed a cup of tea to calm her nerves.

The little cuckoo clock on the wall chimed, and the cuckoo came out, announcing it was nine p.m. Closing time if she worked anywhere else, but her grandfather had kept the little shop open to midnight on Thursdays, Fridays, and

Saturdays. He claimed there was no bigger horror than facing a weekend without something to read. She could have told him there were much bigger horrors out there, as she'd discovered this week, but he wasn't here anymore, and she missed him more than she thought possible.

His presence had always been calming for her and she treasured the late nights she'd sat with him, keeping him company until he was ready to close. She was quite sure he kept the shop open because he was a night owl and would rather be sitting in the shop than upstairs in his apartment. It made him feel more connected to the rest of the world. She smiled at the memory of him sitting behind the counter until all hours of the night, reading whatever latest author interested him.

An ache rose in her chest, and she let out a shaky breath. He'd been gone six months, and she missed him every single day. Her parents had died in a car accident when she was in her late teens, and he'd taken over being both parent and grandparent all in one.

He'd been thrilled when she chose to become a librarian instead of using her law degree. She liked books, and he thought it was a good fit. In the end, she wasn't so sure. Being a librarian is more about online resources these days, and although she liked research, she only liked it when she was interested in what she was looking up. Otherwise, time spent investigating a topic was deadly boring to her.

Not that she thought she'd like law any better. Her father had been a lawyer and looking back now, it was obvious that's why she'd gone to law school. Trying to keep some connection to him. Either way, she wasn't happy, and she'd been thinking about a career change when her grandfather had passed away unexpectedly.

Okay, at ninety-seven it wasn't really unexpected, except that it was. He had always been so young, so vital. She'd never really thought he would go away and leave her alone. She'd thought he would live forever. But now, she was an orphan. Shaking her head at her own silliness, an orphan at her age, she poured the heated water into her teacup and added a bit of milk.

She left the room and made her way back to the front of the shop. Setting her cup on the counter, she sat down and made herself comfortable on the high-backed stool. Thinking her grandfather would live forever was a product of not having anyone else. She'd thought that Drew, her former boyfriend, would be the one. They'd dated for four years but he'd ended up cheating on her with one of her colleagues and then running off and marrying the other woman instead.

Remy let out another sigh. Looking back, she should have realized sooner that Drew was cheating and probably subconsciously she had, but she'd lost her parents and her grandmother, and she didn't want to lose anyone else. That fear of being all alone had blinded her to the truth.

And yet… she was all alone. The thing she hadn't wanted and, in the end, as much as she missed her grandfather, there was no way she was opening the door for anyone else to come into her life. She couldn't take anymore loss. She'd gone on dates since the breakup, but none of those men seemed to click any buttons for her, not even the sex button. She'd decided that she was fine on her own. And when it came to sex… well she had a box of toys that could deliver the same thing any potential partner could. Just as she reached over and picked up her cup, the door burst open, and a fresh-faced uniformed cop entered. She swore as she spilled some tea.

"Are you the one that made the nine-one-one call?" he demanded.

She grabbed a cloth she kept beneath the counter and mopped up the spill. "Yes, I am." Good thing the weird stranger had already left, if this was the police response time. She'd have been long dead. Of course, she had cancelled the call so it wasn't really fair to judge them, she reminded herself as she put the rag back under the counter.

"Do you know his name, the guy that was in here?"

She frowned. "No. I have no idea who he is. Why? Can't he tell you? He has an accent, and his English didn't seem strong. Maybe he doesn't understand you."

"Lady, he doesn't understand anyone. He's dead."

Blood rushed to her head and, dizzy, she leaned back on the stool. She blinked. How could he be dead? He was just here, yelling at her. "I… How…" With the amount of blood on his sweater, he must have bled out.

"Can you tell me what happened exactly?" the officer asked just as the door opened and a man walked in. He was wearing a suit and a long overcoat. He had startlingly blue eyes.

"I'm sorry, Officer," she said, and then turned to the stranger. "Can I help you?"

"Er, I think I'm here to help you. Lacy Carmichael asked me to stop by."

Lacy. Right. She'd forgotten all about that with the events of the evening. Shit. "Um, right." She didn't feel like dealing with that right now. "Tell Lacy thanks, but we can pick this up another time. I don't want to keep you."

He glanced at the cop and then back at her. His gaze seemed to be asking her a question, but she had no idea what it was he wanted. "I've got time. I'll just keep out of your way until you're free." He gave her a brief smile and wandered off into the shop.

Great. Just what she needed. She turned back to the cop just as another uniform officer entered the shop. The first one nodded to the second one and then turned back to her. "You were gonna tell me what happened."

"Right." She drew a breath and then launched into her explanation. "So then, he just lurched out the door."

"I see," the first officer said. "You didn't notice he was hurt when he came in?"

The second officer started moving around her shop. She wasn't thrilled that he was inspecting things, but she supposed it couldn't do any harm. "No. His coat covered most of his chest. I didn't notice."

"And he kept asking about shoes?"

She shook her head. "No. He said he had *a* shoe."

The cop frowned. "He didn't say anything else?"

She shook her head. "No. He just said he had a shoe and demanded help. I thought maybe he was struggling with the words. He had an accent. Maybe he was mixed up and used the word shoe for something else he really wanted. Either way, I couldn't figure out what he was talking about."

"And you didn't know him."

"No. Never saw him before."

The cop gave her a look. "He wasn't a boyfriend or anything?"

She frowned. "What? No. I told you. Just some random stranger."

The cop studied her. "Why are you open so late? Are you normally open this late?"

"Yes, actually. My grandfather liked to be open late."

"And where is he?" the cop asked as he looked around the shop.

She ground her teeth. "He's dead. He passed away about six months ago."

The cop's head came up. "How did he die?"

She suddenly realized the cop was looking at her like she might have done something to the dead guy. Like this was all her fault somehow. "Look, my grandfather was ninety-seven. He died. It happens. I've told you everything I know about the dead guy. I can't help you with anything else. If there's nothing else, I'd like to deal with my customer." She was suddenly quite grateful that the man in the suit had stayed.

"You're sure you don't know the dead guy?" asked the second cop as he returned to the counter after snooping around.

"Positive."

"We're not going to find your number in his phone or anything?"

She clenched her teeth. "No. You won't find my number in his phone. I don't know him. I don't know what he wanted."

The first cop asked, "Do you have a kitchen in here?"

"What?" What the hell did they want now? Her frustration was boiling over. She didn't have the patience for this any longer.

"A kitchen." He pointed to her mug. "I see you made yourself coffee. Where did you do that?"

"It's tea, and why does that matter?" she demanded.

The first officer gestured to his partner. "You mind if my partner checks out your kitchen?"

"The lady is not inclined to show you the kitchen at the moment, Officer"—the man in the suit and wool overcoat glanced down at the officer's name tag— "Harrison. Ms. Tanger is, in fact, finished answering questions for the evening. Should you require her to answer more questions, please reach out, and we'll be happy to set up a time and place for that. If you want to see the rest of the premises, you'll need a search warrant."

"Who the fuck are you?" the second cop asked.

"I'm Ms. Tanger's lawyer."

Harrison snorted. "She didn't know who you were when you came in, so how can you be her lawyer?"

"I have been retained to help Ms. Tanger in another

matter, and I am her lawyer." He offered them a conciliatory smile. "Now, gentlemen. I believe it's time for you to leave. Please be in touch if you require anything else from my client." He offered the first guy his card.

The cop took it. "This says you work for Drake Industries."

"Yes, I work for all kinds of people. Now, if you'll excuse me, I would like to chat in private with my client."

Harrison snapped his notebook closed and glared at the man. "Fine," he growled. "But we'll be back if there are any more questions."

"Of course." The man inclined his head to the cops.

They grunted almost in unison and headed out of the shop.

Remy turned to the lawyer. "Thanks for that Mr...I'm sorry I've forgotten your name. I know Lacy told me but with everything"—she gestured toward the door the police just exited through—"it slipped my mind." More like his good looks had her mind going blank. It wasn't often she had a man this attractive in her store or anywhere in her life for that matter.

He immediately offered his hand. "Thane Hawkins. Most people call me Hawk."

She shook his hand, and she could have sworn a small shiver of desire went up her arm. She was losing it. After clearing her throat, she said, "Remington Tanger." His hand was warm and totally engulfed hers. His grip was firm, but he didn't try and squish her fingers or anything. She studied his face. He was so much bigger up close and there was an undercurrent of...danger, maybe...about him. It was hot as hell. Not only was he damn fine looking, but it was those vibrant blue eyes that captured her gaze. They seemed to know what she was thinking.

"Er, Lacy sent you?"

He nodded. "She asked me to drop by and talk to you about the lawsuit you want to file. I'd be happy to skim it and give you some suggestions. I should tell you I run the legal department for Drake Industries, so I have a bit of experience in the lawsuit game." He smiled at her as he recited his bona fides. He was trying to reassure her that he wasn't some beginner, but he could have saved his breath. Lacy wouldn't have sent him if he wasn't good.

Exhaustion washed over her. She couldn't deal with anything else tonight and this man was throwing her all off balance. She just didn't have it in her. "Right. Listen, I really appreciate your help. You were so kind to come and help me out, but it's been a tough week and I think I'd just like to close up. I'll call Lacy to go over the lawsuit another time. It's Friday night. I can't file tomorrow anyway."

Hawk leaned against the bookshelf behind him. "Well since I'm here, why don't you tell me what happened tonight?"

She shook her head. "Again, I appreciate all your help but it's unnecessary. I don't want to keep you any later than I already have." He had to go. She needed to sit for a few minutes and drink her tea. Get her equilibrium back.

"Indulge me."

Those words triggered a small flutter in her belly. She'd like to indulge him alright. Spend the rest of the night in bed with him. Wasn't that what everyone was after these days? Now she understood it so much more. If every man looked like him, she'd be all good with having one-night stands or in his case, maybe a whole weekend. She swallowed. *Get it together.* "Look—"

"Do you know why they wanted to see your kitchen?" Hawk interrupted.

She blinked. "What?"

"Because they wanted to look for the murder weapon.

I'm guessing the victim was stabbed, and they want to know if you did it. A crime of passion. Your boyfriend comes over. You two have a fight. You grab the knife, stab him, and then push him out the door and call nine-one-one to cover it up."

Those words sobered her right up and snapped her back to reality. "Are you crazy? That's insane! I don't know who the guy is, er, was. I've never seen him before." This was all too much.

Hawk nodded. "I believe you, but I'm not sure the cops do. You have to admit, your story sounds a bit weird."

"But that's what happened," she said through gritted teeth. How had everything gone so horribly wrong?

"I'm sure it is. All I'm saying is you need to be very careful. Do you have video cameras?"

She shook her head. Her grandfather had been dead set against them.

"Consider installing some. Supporting camera footage would make it easier to show the police exactly what happened, so they leave you alone."

He had a point. If she was going to continue to run the shop, who knew what other encounters she would have? "I'll take that into consideration," she murmured.

Hawk's eyes narrowed at her. "Why don't you tell me about your lawsuit? We might as well get it done since I'm here."

The last thing she wanted to do right now was talk about the suit. Frazzled beyond belief, she wanted him gone, but she could hear her grandfather's voice in her head. *"Treat others as you would want to be treated."* This man had come to help her. She couldn't very well push him out the door now. Letting out a sigh, she squared her shoulders. "Would you like a cup of tea? Mine seems to have gone cold."

Ten minutes later, tea in hand, and calmer in spirit, she sat on her stool at the counter. He stood across from her, his overcoat still on, and studied her intently as she began to speak.

"The name of this shop is Under Lock 'n Key. In the early nineteen hundreds, my great-grandfather opened up shop as a locksmith. When my grandfather took over the shop, he kept the name but switched the business to a bookstore. He wasn't much good as a locksmith apparently. Always said he didn't have the touch. Books were more his speed. He built a reputation around the city for being able to find rare books, but also for being a place where you could come and hang out and read for a while with no one bothering you."

She swallowed a mouthful of tea. It was hard to talk about her grandfather in the past tense. "Anyway, about three months ago, a store popped up around the corner and down the block. It's a locksmith shop. The thing is, it's called Lock and Key and their logo is almost a dead ringer for mine. I asked the owner about it, a man named Lawrence Patterson. I pointed out how close the name was to mine and that his logo was almost an exact copy. He got belligerent and kicked me out of his shop." She shuddered at the memory. It had been scary at the time and looking back at it didn't make it any less so.

"I don't really care about the name. We don't sell the same things, but the logo, well, my great-grandfather designed it, and my grandfather was enormously proud of it. I won't have it stolen by some asshole locksmith."

Hawk took a sip of his tea. "What's the rest of the story?"

"What do you mean?" she asked.

"When you mentioned Patterson you...reacted. Did Patterson do something to frighten you?"

She stared. This man was way too perceptive. Those damn gorgeous eyes studied her. "I...that is he's a big man and he got in my face to intimidate me. It was...scary."

"Did he do anything else? Did he get physical with you at all or anything?

Remy hesitated. "No…he didn't touch me."

"But someone did." It was a statement of fact.

Jesus, how had he known? She hadn't told anyone about what happened. It was…humiliating. "I…" she ran a hand over her face. She had no intention of telling anyone about this but as she met Hawk's gaze, she knew he wasn't going to let her off the hook.

She swallowed a sip of tea. "I was locking the door on Wednesday night when someone came up behind me and smashed me against it. He twisted my arm behind my back and told me to stop causing trouble and that if I didn't stop, he'd come back and make me regret it."

There she'd said it. Heat filled her cheeks as she stared into her tea. Hawk's piercing gaze didn't seem to miss anything. He seemed to be able to read her too well and she didn't need him to know how ashamed she felt. It was stupid. Instinctively, she knew the episode wasn't her fault, but she couldn't stop the feeling that she'd somehow failed.

"You didn't report it to the police?"

She did glance at him then, feeling judged. "There was no point. By the time I got myself together, whoever it was, was gone. I couldn't describe him and had no way of identifying him."

His jaws seemed to be clamped together and his eyes glittered. He wasn't happy. "I see. You think this has to do with this Patterson guy?"

She nodded. "I sent him several cease and desist letters threatening him with a lawsuit if he didn't change his sign."

"There's no one else that you…"

She arched an eyebrow. "Pissed off lately?"

He nodded once.

"No," she said. "I'm not in the habit of causing problems." Shifting in her seat, she glanced out the window. "There's something shady about that locksmith shop. The people that go in and out of there, it's not…normal. I don't know how to explain it other than that. Other shop owners have noticed it too, but no one wants to say anything. They think it could be a mob front."

"What do you think?"

She shrugged. "It's a possibility."

"But you're going through with the lawsuit anyway."

"Yes. As I said, that's my great-grandfather's logo. He created it, and it's been on this shopfront for generations. I can't just let this guy use it."

"Do you have any paperwork to prove your great-grandfather created the logo? Did you have it trademarked?"

"He designed it back in the early nineteen hundreds so there's no paperwork, but this shop has been here since then, and the logo is outside on the sign. It's been hanging above the door for almost a hundred years. My grandfather did have the logo trademarked but it was a long time ago. I'm still trying to find all the paperwork on it."

He put his own mug down on the counter. "It might make more sense to wait until you have all of the paperwork in order before you file your suit."

"Yeah, I know. I am jumping the gun a bit. I was just so rattled with the…thing the other night. I wanted Patterson to know his intimidation tactics weren't working."

"How about you show me the signs with the logo on it? Both yours and the other shop."

She blinked. "What? Now? Why?"

He cocked his head. "I would like to see it before I read all the documentation."

"You don't have to do that. Read everything, I mean. I know you're right. I probably won't do anything until I have all the necessary paperwork."

"Humor me." He offered her a soft smile.

She cursed silently. He was only trying to be helpful, but it was really starting to annoy the hell out of her. She was all jittery and just wanted to go home. Staring at him for a moment, she finally decided she might as well get it over with.

"Okay," she said as she stood and pulled her jacket off the back of the stool and tugged it on. Turning, she gestured to the door and waited for Hawk to go outside. She was damn tempted to lock the door after him and pull down the shades. Then she could hide from those eyes. She could go upstairs to her grandfather's apartment and spend the night there, face this mess in the morning when she would feel stronger and more equipped to deal. *As if that was going to happen.*

That was the real reason she wanted to see Lacy tonight. She was off-kilter before all of this happened and just wanted her friend to make her feel better. Instead, she had this man trying to help her with her legal problems. Served her right for not just telling Lacy that she was struggling. Telling people about her feelings had always been hard for her but admitting someone had assaulted her, tried to intimidate her was, for some reason, humiliating. And now, her emotions zoomed past the scope of her ability to deal.

Instead of hiding, she followed Hawk out and then paused to lock the door. She checked the lock and then stepped back. She pointed. "See? That's the logo." It was an old-fashioned skeleton key in a round hole that was supposed to be a lock. It was done in gold and the head of the key was a winking skull with a grin. It was like her great-grandfather she'd been told... stately with a dry sense of wit and, more importantly, very distinctive.

Hawk held up his phone and took a picture. He turned to her and nodded. "Got it."

Without another word to him, she turned and strode down the block. The scuff of shoes on cement told her that he'd followed her. Sure enough, a moment later, he was abreast of her, and it was then she realized how much taller he was than she was. Remy barely came to his shoulder.

When she turned right at the corner, the wind took her breath away. She hadn't realized that it was so damn cold and windy outside. That was the thing about New York. Sometimes turning the corner led to a brutal surprise. She immediately wished she'd brought her scarf, hat, and mittens. Her hands, in particular, were freezing. She jammed them into her pockets.

Hawk must have noticed because, in the next minute, he was offering her his gloves. "Here, take these."

"Thanks, but I'm okay," she said, fighting to have her voice heard above the wind.

He smiled down at her. "Your hands will hurt and get chapped. Take them." He held the gloves out to her.

She could keep refusing, but it was *really* cold, and he was right, her hands ached with the wind. She pulled on the gloves as they walked along. She was a mitten girl, but the gloves were warm and soft. Were they cashmere lined?

"Thanks," she said, and he offered her another polite smile.

Lock and Key was at the end of this block, and when they reached the store, she turned and pointed up at the front of the building. "See?"

Hawk looked up and squinted at the sign. It wasn't illuminated like hers was at this hour. He pulled out his phone and zoomed in on the logo. He snapped a couple of pictures of it.

Suddenly, his opinion mattered. "What do you think?" she asked.

She knew he was right about the lawsuit. She'd graduated

from law school even if she didn't pursue a career in law. But she'd let her emotions get the best of her and she wanted to file as quickly as possible, so Patterson knew she wasn't frightened off.

"It certainly looks like yours," he said.

"It's identical."

He nodded. "We need to establish when they designed it."

"What do you mean? They just opened about a month ago."

"Yes. Here. But did they have that logo on a shop somewhere else in the city? Has it been there for more than a hundred years? The trademark information will be vital to your case. I need to do some research on all of this before I can do anything else. We have to know what we're up against."

Dammit! Why hadn't that thought occurred to her? Stupid. He was right, of course. That just annoyed her more. This just couldn't be happening. Why did everything suddenly have to turn to shit? And what was this 'we' business?

"I'll poke around a bit tomorrow and see what I can come up with."

She tried to rein in her temper. She was mad at herself for not seeing the obvious. But yelling at Hawk wasn't going to help. "You don't have to. Really. I'll put everything together and then I'll get Lacy to look it over. You've been too kind, but I can't impose on you like that. Besides, tomorrow is Saturday," she said. "I thought lawyers didn't work on the weekend." She tried to smile up at him, so he understood she was joking.

He snorted good-naturedly. "We work all the time. There's some stuff I can do even though it's a weekend. I'll let you know what I find out."

This man and his willingness to help affected her in ways she didn't understand. It was too damn cold to argue anymore. If he wanted to do the work, that was on him. "Okay then."

He gestured for her to start walking back in the direction they'd come. She moved along the sidewalk. It was so damn cold, maybe she should stay at her grandfather's apartment. The thought of walking the twelve blocks to her own place seemed daunting and cold wasn't her thing at all. But she hadn't cleaned out her grandfather's place. It would be difficult to be in there with all his stuff. It was why she hadn't done anything with it over the last six months. She couldn't bring herself to throw anything out just yet.

There was another matter that she just didn't want to deal with either. Going through her grandfather's papers would mean she would find out all the details of his life and she wasn't sure knowledge in this case was a good thing.

They rounded the corner and came to a stop in front of the shop. "Well, thanks for coming," she said.

He nodded, but he wasn't looking at her. He was looking over her shoulder into her shop. "You locked the door, right?"

"What?" Yes, she'd locked the door. She whirled around and stared into her shop windows. She didn't see anything, but she moved over and pulled on the door handle. It opened. A chill went down her spine that had nothing to do with the cold.

Hawk gripped her arm and moved her away from the door. "Call nine-one-one and report a break in." He stepped forward and pulled the door open slowly.

A frightened twist in her gut almost doubled her over and sweat broke out across her skin. She wanted to let him go in and check the shop, but it was her responsibility. She couldn't let him take that kind of a risk for her. She didn't even know him. "You're not going without me," she said as she moved in close to him.

He shot her a quick glance, but he was more focused on entering the shop than on what she was doing.

"Stay behind me," he said in a quiet voice as he entered the shop.

She wanted to argue but she was, in fact, a small woman, and if the intruder was large, well, it wouldn't go well for her. Maybe letting this guy lead the way wasn't such a bad idea, but she'd stay close on his heels.

Hawk moved silently and took the steps cautiously. He walked past the counter toward the back room. A flash out of the corner of her eye made Remy yelp, and she whipped around to see a book sailing through the air directly at her face.

Hawk stepped in front of her and knocked down the book with his hand, sending it crashing to the ground. Then someone wearing a ski mask came flying out from one of the aisles of books. With a yell, he threw another book that glanced off Hawk's shoulder. Hawk rushed forward, and he and the masked man crashed together in the middle of the aisle.

As they struggled, Remy looked around wildly for a weapon, anything to stop this guy. What the hell was he doing in her shop? Her gaze landed on a copy of the Oxford English Dictionary. She heaved the heavy tome off the shelf and held it up in the air. The two men were still struggling. Hawk was facing her now, and the masked man had his back to her. She let out a piercing yell and brought the book down with all her might.

The masked intruder turned at the last second, and the book ended up clipping Hawk's ear and crashing down on his shoulder. He swore and let go of the man. The guy pivoted and pushed her with both hands, sending her sprawling into the shelves. She lost her footing and ended up on the floor with several books falling on top of her. She tried to get to her feet, but by the time she got herself untangled, the intruder was gone.

She leaned back against the shelves and took deep breaths to steady herself. She was woozy. She must have hit her head as she fell. She glanced over at Hawk, who was leaning on the shelves almost opposite of her, holding his hand to his ear. When he dropped his hand, it was red with blood.

"Are you okay?" she asked.

"Yes," His scowl told her he wasn't happy. After a deep breath, he asked, "Are you okay?"

She nodded but then regretted it when the room swam for a second. Her head started throbbing and she lifted a hand and winced as she prodded a small knot forming on the back of her skull. At this point, she couldn't be sure whether the injury came from falling against the shelf or from the falling books, but she suspected it was a result of both. Her hand shook as she reached for the shelf to steady herself.

Hawk had pressed a tissue against his ear to stop the bleeding. "Perhaps, in the future, you could call nine-one-one rather than try to help. Safer for both of us."

And just like that, the camel's back broke. She'd had enough. Her day had turned to shit, and now she had a big-ass headache. She glared at him. "I distinctly remember telling you thank you for your assistance and you could go home. You chose to stay."

He looked over at her and cocked an eyebrow.

She was being unreasonable and she knew it, but goddamn it, she'd had a hell of a day. If she felt like being unreasonable she'd goddamn indulge *that*.

Immediately contrite, she let out a long breath. "I'm sorry," she mumbled. He was only there to help her, and she'd gotten him attacked by a masked guy and beaned him with the OED. Truthfully, he had every right to be pissed.

There was a crash at the door of the shop. Hawk immediately jumped in front of her and stuck his head out of the aisle. She peeked around his shoulder to see what was going on. It was the two uniform cops from earlier. They were standing there, hunched down, guns drawn.

"Fuck," she mumbled. Somehow her night had gone from bad to horrendous in the blink of an eye.

CHAPTER THREE

H awk leaned back against the shelves and cursed silently. *Fucking idiot.* He should have left when he'd had the chance. Just walked her to the door and said, "We'll be in touch." Instead, he had taken one look inside the store and knew instinctively something was wrong. When he'd been a SEAL, his team used to tease him about being psychic. It hadn't taken long for him to become the first one sent in to suss out a situation. If he said it was all good, they believed him. More often than not, he could tell when there was going to be a problem.

He'd tried to play his instincts off as mere luck. Like he'd seen something that had given away the booby-trap or some such, but his team were fucking SEALS…they caught on quick. His *skill* stopped being a joke and became something they relied on, more than he was comfortable with, if truth be told. It was one of the reasons he left the SEALs. He was burnt out, and he was afraid his sixth sense would fail him and lead them all to disaster. He couldn't have lived with himself if that had happened. It was better to get while the gettin' was good.

But standing in front of that store, he had known in his bones that someone was inside. Someone who shouldn't have been there. No way in hell could he leave Remy to face that alone. It went against his nature. It didn't hurt that she was attractive, and her big gray eyes intrigued him. If only she'd listened, then he wouldn't be standing there with a stinging cut on his ear, a raging ache in his shoulder, and nothing to show for it.

"No, I didn't see his face," he said for what seemed like the fifth time. Officer Harrison narrowed his eyes at Hawk's tone, but he really didn't give a fuck. This rookie cop needed to finish up because Hawk was fucking done. He wanted to go home, put his feet up on the coffee table, and have a large scotch.

"How did you know the guy was inside?" Harrison asked again, conveniently forgetting Hawk's answer from the first three times he'd asked.

Hawk released an exasperated sigh. "As I said before, I saw the door move slightly. I was here when Ms. Tanger locked it, so I knew something had happened, and now it was open." He caught Remy looking at him over the shoulder of the cop questioning her. She frowned. She knew he was lying, but at least she was holding her tongue, not ratting him out.

He turned back to the cop. "Officer Harrison, I think we're done here. I've answered all your questions and so has Ms. Tanger." He straightened from leaning against the bookcase and took the cloth away from his ear. "Ms. Tanger will get you a list of anything that's missing, and we'll both be happy to come down the station tomorrow and sign the report but right now, I think it's time for you to go."

Harrison shifted his weight and exchanged glances with his partner. "So, you're refusing to answer any more questions?"

"I'm calling it a night for all of us. We'll be happy to answer whatever other questions you might have in the morning. How does ten o'clock sound?"

Harrison's partner, one D. Purdy, shook his head. "You can come by the precinct on Monday. This is our weekend off."

"Fine, Monday it is."

Harrison flipped his notebook closed and nodded to Purdy. The two of them glanced over at Hawk but made their way to the door. "See you Monday," Harrison said in what must be his menacing tone. Hawk just stared at him. The two cops left.

"Finally," he said, "I thought we'd be here all night." He turned to find Remy glaring at him.

Her hands were balled into fists and rested on her hips. "Why'd you get rid of them? Now they won't help me."

Was she crazy? "Help you? How exactly do you think they're going to help you?"

"They need to call in the fingerprint people. You know, the crime scene techs so they can track down who the guy was. Maybe he left fingerprints or DNA."

"DNA?" He burst out laughing but then immediately regretted it. It made his shoulder hurt, and now a dull throb kicked up in his head. "This is New York. No one is going to fingerprint anything. DNA? That takes months to process in real life, and they won't do it unless there's a dead body involved, and sometimes not even then. Don't kid yourself. These two will take the report, and that will be the end of it."

"So then why bother calling them?" she demanded.

Remy had him there. "Because we're supposed to for insurance purposes. If anything is missing or damaged, you won't be able to claim it if you don't have a police report," he responded.

She snorted. "Insurance? I don't plan on making any

claims. It won't be worth the cost of my rising premium." She started down an aisle toward the back of the shop.

"Where are you going?" he asked as his eyes were drawn to her ass. Her jeans fit like a second skin, and they only emphasized the roundness. A small wave of desire hit him.

"I'm making more tea. I'm in desperate need of a cup. Then I'm going to start putting my grandfather's shop back together. That asshole made a mess of things."

Hawk glanced around. It hadn't been evident from the front, but she was right. The intruder had hauled all kinds of books off the shelves and left them on the floor. It looked like a cyclone had gone through, but only in certain aisles.

He watched her disappear around the corner. She was a cute little thing, but what a pain in his ass, which of course, only had him thinking about her ass again. Her chestnut hair hung in loose waves around her shoulders, and earlier he'd found himself wondering what it would be like to run his fingers through it. Yes, she was attractive. Her large gray eyes were mesmerizing, and she had a wonderfully curvy figure, but she also had a smart mouth and a whole lot of attitude. She'd done her best to keep it hidden but her eyes didn't lie and those were two things he didn't need in his life. No, it was time for him to take his leave.

"Remy," he called.

She stuck her head out of what he assumed was the little kitchen.

"I'm leaving. You should go, too. Where do you live?" He didn't want her taking the subway at this hour on her own. After everything that had happened this week, a blind man could see she was a target. Going anywhere alone, especially at night, was a big mistake.

"Why?" she demanded.

He closed his eyes and quietly muttered a long string of curses. He opened his eyes again. "I was going to suggest that you take a cab or Uber home if you don't live within walking distance. You've had a long night, and it's late to be taking the subway."

"Thanks, Dad," she said, her words dripping in sarcasm. "But I think I can handle it."

He wanted to say, *like you've handled everything else this week?* But he knew better. She'd done her best. Just telling him about being assaulted had been humiliating for her judging by the shade of red her cheeks had become as she told the story. Living it had to be ten times worse. He felt for her, he really did, but his patience was gone and, in his estimation, she was being stupid.

He strangled his urge to throttle her and asked, "Do you keep a set of keys to your apartment here in the shop?'

She frowned at him. "Why?"

"Because someone just broke in here. If your house keys were here, then they could have those and go to your apartment," he said bluntly.

Her mouth opened into a small *O*, but then the kettle screamed, and she stepped back into the kitchen. She reappeared a minute later, tea mug in hand. Her face had gone pale, and her hand shook slightly. Shit, now he'd scared the crap out of her. Not his intention, but she did have to be careful. He wouldn't want something to happen to her. *Something else,* he amended.

"Um, yeah. I have a set of keys here."

Her eyes were huge, and the color had yet to come back into her face. She was definitely scared, and he wanted to kick himself for being so blunt. "Why don't you make sure they're still here?"

She nodded and put her mug down on the counter. She ducked down behind the cash register and then came up a second later with a small box. She opened it, and her shoulders sagged in relief. "The spare key is still here."

He nodded. "Good. Why don't you go home now? You've had a long, trying day by the sounds of things. You can come back and clean up in the morning. People will understand if you open a couple of hours late."

She glanced down at the now closed box. She started to nod but then her expression changed. She squared her shoulders. "I'll stay and clean up tonight. My grandfather never opened the store late a day in his life. I can't let him down now."

Hawk wanted to remind her that her grandfather was dead and beyond caring now, but it wasn't worth another argument. He needed to go home and ice his shoulder. But then he found himself asking, "Do you want help?" *What the hell?* Staying to help her went against his better judgement, but this woman intrigued him. The idea of her struggling in the shop, on her own, grated on his nerves.

She glanced up at him. "No. But thank you for offering. You don't know where things go. It will be faster if I do it. It won't take me long."

He thought about pushing the issue so he could stay and make sure she was safe. On the other hand, she'd made it quite clear she wanted to do it herself. He didn't want to force his presence on her in any way. If she wanted his help, she would have to ask for it.

"If you're sure?" he said, leaving it open.

"Yes, I'm sure. I'll clean this up and then go home." She gave him a quick smile. "Thank you for all of your help."

He nodded. "I'll poke around a bit about the locksmith shop and see what we can do about that logo."

She gave him a brief nod and extended her arm. He took the small, finely boned hand and watched as it disappeared completely within his grasp. "It was nice to meet you, Remy."

She snorted. "No, it wasn't. You had to deal with the cops

twice and got beat up by an intruder. There was nothing nice about tonight."

"I didn't get beat up," he protested. This woman was impossible. "Good night," he said stiffly, and then turned on his heel and left the store.

He was halfway home before he'd calmed down enough to breathe normally. That woman pushed all his buttons. It had been a long time since he'd been that pissed off. He sucked in a breath as he made the light on the southeast corner of Eighty-Second and Broadway. He continued north on Broadway weaving around the few brave souls on the sidewalk. The frigid air kept all but the most dedicated dogwalkers inside. Most of the stores were closed at this hour and traffic was minimal. He turned on to eighty-fifth street and walked toward the river. The cold was bitter, and his hands were killing him.

His gloves. She still had them. He'd totally forgotten about them until just this minute. He swore. He was going to have to go back tomorrow and get them. They were his favorite pair. It was like the universe was conspiring against him.

Ten minutes later, he walked into his apartment and closed the door behind him. It had been a hell of a day in all kinds of ways. He winced as he took off his coat. His shoulder was going to hurt for a while. What the hell kind of book did she hit him with? Jesus. He was tired of being cold. No fucking way was he putting ice on his shoulder.

He went into his bedroom, peeled off his clothes, and got into a hot shower. He needed the heat. His hands hurt from the cold. What had possessed him to give Remy his gloves, he didn't know. Actually, that wasn't true. He wanted to treat her well because he didn't want to annoy the Callahan brothers in any way. They just might hold the key to his future. At least, that was what he was telling himself. Her large eyes and nicely rounded ass didn't have anything to do with it. *Much.*

But who was he kidding? He let the heat work its magic on his tired muscles. If he went into security work, this would be a common occurrence. He'd feel beat up on a regular basis. Or, at least, he had in the SEALs. It couldn't be too bad working personal security, could it? He thought about what had happened in Florence when the Callahans had reached out to him to help Jake and Monty. Shit, if that was the norm, he'd need to get back in fighting shape.

He looked down at his body. There were a few scars here and there, but overall, he was still solid. Maybe not as good as he once was, but he hadn't let anything go to seed. It wouldn't take long to get back to peak physical condition. A few more hours at the gym each week, and he'd be back up to the size he used to be. The question was, did he want to do that?

He had left the SEALs for a reason. He'd needed a break, but that was then, and this was now. Maybe going into the security game was just the thing he was looking for.

He toweled himself off and put on a pair of pajama bottoms and then wandered out to pour himself a drink. Tumbler in hand, he stared out the balcony door at the darkness. Riverside Park was out there and then the Hudson River, although from this angle and at this time of night, he couldn't see it. Just inky blackness between the lights from Riverside Park and the lights of New Jersey on the other side.

He loved his place. This apartment was home. The balcony with a view of the river had sold him on it in the first place. He could barely afford it when he'd graduated from law school, but with Drake's help, he'd gambled on it anyway.

He had known he'd do well working with Drake. They'd hit it off immediately during the interview. Hawk never had a doubt he'd be hired, nor had he ever paused to wonder how he was going to climb the ladder. He had just known he'd be in the top spot one day, and he was.

Jameson Drake was a brilliant man. Hawk had learned a lot from him, but theirs was also a symbiotic relationship. Drake had gotten his money's worth from Hawk, and then some. It was no wonder Drake knew Hawk was struggling. They were similar in many ways.

Hawk dropped his gaze at the tumbler of scotch for a second before he moved out from behind the bar and went into his galley kitchen. He searched his pantry, letting out an *ah ha!* when he found an old box of tea bags. When the kettle boiled, he made a cup of tea. He hadn't really had tea in years, but somehow tonight, it felt right.

He took his mug and sat down on the sofa, staring out at the darkness. He shouldn't have left Remy alone. He tried to relax, but his mind wandered. Was she in danger? His instincts told him there wouldn't be any more trouble tonight. And that was truly why he'd left. She was fine. For now. But just as he knew she was safe for tonight, he knew more trouble was coming. The sense of disquiet that ran across his skin told him that something was brewing. Remy Tanger was in trouble. He had no idea from what or whom, but he knew she was way in over her head, and she was going to need help. His help. Whether he wanted to give it or not. She was now his responsibility somehow, and life was about to get difficult. For both of them.

CHAPTER FOUR

Remy shelved the last book with a groan. Her back hurt, her head ached, and she was beyond exhausted. What had looked like a small mess had turned out to be more like a mountainous one. Once she started restoring items to their rightful places, it became obvious that most of the books remaining in the stacks had been out of order as well. She glanced at her watch. Two a.m. No wonder she was so damn tired.

She sighed as she started down the aisle to the kitchenette. She dumped her cold tea in the sink and then rinsed out the mug, putting it on the rack to dry. She turned out the lights and headed to the front of the store. She could stay in her grandfather's old apartment, but she just didn't have it in her to face all his stuff on top of everything else. She'd cried the last time she'd gone up there, and today had already sucked beyond measure.

Except for meeting Hawk. He was something else. Annoying as hell but so damn hot. She'd have to ask Lacy about him.

She pulled on her coat and stuffed her hands in her

pockets to get her mittens. She closed her eyes and swore. She'd forgotten to give Hawk his gloves back. She pulled them out of her pockets and studied them. The gorgeous black leather suited him. Very refined. Like the man himself, but somehow not.

He was a handsome man, no doubt, with short, dark hair and gorgeous blue eyes. The stubble on his jaw by the end of the night had led to all kinds of interesting thoughts for her. If she'd met him another way, or even if she just saw him on the street, she'd think he was the hottest thing. Tall, dark, and handsome, for sure. Too bad he was a jerk. *Was he, though? Or was she the jerk?* She groaned again; she was toast for the night. It didn't matter who the jerk was. Then again, it had been her experience that most men were jerks when it came to it.

She put Hawk's gloves on the counter and then bent down and retrieved her own from the shelf behind the counter. She'd leave his gloves here and find a way to get them to him in the morning. Just one more thing to do. She grabbed her purse and then headed out, making doubly sure to lock the door behind her. She pulled down the iron grate over the store front and locked that as well. Hopefully, everything would be fine when she returned in the morning. Or rather, in a few hours.

She walked down the street, and as she turned the corner away from the store, she saw the crime scene tape left on the sidewalk from earlier in the night. This had to be where the man had died. A wave of sadness washed over her. Why hadn't he stayed for the ambulance? If he'd just told her he needed medical help when he'd first come into the store instead of yelling about a shoe, then he might still be alive. It was just stupid.

At least Lacy came through. They'd been close in law school and stayed that way all these years later. She'd done some legal work for Remy's grandfather too. Lacy was the first one Remy had thought of when she saw the locksmith shop's sign. She had no doubt that Hawk was a good lawyer too. Not just because Lacy sent him, but if he ran the legal department for Drake Industries, then he had to be top notch. Everyone knew Jameson Drake by reputation. He was not the sort to hire anyone but the best. A small wave of guilt plagued her as she turned onto Seventy- Fourth Street. She'd really whoomped him one with the OED. She grinned. No better weapon than the Oxford English Dictionary. That thing was huge. Probably part of why she was so sore.

She glanced around her once again. The sidewalks were empty, and traffic was non-existent. Maybe walking hadn't been such a good idea. With the bad luck she'd been having this week, it was probably riskier than she first thought.

Before this mess with Patterson, and she was sure the owner of the other Lock and Key was responsible for every-thing, she'd never been afraid to walk home on her own no matter what time of night. An old song had declared her hometown the city that never slept, and it was true. There were always people around doing their thing. New York was a relatively safe city. At least she'd always felt that way until now. She took one last sweeping glance at the sidewalk behind her and then turned onto her block.

With a bit more pep in her step, she entered her build-ing. She hadn't meant to hurt Hawk with the OED, but sometimes shit happened. She appreciated his help with the police, both times, but she refused to feel guilty about his injury. She'd told him he could go, that he didn't need to help her. Although, if truth be told, she'd been damn glad he'd chosen to stay when they came face-to-face with the intruder. She didn't need rescuing, but a little help now and then was sometimes a good thing. And when the help looked like Thane Hawkins, well, that was alright, too.

Her apartment was in the back corner of the ground floor. She paused in front of her door, her heart thudding against her sternum and her palms slick with sweat. What if someone had broken in while she was out? She held her breath and twisted the knob. *Still locked. Thank God.* She put in her key and opened the lock.

Her apartment was exactly as she'd left it. The small one-bedroom was tidy and cheery thanks to the red and purple throw pillows on the beige sofa cover across from the TV and the big windows overlooking the small yard that only the landlord was allowed to use at the back of the building. Her long, narrow kitchen had a window at the end that over-looked the alley, but it provided some light and she'd chosen to hang the red and purple flowered curtains that matched the sofa pillows. The galley kitchen was also open to the living room with a counter in between the two. It felt homey to her, and she liked it.

She made sure the door was locked and flicked the security bar over as well. It was the same kind of thing as they had in hotel rooms. New York City was a safe place, but the added precaution made her feel just a bit safer. After dropping her purse on the kitchen counter, she shrugged off her jacket and draped it over the back of the stool that stood beside the island. She headed to her bedroom. She desperately needed sleep. She had to be back at the store by nine a.m.

She got undressed, climbed into bed, and closed her eyes. The image of the door of the shop came into her mind. How had Hawk known there was someone inside? She'd heard him lie to the police that he'd seen the door move a bit, so he knew it was open, and he was sure she'd locked it when they'd left. But the door hadn't moved. It fit solidly into the frame. Not even on the windiest of days did it rattle, so what the hell was he playing at? Did he have something to do with the break-in?

Don't be silly. He was there to help her, wasn't he?

The next morning came way too early, and Remy cursed the clock before she got out of bed. She'd hit snooze on the alarm one too many times, and now she would have to have an incredibly short shower if she was still going to have time to stop and get some breakfast from the bodega on the corner before she opened the shop.

She rushed through the shower and ended up pulling her wet hair into a bun at the top of her head. She pulled on a pair of jeans and a snowy white blouse with a gray cashmere sweater that matched her eyes. The forecast said it was going to be a cold one again today.

Twenty-five minutes later, after a quick stop for an egg and cheese roll and black coffee to go, she rocked up to the shop gates with three minutes to spare.

After lifting the security gate, she made to open the front door but stopped dead. She stuck her nose to the glass. Someone had pulled all the books off the shelves in the shop. There wasn't a surface that hadn't been trashed. Nothing had survived the destruction. Not one book remained in place.

Her knees buckled just as strong arms grabbed her around the waist. "Are you okay?" Hawk's voice sounded in her ear.

"N-no," she stammered. She pointed with her key, unable to form the words to describe the horror.

"Shit," he murmured. "Someone broke in after you left."

She nodded as she leaned against him. She didn't have the strength to stand up right just yet.

He turned her slightly, so she was looking up at him. "Are you okay?" he repeated.

She nodded once and bit her lip. "I'm— I'm fine." Her voice came out as a bit of a croak, but at least she'd been able to form the words. She leaned into him. She seemed to be unable to make her legs work on their own, and he was so solid.

"Let's find a place for you to sit for a moment." He kept his arm around her and guided her over to some chairs that were on the sidewalk in front of an intrepid little cafe a few doors down. Like they expected people to want to sit outside and eat in the freezing cold.

"Sit here. I'll call the police."

She dropped down into the chair, missing the strength and warmth of Hawk's embrace, and put her stuff on the little cafe table. She stared at the sidewalk, unfocused as if surrounded by a dense fog. How could this happen? It was just insane. She'd just cleaned up yesterday's disaster, and here she was all over again. Was this Patterson?

"This wasn't random," she said out loud.

Hawk glanced down at her. He had his cell to his ear, and he was speaking to the nine-one-one operator. A moment later he said, "No, you're right. It wasn't random."

"Is this Patterson trying to intimidate me again? What does he gain by doing this??" Her hands were shaking. She flexed her fingers to get them to stop.

"Do you deal in rare books?" Hawk's deep voice cut through her brain fog.

She nodded. "Sometimes, but not lately. That was more my grandfather's thing. I dabble a bit here and there, but it has to be a request from a good client, and I don't have anything in the shop that's worth the risk of breaking in and tossing the place. Most purchases are on credit cards these days. I don't even have more than a few hundred in cash."

He stared at her. "And there's nothing that comes to mind, nothing at all that would make someone want to break in?"

She shook her head. "It's a book shop. There's nothing there but books. Other than Patterson, it doesn't make any sense and even that seems like a stretch. What does he gain by doing this? It's not like I'm going to close my shop." That idea suddenly had some merit, but she shook off the thought. "He must know that. It seems like a waste of time. Does he think if he keeps doing something like this, I'll stop trying to get him to switch his logo? And why does the logo mean that much to him? It's crazy."

It was completely bewildering. She could not fathom why someone would do that to her shop. There was no logical reason. No upside to it. She propped her elbow on the table and rested her forehead on her cupped palm as her heart rate slowed. The whole thing just didn't make any sense but sitting out here wasn't going to fix it.

She looked up at Hawk. "Hang up."

"What?"

"Hang up. You said yourself they aren't going to take fingerprints or do any forensic testing. What's the point in calling them? They'll just waste my time questioning me instead of doing anything helpful." She stood. It hadn't taken long for rage to replace shock and fear, making her knees steady again. "Hang up," she demanded and then, grabbing her stuff off the table, she stalked toward her store. Hawk followed her but stayed outside. He seemed to be making another call.

She opened the door and immediately growled. It was going to take days to get everything back the way it had been. Books were strewn all over the floor and hanging off shelves. Pictures had been yanked off the walls as well and smashed on the floor. No section of the store had been left untouched by violence except the two tapestries. They still hung on the walls like book ends. It made her feel immensely better that the one covering the doorway to Gramp's apartment was still hanging straight with no signs of damage. Everything could be fixed. This was going to be costly for her, but it could all be put right again.

She dumped her stuff on the checkout counter and made her way behind it to hang her coat on the stool. Turning around, she let out a long breath. For the first time ever, the shop was going to have to be closed. There was no way she could keep it open. She mentally ran through what she had on the calendar for today. Shit, she had a story time for the little ones that was always popular, and she had the teen writing group that liked to come in and hang at the back.

She thumbed through her phone and made the requisite calls to cancel the events the best she could. She posted the temporary closing on social media and hoped between that and word of mouth most people would find out that she was closed before they left home.

She wanted to call Emily, who worked the cash on weekends, but the young woman was on vacation. She'd left town on Thursday and wouldn't be back for a week.

Putting down her phone, Remy looked out through the window. Who was Hawk talking to? His mobile was pressed against his ear and he was scowling. Not that whom he was speaking to was any of her business. She had enough on her plate. Still, he looked damn fine in his jeans and black winter jacket. Even with the harsh look on his face, he was fine. He'd been so solid when she'd leaned against him. His warmth had helped to keep her on her feet. She owed him one for sure after all this. Maybe she'd offer to take him out to dinner as a way of saying thanks assuming he didn't have a girlfriend. She snorted. A man that good looking, no friggin' way someone hadn't snapped him up.

She shook her head as if to clear her mind and turned on some music. Usually, she had the satellite radio tuned to a top forty channel, but instead the harsh twang of Austin Davis came through the speakers. He was doing some sort of interview. God, but he was an annoying asshat. Way too right leaning for her. Like into the weird conspiracy theory zone. He'd been in the senate for a couple of terms now as she understood it, but he'd just started gaining momentum in the last few years. He was everywhere these days. With a grimace, she tuned it to a new channel and soft jazz came through her speakers. Squaring her shoulders, she immediately got to work picking up books and stacking them on any flat surface. She put the damaged ones on the front window seat after moving the pillows and the rest on top of the shelves. Once she got a section off the floor, she'd put them on the shelves in order. She needed to be able to walk around the room first.

Remy glanced at the book in her hand. A thriller. She snorted. Her life resembled a thriller novel at the moment. Too bad she couldn't just put the book down, or even turn the page.

She stacked another pile of books on a shelf and then leaned against the shelves for a moment. The floor in this area was clean. Now she just had to put the books in order. It was going to be a long day, or possibly two.

The sound of the door opening reached her ears. She turned to find Hawk standing in the doorway.

"Do you want some tea?" she asked instead of, '*who were you talking to?*' Which was what she really wanted to ask.

"I called Lacy, who put me through to Gage Callahan. Do you know him? He's Logan's brother. They run Callahan Security along with a third brother, Mitch." Hawk closed the door behind him and descended the stairs. "Sorry, didn't think. Of course you probably know that since you're close with Lacy." He came to a stop beside the checkout counter, where she stared at him, her mouth agape. Once again, she was very conscious of his size. He seemed huge to her.

Her thoughts switched back to Lacy. She hadn't told her friend any of this and now he'd ratted her out. *Great.* Lacy was going to be wild at her. "Um, I haven't met him, but I know the name." She jammed her hands into her pockets while she tried to remain calm.

"Anyway, I talked to him, and he's sending some video equipment over. I think it's only wise to install some in the store until we know what's going on."

Okay, now he'd done it. This was just too much. "*We* can't afford it. Besides, my grandfather never wanted cameras. He used to say that no one wanted to be spied on while they were picking out a good book."

Hawk narrowed his eyes. "That might have been your grandfather's stance on it, but he's no longer here, and you've been attacked and broken into twice in the last two days. You need some security in here."

She glared at him. "As I said, I can't afford it. The business does well enough, but I can't do anything crazy, or I'll go under. Security systems are too expensive." She wasn't going to think about the money her grandfather had left her. It gave her hives every time she even contemplated where he could have gotten that kind of cash.

Hawk sighed. "I really think—"

"I don't care what you think," she snapped. *Enough!* Where the fuck did he get off sticking his two cents in. She was done with being nice.

"That's no way to speak to someone," a voice said from the doorway.

"Gus," Remy said, immediately chagrined. "What are you doing here?"

He looked around bewildered. "Carol from the dry

cleaners down the block called. She said the police were here last night. She didn't call until this morning or I would have come over sooner. What happened here?"

She quietly fumed. Carol was the nosiest woman on the block. She should have kept her mouth shut. Remy cleared her throat. "Someone broke in." Just looking at the mess made her heart burn in her chest. Her grandfather would be so upset.

"Why didn't you call me?" he looked at her accusingly.

She frowned. "I didn't want you to race down here and try and help. You should be taking it easy. I know how much the store means to you too and seeing it this way is…hard." Devastating was the word she wanted to use but she didn't want to upset Gus. He was the same age as her grandfather and quite frail. He was also the closest thing to family that she had left.

"They made a mess, didn't they?" He turned to her. "Do you have any idea who did it?"

She shook her head. "No." She hadn't mentioned anything about Patterson, and she shot Hawk a thunderous look to make sure he did the same. "Just some random person out for kicks, I guess." She wasn't going to share that she'd been attacked, and someone had broken in twice.

That thought stopped her cold. How had they gotten in? The security gate was still locked when she arrived. She would have to ask Hawk later when Gus wasn't around. To say it was troubling was the understatement of the century.

Hawk sent her a questioning look, but she ignored it. He turned and took a step toward the elderly man. "I'm Thane Hawkins, Hawk to my friends."

"Hi Hawk. I'm Gus." The men shook. "Are you a friend of Remy's?" He glanced at her and cocked an eyebrow.

Remy blinked. Gus had the wrong idea. He was always

trying to get Remy to settle down, find a good guy and make a life together.

"No," she said.

"Yes," Hawk answered.

He looked at her, and she shot him another look. "That is, he's a friend of Lacy Carmichael. You remember her, don't you, Gus? Anyway, Hawk here just stopped by to help me with some legal stuff."

"On a Saturday?" Gus frowned. He didn't believe any of it.

Hawk shifted on his feet, and for the first time since Remy had met him, he seemed a bit unsettled, not the austere calm that drove her a bit nuts. He cleared his throat and said, "I, er, started to do some work for Remy, and I had some questions. I live in the neighborhood so I thought I would drop by and get the details I needed. Once I saw this, I thought I should maybe stay and help."

Gus nodded approvingly. "That's mighty nice of you. I'm sure Remy appreciates it." He looked around again. "Well, I guess we'd better get down to work."

"No, Gus, the place is a mess. It's too..." she'd been about to say dangerous but he was already glaring at her. "That is, I wouldn't want you to strain yourself. You know you're still getting over that fall from last spring." He'd fallen and it had almost been the end of him but her grandfather had helped him get back up on his feet and he'd bounced back as well as any ninety-seven year old could.

"You never mind. I'm here to help out." He went down the stairs and set his hat and gloves on the counter. He took off his coat and slung it over Remy's on the back of the stool.

She wanted to argue with him but she knew it would hurt his feelings. Maybe if he just stayed in one area and didn't do much.

"Why don't I clear a path to the kitchen and make us all a nice cup of tea?"

She shot Hawk a look. *Help!*

"I'll help with that," Hawk volunteered.

Remy just stood there staring at the two. How had this happened? The elderly gentleman should not be doing too much physical labor, and she didn't want him to know the truth. Also, she wanted Hawk to leave. Having him around just put her on edge. She was too aware of him standing there in his ass-hugging jeans and soft blue sweater that made his eyes seem brighter.. Now, he and Gus were getting on like a house on fire, as her grandfather used to say. There was no way in hell she could ask Hawk to leave now. Gus wouldn't let her and in truth she needed all the help she could get.

"Shit," she mumbled under her breath. This day was just not getting any better. What else could go wrong?

CHAPTER FIVE

Hawk helped the elderly gentleman stack books so he could make his way to the kitchenette. The problem was the kitchen was also a disaster.

"Um," Hawk said, "you know what? Maybe you could put the books in order for us? I'll bring you a stack and you can put the books in order and tell me what shelf to put them on." He smiled encouragingly.

Gus snorted. "Young man, I'll have you know I was a cook in the Navy. I can handle kitchen cleanup."

Hawk tried not to smile. "I'm sure you were very good, too, but it's a lot of work and—"

"I've got it. You just go help Remy with the books."

Coffee grounds, tea bags, and cookie bits were strewn over every surface. It was like they pulled everything out and jumped on it, then kicked the debris over everything. He was worried the old guy would slip and fall on all the crud on the floor.

"Go on." Gus made shooing motions with his hands. "I've got this."

It wasn't Hawk's place to argue, but he was not too

pleased about the whole thing. He went back out to the front of the store to start stacking books on the top of shelves. Why he was still here was a bit of a mystery. He should have left her to clean up her own mess. It had nothing to do with him.

Except Lacy had asked him to help. Of course, she had no idea that all this would happen. She wouldn't expect him to stay and do all this work, and his shoulder still ached from yesterday. The last thing he needed to do today was physical labor. He straightened, stretched his back, and glanced around the store. It would take days to get back in order.

Remy was standing in the corner sorting books. Her shoulders sagged, and she looked sad. There were already dark circles under her eyes. She was all alone in this. He needed to stay and help her if for no other reason than she'd never get it done if she didn't have help. He went back to picking up books.

Sometimes he cursed his protective nature. A woman in trouble was his weakness. It had gotten him into predicaments more often than not when he was younger, but he'd managed to curb it since working for Drake. But…there was something about Remy, something that pierced his armor and didn't bear thinking about.

In what seemed like years later, he picked up the last book off the floor. He'd consumed at least fifteen cups of tea and even eaten cucumber sandwiches without the crust, which he had to admit were quite tasty. Of course, he'd been working non-stop all day, so chances were good eating one of the books off the floor would have tasted delicious.

He stretched his arms over his head and was surprised to see the sun was just setting. He glanced at his watch. Twenty to five. That was it? He would have sworn it was midnight.

"You want tea?" Remy called from the kitchen.

"God, no—, um, no thanks."

Remy came out of the kitchenette with two tumblers full of amber liquid. "Good, me neither." She handed him a glass. "Bourbon," she said and took a sip.

He took a sip and enjoyed the burn that went down his throat. "Thanks."

She looked at him appraisingly. "Thank you. You stuck it out. I didn't think you would. I appreciate it."

"No problem." His shoulder said otherwise, but he didn't feel the need to share that. He cocked his head. "Where's Gus?"

"I sent him home a couple of hours ago. You seemed engrossed so he said to tell you it was nice to meet you."

He nodded and took another sip of bourbon as he leaned against the shelves. He'd been engrossed alright. Trying to avoid looking at Remy's ass every time she bent over. It had been a losing battle.

He glanced around the store. The pictures that had been on the walls were now on the front counter. Some of them were in need of repair. The shelves in the front were put back together the way they should be and the ones at the back had the books stacked on them at least. All in all, it was a good day's work.

He said, "I've spent the day wondering what they could've been searching for and if they found it."

She looked up at him and narrowed her eyes. "Searching for? You don't think this was Patterson just making a mess?" She'd decided earlier that it must be him. Another intimidation tactic.

"No." He swept an arm around the place. "Whoever did this was definitely after something."

Her shoulders sagged once more. He was sure she'd been fighting that thought all day. If he were in her shoes, he'd want it to be Patterson, too, because then at least it was a known entity.

She tapped a finger on the glass she held. "Yeah, I know, and I have no idea what."

"Was your grandfather into anything…sketchy?"

"Sketchy? Are you serious? No! He ran a bookshop. He didn't even do that much in rare books. He just loved to sit here and read and sell books to other readers."

And just how did he make enough money doing that? Hawk didn't say anything, but he was sure Remy's grandfather had to be into something illegal in order to make ends meet. It didn't matter that the book shop was in a prime location on the Upper West Side, with the major chain bookstores around and online shopping, he couldn't imagine that a small bookstore was making that much money. He didn't have the space to carry all the titles that the big stores did. People didn't want to wait for things to arrive either. Why order from him when they could get it delivered within two days? Even with loyal customers it would take a hell of a lot of book sales to pay the bills and eat. No, there was something else going on here or, at the very least, her grandfather had an alternate source of cash. Whatever it was, it seemed to be coming back on Remy.

He hadn't wanted to ask her earlier, and he certainly didn't have the energy to fix anything now, but he knew it needed to be done. "Did you check out your grandfather's apartment?"

"No. The tapestry covers the door. It's still in place, so I assumed it's all good."

He grimaced. "Well—"

"What?" she demanded.

He walked to the back corner of the store, and she followed. He pointed to the makeshift curtain. "The bottom is torn."

All the blood drained from her face, and she swayed on her feet. He reached out and grabbed her arm to steady her.

"I...guess I missed that. Now, I have to go check," she said, but didn't move.

"It'll keep. You've had a lot of shocks in the last twenty-four hours. Give yourself a bit of a break."

She shook her head. "No, I need to know." She took a bracing swig of her drink and then set the glass down on the shelf. She lifted the horse tapestry to the side and put her hand on the doorknob behind it. She turned the knob and gave the door a shove. It opened. "Fuck," she said. "That should've been locked. They've been here as well."

He wanted to reach out and give her shoulder a squeeze as a sign of support, but he wasn't sure she'd be open to that. It wasn't something he normally did, but Remy just seemed so lost, so alone that his protective instincts went into overdrive. He gave himself a mental shake.

She started up the stairwell, so he set his glass next to hers and followed.

Hawk thought about leading the way. Actually, what he wanted to do was make her wait downstairs while he checked the place out, but he knew for sure she'd never agree to that. She was fiercely independent and would no doubt take it as some kind of insult. The chances someone was still upstairs were practically zero at this point, and he didn't feel any danger lurking, but it still rankled him that she was charging in and not being more cautious.

"Maybe we should take it easy. Let me check—"

She threw open the door at the top of the stairwell.

"Or maybe not," he mumbled under his breath and shook his head.

The place had definitely been tossed. It wasn't as messy as downstairs, but someone had gone through it. Remy and Hawk entered at the end of a hallway. There were rooms off the hall. The first one was the kitchen, which was like the kitchenette downstairs, a total disaster area. The next room was a TV room, which wasn't too bad. The books were on the floor and the cushions were strewn about, but they hadn't been cut up and the stuffing was still inside them.

"Fucking assholes," Remy said as she moved down the hallway. The next room was a bedroom, which was a mess but again, they hadn't slashed the mattress or pulled the stuffing out of the chair. The last room on the left was a den of sorts. It had a desk and a hard chair along with shelves of books, which were now all on the floor like downstairs had been. Papers were scattered around the room, and the pictures had been pulled off the walls and smashed on the floor.

At the head of the hallway was a bathroom. That, too, had been tossed, but they hadn't emptied the shaving cream or shampoo bottles or anything. They knew the place hadn't been tossed for shits and giggles. Someone was definitely looking for something specific. All in all, Hawk had seen much worse.

Remy stood near the doorway that led downstairs, her arms crossed. "If I find these fuckers, I'll strangle them with my bare hands."

Hawk leaned against the wall and said nothing. There was nothing he could say at this moment that would make anything better, but the truth was those words coming from her mouth were all kinds of hot and he needed to take a moment to clear the thought of taking Remy to bed out of his mind.

"Do you want to call the police about this?" he asked in a quiet voice.

She shook her head. "What's the point?'

"Insurance claim. You'll need a police report to claim any damage."

She snorted. "We've been through this. What these fuckers damaged isn't something that can be fixed by insurance." She leaned back on the wall next to him and put her hands over her face.

"You can hire a cleaning service." He didn't want to upset her, but she was exhausted. The lines of her body screamed that she was beyond tired and stressed. The fine lines around her eyes had deepened and the dark circles beneath seemed to have turned black just since they came upstairs.

"I…"

"They can do the kitchen and the bathroom. I'll help you do the other rooms." He studied her.

She dropped her hands and gave a nod. "Maybe that's what I'll do. I'll take a pass through and pick the stuff up off the floor and put the furniture upright. Then I'll get a cleaning crew to clean the whole place."

At least she was seeing reason.

She bit her lip, lost in thought. "I think I'll start cleaning now, then I can stay here tonight."

So much for reason. "Ah, I'm not sure that's a great idea."

She turned to stare at him.

He hated to point out the obvious, but she had to understand what was going on. She would be putting herself in danger otherwise and he couldn't allow that. He wanted her as far from danger as she could get. For his own peace of mind. "Look, this place has been broken into twice in the last twenty-four hours, and you were also attacked. I think—"

"That's exactly right. Whoever it was has already been through here. They probably found what they were looking for, so it's not like they'll be back. If I stay here, I can work later and be up earlier to get everything up and running again. It's just easier."

He ran a hand through his hair. He was tired and didn't want to pick a fight, but she wasn't thinking straight. "You don't know if they found what they were looking for or not. To be honest, I don't think they did."

Her brows dipped with a frown. "What makes you think that?"

He bit the bullet. Time for some hard truths. "Look at this logically. If they found what they were looking for, then the whole place wouldn't be a mess, would it? They would have stopped searching once they found it. The fact that the whole place is trashed leads me to believe they didn't find it.

"Also, if you stay here, you are on your own. No one will hear you if you yell. No one will notice if you're in trouble. Say what you want about thin walls in the apartment buildings in Manhattan, but if you're in trouble, someone is bound to hear it."

Remy let out a puff of air. "I still think I should stay here. It's been searched. Even if they didn't find what they wanted, they know it's not here, so why bother coming back?"

"Unless they decide they need to check again. If they didn't find it, where else could it be?" He straightened off the wall and turned toward her. "If they think your grandfather has something they want, where else could he possibly have hidden it?"

"Nowhere. I mean"—she raised her arms— "this was his whole life."

"Exactly. So where else can they search? This is the most logical spot, unless..." He frowned. "Do you have any siblings? Did your grandfather have any other relatives?"

"No, it was just the two of us. Why?"

"Because..." He didn't want to scare her, but it had to be said. "Because if they didn't find whatever it is here, then the only other logical place to look would be..." He hesitated again.

Her eyes got big. "My place? You think they're going to search my place?"

He gave a small nod. "It depends. You live in an apartment, right? In a building?"

"Yes."

"Does it have a doorman?"

"No."

He hated to keep asking questions, but he had to know what the likelihood of success was if they decided to break in. "What floor are you on and in what part of the building? How many neighbors do you have on your floor?"

She wrapped her arms around her stomach as if to hold in her growing fear. The news was not going to be good. His gut tightened.

"I live on the ground floor. There are only three of us on the floor. It's a small walk-up." She swallowed hard. "The windows are on the alley and face the backyard."

His gut was well and truly knotted now, and his heart rate had ticked up a notch or two. His biggest nightmare. "Okay, do you have security bars on the windows?" *Please say yes.* That would be something at least.

She shook her head. "No, the building won't put them on. I've asked, but they say it's not necessary." She cleared her throat. "And to be fair, it hasn't been so far."

"So far," he mumbled. He'd like to meet the owners of Remy's building in a dark alley and show them what was necessary. His blood roared in his veins. His entire body was going into fight mode for a woman he'd only just met. He needed his head examined. "I'm going to make some calls and get you set up with a security system. It'll probably be a day or two before it's done, so we'll have to plan for that." He pulled his cell out of his pocket.

"I really can't afford a security system. Up until six months ago when my grandfather died, I worked as a librarian at the New York Public Library. They don't exactly pay fabulously. I have some savings, but nothing that would cover some high-tech security setup."

"It's fine. I'll take care of it, and we can work out something later." There was no way in hell he was going to let her turn him down. She needed protection, and he was damn well going to make sure she had it in one form or another.

Her eyes narrowed. "Just what do you mean—"

"Hey, Logan," he said when the man answered, purposely cutting her off. He didn't want to get into an argument with her. She needed security whether these people broke in or not. Ground floor apartment without security bars. *Jesus.* "I need a favor." He went on to explain what he needed and then got her to provide the address. It would be Monday before Logan could get anyone over to her place. He apologized for it, but Hawk brushed him off. "I get it. Monday is fine. And thanks. Tell Lacy I've got this, and Remy will be okay. I don't want Lacy to worry. Also tell her I started doing some research as we discussed and it's not looking so good."

"She trusts you, Hawk. We all do. We know you'll help Remy with whatever she needs. Consider it a trial run with us. Your first job at Callahan Security. If you like it, then you come to work for us full time. Call with anything you need. We'll get it to you."

Shit.

He paused. "That's …great. Thanks, Logan." He signed off and put the phone back in his pocket. Was it great? Suddenly he wasn't so sure.

Remy stood there in the hallway, glaring at him. "You just ignored me. How am I going to pay for this?" She folded her arms across her chest. "And what research are you talking about that doesn't look so good?"

Right. Of course she'd caught that. He'd come over this morning to get his gloves back and to tell her that his initial poking around about the locksmith company had turned up the fact that they incorporated the year before her great-grandfather had. He had no idea if they'd already had the logo at that point but, technically, they were around first. She was going to need that trademark paperwork if she had a hope of winning her case.

"Don't worry about the cost of the system. I'm sure Logan and Lacy will work with you on it." He wouldn't let that happen. He'd pay for the damn thing himself. "It should give you some warning, at least, if someone tries to break in." He took in her fighting stance and decided he might as well tell her everything and give her a push while he was at it. No point in beating around the bush. "You need to move."

She blinked rapidly, trying to process what he'd just told her.

He held up a hand. "Before you yell at me, I'm just being logical. A bottom floor apartment that's on an alley without bars on the windows is like an open invitation for criminals. You need to be in a more secure location. I know Manhattan apartments are expensive, but sacrificing your safety is not a good plan."

"No shit. I never would've thought of that," she fumed at him. "I don't know what you earn, but I don't make a lot of money, and I needed an apartment near my grandfather. My place is what I could afford." She put her hands on her hips. "I don't need you to lecture me on how unsafe it is, thank you very much."

He lifted his hands up again, a conciliatory gesture. "I didn't mean to lecture you. It's just…it bothers me that you are living somewhere that isn't the safest." A serious understatement.

"Well, it bothers me, too, but that's fucking life sometimes."

He stared at her. It was true. He'd been mansplaining to her. She didn't need him to tell her what was wrong with her place. She needed him to help her fix the problem, whether she admitted it or not.

"I'm sorry. That came out all wrong. You're right. You know the dangers. We'll get the security system up and running and then see what we can do to get the building owners to put some bars on the windows." He'd go after them and force them to do it no matter what it took.

"So…since they could break in here again and might possibly hit your apartment, I think it's best if you stay somewhere else for a few days."

All the fire went out of her, and she slumped against the wall. "I have no clue where else I could stay other than a hotel, and I'd rather not spend that kind of money."

She looked so sad. Her gray eyes were the color of clouds before a rainstorm. She had to be exhausted and feeling way out of her depth. And alone. She most likely had friends, but it's not like she'd want to drag them into this mess.

"I'm sure you could stay with Lacy or even at Callahan Security. They have some bedrooms there." That wasn't what he wanted but at least then he knew she'd be safe. No, he wanted her to be with him. And that thought bothered the hell out of him.

"No," she shook her head. "I don't want to ask for anything more than I have to from Lacy. I feel like I'm taking advantage of our friendship. It means too much to me to do that."

So, no telling her that Logan just hired him to look after her then.

"I'm sure she wouldn't see it—"

"I said no." Remy straightened. "I'll get an Airbnb here somewhere or stay at a hotel."

Oh hell no! He couldn't believe he was about to do this. It went against all his rules—every single one he lived by. No fraternizing with clients. Mixing business and pleasure was always a bad move. No overnight guests. He didn't like women to get comfortable in his space. But this was different. Remy was in desperate need, and something about her tugged at him, made him want to protect her fiercely. He took a deep breath. "Why don't you come stay with me? I don't live too far from here, and I have a spare bedroom."

She glanced at him, a surprised expression on her face. "I'm not sure..."

"I live in a high-rise with a doorman. It's a safe building, and it's close enough to walk to from here. It also has an en suite, so you'd have your own bathroom. It's just for a few days until we can make your place more secure." He braced himself to argue if she said no. Hell, he'd throw her over his shoulder and carry her there if he had to. This was a job now. Not just a favor for a friend. *Sure, that was the reason.* He didn't look too closely at his justification. He knew it wouldn't hold water.

She let out a long sigh but nodded. "Thanks. That would be good."

Hallelujah. His gut unknotted slightly. He didn't know why it mattered so much to him, but it did. He had to know she was safe. He wouldn't be able to sleep if he didn't. "Let's go get some food and then we can swing by your place and get your stuff."

She nodded. "Let's go. I'll start on this tomorrow."

They went back down the stairs and into the store. She locked the door and put the tapestry back in place.

"Where does that one lead? To a storeroom?"

"What?" Remy asked.

Hawk gestured to the other tapestry. "That door. Does it lead to the storeroom?"

"No. There is no door there. The tapestry is for show. A way to add symmetry and balance the space. You have to access the basement through the doors on the sidewalk. My grandfather didn't use it. He always just put the book deliveries next to him and worked on them in the store. Anything else, he did up in his apartment."

He frowned. That didn't make sense. He'd noticed a small seam in the wall right there when he was picking up books from the floor around it. He walked over to the other tapestry and tried to move it.

She snorted. "What? You don't believe me?"

"'Trust but verify.' My dad taught me that, and it's come in handy more times than I can count." He tugged at the tapestry again, but it still didn't move. "This one doesn't move?"

"Like I said, it's just a tapestry. He anchored it."

Her tone suggested she wasn't pleased with his actions, but he just couldn't help himself. He was positive he'd seen something earlier. He squatted down and studied the pole that the tapestry was attached to at the bottom. It was pulled tight so he couldn't slide the tapestry in one direction or the other, but if he lifted the pole out of the holder...

There was a *clunk* sound, and he had the pole out. Then he pushed the tapestry to one side.

"What are you doing?" Remy demanded. "Don't damage it. I don't want to lose it."

"I won't." He peered down at the baseboard. There was a definite crack in two places about the width of a small door. The wall itself didn't look like it had any seams, but with the busy wallpaper, it was hard to tell. He stood, still holding the tapestry to the side. What if he pushed the wall? He tried, but nothing happened. He moved his hands over the wall, pressing down in different places, but it wasn't moving.

Remy stood behind him, arms crossed over her chest, foot tapping. "Are you satisfied now? I told you it's just for show."

Hawk took the end of the tapestry and put it up on a

high shelf so it was mostly out of the way, and took a step back for a wider look. On either side of the tapestry were bookshelves that had stacks of books. Except one. On the right, at about shoulder level, there was a shelf that had one book still upright. The book was green but had no writing on the spine. He reached up and pulled the book. It gave at the top but not the bottom, so it came out at an angle.

The wall behind the tapestry slid back to reveal a staircase. "Open sesame," he murmured.

CHAPTER SIX

All the breath left Remy's lungs as she stared into the darkness. *What the hell?* When her head began to spin as if her whole world had shifted on its axis, she latched onto a shelf to hold herself upright.

How could she not know this existed? How could her grandfather not have told her? Wrapping her brain around this felt as futile as trying to wrap her arms around the Rock of Gibraltar. Her grandfather, her only living relative, had lied to her. *Her entire life.* He'd lied. There was nothing behind that tapestry, he'd tell her when she would ask to move it. *Nothing at all.*

"Remy." Hawk's voice finally broke through her thoughts.

She pulled in much-needed oxygen. "I—I had no idea. He always said there was nothing behind this tapestry. He never mentioned the door. Not once." She let go of the shelf, but her hands continued to tremble. *This couldn't be happening.* She wrapped her arms around herself when a cool dampness seeped out from the stairwell. "Where do you think it leads?" Her voice came out in a whisper. She cleared her throat. *Okay, now she knew she was discombobulated. Of course it led to the basement.*

She stared into the dark hole. A dank, musty smell burned her nostrils. The stairs were stone, as were the walls. The stairway was quite narrow as well and there wasn't a handrail of any sort. It was just stone leading down into darkness.

Hawk shrugged. "New York has all kinds of hidden underground spaces. There are old subway stations that went out of use, and they just blocked them up. They say there are even people living underground in parts of the city."

She shuddered. None of that sounded like anything she wanted a part of. "Maybe that's why my grandfather never told me about this. Maybe it leads to one of those spaces, and it's not safe." But if that was the case, wouldn't Grandfather have sealed the space better? Boarded it up, or bricked it in?

"Maybe," Hawk said, but his tone was doubtful. "There's only one way to find out. Got a flashlight?"

Was he crazy? "You're going down there?"

He smiled at her. "Why not? We need to know where it goes."

"Why? He kept it hidden for years. Do we really need to know anything about it now?" Panic gripped her throat, driving her voice high. Her palms were sweaty. The last thing she wanted was to find out something horrible about her grandfather.

She'd been able to fool herself for a long time about how he made money, about how he lived. She'd even fooled herself into believing the break-ins had nothing to do with him. But deep down she knew the truth. Grandfather had a shady side—one she wasn't keen to explore. He'd been the last relative she'd had. Finding out he'd been less than perfect hadn't been an option when he was alive. Was it an option now that he was dead?

Hawk was staring at her, waiting. She closed her eyes. Logically, they had to know where the stairs went. Her curiosity would get the better of her at some point in the future, and she would have to check it out. Better that she did it now with Hawk holding her hand as she climbed down the stone steps to an awareness she might not want. As much as the man could be insufferable, she knew instinctively he'd protect her. And the literal last thing she wanted to do was go down those stairs on her own.

"I think I should probably tell you that my grandfather may have been into something shady." Merely saying those words out loud grated on her, leaving her raw.

He cocked an eyebrow at her. "May have been?"

"Okay," she snarled. "He was, all right? He was into something shady." She bit her lip as she tucked a stray hair behind her ear. Getting mad at Hawk wasn't helpful. She needed to direct that anger where it belonged... at her grandfather.

"How do you know?" Hawk asked.

"Because he died a very rich man." At his blank look, she heaved an exasperated sigh and continued. "There's nothing here in the bookshop or anywhere else in his life that could account for the amount of money he had. When I questioned the bank about the sum, or the source of the funds, they said the income came from some company I'd never heard of. I didn't find any paperwork about it in the store." She hadn't been able to search the apartment upstairs, not just because it was his home and she missed him, but because she was terrified of the truth she might find there.

Hawk leaned against the bookcase. "That's why you kept the bookstore as is and never cleaned out his place. You were afraid of what you might find."

She nodded slowly. "He was all I had." Her words came

out whisper-thin as she rubbed her arms trying to warm herself from the sudden coldness filling her chest.

Hawk reached out and pulled her into his arms, wrapping her in a big warm hug. "It's going to be okay. It doesn't matter who your grandfather was to the rest of the world. He was good to you and took care of you. That's what you have to remember. The rest just isn't important, Remy."

She wanted to believe that. She let the warmth from Hawk's embrace seep into her, body and soul. If someone had told her this morning that she would welcome a hug from this man, she would have told them they were crazy. But somehow, she seemed to draw strength from the man who had annoyed her all day and it felt so damn good.

Finally, she straightened. "I think I have a flashlight at the front." She moved out of the circle of his arms and immediately missed his touch. All this had thrown her for a loop. That had to be why her heart was pounding, right? She stepped around the front counter, mentally chastising herself... *get it together, girl.*

Bending down, she retrieved the flashlight from the back of the shelf. She tested it, to be sure it was working, then started toward Hawk, but changed her mind halfway there, pivoting toward the front door to make sure the lock was engaged. She pulled down the blinds on the door and the window seat. No one had to see them going through the hidden staircase. Somehow, she knew that would be a bad thing.

She walked back over to Hawk and handed him the flashlight. "Here." She glanced through the doorway. "Let's do this."

He nodded once and turned on the flashlight. Her stomach rolled as she followed him down the old stone steps. The dank smell eased as they went lower. She kept her hands running along the old stone walls as she descended.

The staircase was longer than she'd assumed. There was a landing and a turn she hadn't seen from above. The walls widened out at the landing, alleviating some of the claustrophobia crushing in on her. When they arrived at the bottom, Hawk reached out and hit a switch on the wall. The area flared into light, revealing something resembling a foyer but larger. She guessed maybe fifteen by ten feet, more like a large closet. Four wall sconces, one per wall, banished all the shadows.

She looked around, and any denial she might have harbored that her grandfather couldn't have known about this place disappeared. His sweater hung on a hook by a steel door. Her stomach churned... he had lied to her. Her heart hurt with the knowledge of his betrayal. It was past time for her to admit her grandfather wasn't the man she'd thought he was. No, that was unfair. She still didn't know anything yet. And that was the problem. It was like she didn't know her grandfather at all.

Hawk studied the door. He tried the knob, but it didn't turn. There was a keypad with some sort of screen next to the door, and at about eye level, there was another device. "That's a biometric set up using both eye scans and handprints to grant access."

"What do you mean?" she asked.

He pointed to the keypad with the flat screen. "I'm pretty sure we would need to key in a code and then put a hand on the reader. The electronics inside would read the prints." He stopped and looked up at the wall. "That, in turn, will activate the retinal scanner, which then scans the person's eye. I'm guessing that would unlock the door."

"Jesus," she muttered. "What the hell is down here?" Her heart thundered in her chest. What had her grandfather been into? She was becoming more and more convinced there was a criminal nature to whatever it was.

He pointed to a small cut out in the door. "Or someone on the inside can open the door once they see…someone. That's a window. Like a window to see who's there without opening the door. Maybe people have to be verified before they are let in."

"You mean like showing ID?"

He shrugged. "I have no idea, but I assume whoever is on the inside needs to get a look at who's at the door before they open it."

"How long do you think this has been here?" she asked, dreading the answer.

He glanced at her. "The door is fairly new and in good shape, and the electronics are close to state of the art. Also, the light switch on the wall is brand new by the looks of things." Hawk let his gaze travel along the walls. "But the stairs are old. If you look at the wall hooks, they are also old. So, I think this entrance has been here for a long time but has had some recent upgrades in security."

"Do you think we can find a way in?"

He glanced at her. "At this moment? No. I'd need tools."

"What kind of tools?"

He squatted down to get a closer look at the panel and the keypad. Then he stood and peered at the retinal scanner. "Tools I don't have, but I know who does." He glanced around the foyer they were standing in and then swore. "I don't think we can break in anytime soon."

"Why? I need to know what's behind that door." She'd come this far. She wasn't stopping now.

"Because"—he pointed to the ceiling—"we're on camera."

In the corner of the room, there was a tiny round circle. It blended in so well with the dark stone walls, she could hardly pick it out. Until it moved slightly. "Shit."

"Someone knows we're here." Hawk confirmed her suspicions.

All of a sudden, a wave of pure rage washed over her, and she yelled, "Hey you fuckers! Open the damn door!" She needed to know what the fuck was going on, and she wasn't going to stop until she figured it out. The camera moved a bit again. "Hey, asshole! Open the door." She kicked it for good measure which didn't hurt the door but killed her foot.

Hawk put a hand on her arm. "Yelling and calling them names is not going to work. They're not going to let us in."

"How do you know?" she demanded.

"Because if they were going to, they'd have already opened the door for us. We've been down here long enough, and they've been watching us. No one is going to suddenly open the door now and invite us in."

"So, what are we going to do? I need to know what's going on." She turned back and banged on the door, yelling again.

Hawk grabbed her arm. "Stop. It's not going to work."

"But I need—"

"Not now," he said through clenched teeth, grabbing her attention. "We need to get out of here." She wanted to argue with him, but the tension evident on his face made an impression. He'd gone from lawyer to something else… predator or protector? She didn't know but it set her heart thumping in her chest. His eyes had darkened, and she would guess every one of his senses was on high alert. He'd become a dangerous man. *Thank God he was on her side. Wasn't he?*

He turned her and shoved her back, pushing her up the stairs ahead of him. "Move," he growled.

She took the stairs two at a time and burst into the store again. She turned to see Hawk come out behind her, and then he froze.

She turned around to find three men standing in the middle of her shop. "Who the fuck are you?" she demanded, "And how did you get in here?" She looked at the door, but the lock didn't look broken.

Hawk came up and touched her arm. "These are the men that run whatever is downstairs."

"What? How do you know that?" She stared at the men.

He moved so he was slightly ahead of her. She knew instinctively that he was positioning himself to protect her. Why? What did these men want?

The tallest man wore a black leather jacket and jeans and sat down on her stool, his emerald-green eyes studying her. He flicked his dark hair out of his eyes and offered a cold smile. "Listen to your friend. He seems to know what he's talking about."

"But who are you?" she demanded.

"I'm a friend of your grandfather's." His deep voice sent shivers along her skin.

She stared at him. "What kind of friend? I've never met you, and you didn't come to the funeral, so you can't have been that close. Who are you really?"

"Your grandfather was a good man, if a bit old-fashioned. I'm sorry for your loss. I know this must be a difficult time for you." He glanced around the shop. "It looks like you're making some changes in here."

She snorted. "Like you don't know, asshole. You did this, didn't you?"

His eyes narrowed. "Did what exactly?"

"You and your goons." She gestured to the bald man with the pale scar on his cheek and the blond man wearing the puffy jacket. "You broke in and tossed my shop. Twice! Asshole!" she snarled again.

His face went blank, and she could have sworn she heard

his teeth click together. "That wasn't me or any of my people."

"Oh, sure. Then how did you get into my shop? It's like the last two times. No damage to the lock, but someone who doesn't belong is inside."

His eyes narrowed slightly again. He seemed to have some kind of unspoken communication with Hawk because Hawk gave a slight nod.

Hawk said, "He's telling the truth, I think. It wasn't him, but he knows who, or at least he knows something about it, don't you?"

The man nodded slightly. "Unfortunately, I can't really comment on it. I can tell you I got in with my key."

"You have a key?" Her voice went so high she squeaked.

He nodded. "Your grandfather gave it to me."

"Why the fuck would he do that?" Her grandfather never gave out keys. She had one and Gus. He hadn't even given one to Emily who worked there.

"We were partners, of a sort."

Her stomach rolled. *This has to be about the money. What the hell had her grandfather gotten involved in?* "Could you be any more vague? What is going on?"

He cocked his head. "Your grandfather didn't tell you anything?"

"No, he fucking didn't. So why don't you tell me?" She was so damn tired of being in the dark. She needed answers.

A buzzing noise startled her. The man on the stool pulled a phone from his pocket and glanced at the screen. He looked up and caught the eye of the blond man to his right and then gestured to the outside with his head. The blond nodded once and went out the door.

He turned back to her. "I'm sorry, I can't tell you anything. That would be against the rules."

"The rules? What rules? Seriously, what the fuck is going on?" she demanded.

"What I can tell you is to leave the tapestry in front of that door and keep the door closed. It won't help you to have the door open or to bring anyone down the stairs. You won't be allowed in unless you can show me…" He stopped speaking and stared at her.

"Show you what?"

He gave a small shrug. "Nothing. It doesn't matter at this point. Just keep the door closed and don't come down the stairs."

Adrenaline blasted through her veins. "And what if I don't want to do that? What if I want to go down and bang on your fucking door? Maybe I'll bring the cops down there with me!"

Hawk shifted his weight slightly. "I don't think that would be a wise move, Remy."

The man shoved his phone back into his pocket. "Listen to your friend. He seems quite smart. Informing the police wouldn't end well for you."

Was he threatening her? "Why? What the fuck are you going to do about it?"

"I'd have to kill you. And the cop."

She jolted backward a step or two. Was he serious? He was. She knew it with every fiber in her being. He was deadly serious. There was nothing but coldness in those green eyes.

He stood. "I'm sorry about the break-ins. It may happen again. It will be a few days before things…calm down, or it could be longer. You might want to go away for a while. Might be better for your safety." He looked directly at Hawk. "Finding her a safe place to stay would be advisable. It will take some time for things to…sort themselves out. She will be at risk until that happens." He started to move around the counter. "Oh, and please stop with the cease and desist letters. The logo is ours. Your great-grandfather designed it *for us*. Calling attention to the locksmith shop is not in your best interest, nor is calling attention to yourself, especially now. Don't waste our time and yours or it will end badly for you."

She wanted to throw up. The man headed out of the store. "Wait!" When she moved forward toward the man, the bald guy removed a gun from behind his back and aimed it at her.

Hawk immediately pulled her back and stood between her and the gun. She tried to move around him, but he held her arm behind him. She had to peek around his shoulder. "Wait," she said again. "What's your name?"

He smiled but didn't answer.

"Leave my fucking key!" she yelled.

He looked at her and nodded. He pulled the key out of his pocket and placed it on the counter. "Again, I'm sorry for your loss. I liked your grandfather very much. I miss him." With that, he strode out of the store with the bald guy following.

Hawk finally let go of her arm and hurried to the door and flipped the lock. He turned back to face her. "Are you okay?"

"No, I'm not fucking okay!" She bent and braced her hands on her knees, lowering her head in hopes that her heart would jump back into normal rhythm. "Who was that? What was he talking about? What rules? Why couldn't he tell me anything? What the hell is going on?" Her voice rose in pitch and volume.

Hawk's hand rested on her back, but she shook him off and straightened.

He let out a long breath. "I can't answer any of those questions, but I know a way we might be able to find some answers."

She walked across the store and was reaching for the key the man had left, when Hawk lunged after her and grabbed her arm.

"What now?" God she was all out of fucks to give, and she let that bleed through to her tone.

"Fingerprints. I'll ask the Callahans to run this for prints, and maybe then we can figure out who we're dealing with and get an inkling of what's going on. Do you have a baggie or cling wrap? I want to put the key in something without touching it."

She curled her lips together and then went into the kitchenette. This was insane. *Insane.* How could her grandfather not tell her about…whatever the hell this was? He'd left her vulnerable. How could he have done that to her? She grabbed the edge of the counter as a wave of sadness took her by surprise, tumbling her emotions as if caught in a violent tide. He'd betrayed her. The one person she trusted most in the world had left her lost and in the dark. Tears rolled down her cheeks.

She grabbed a paper towel and buried her face in it. But only for a moment. Then, squaring her shoulders, she grabbed a baggie and returned to the front of the store. "What are you doing?" she said when she saw Hawk down on his knees by the tapestry.

"I'm closing the door and putting the tapestry back in place. You heard him. It's not safe to keep going down there."

She started to argue with him, but he cut her off. "I know you want answers, but there's no point in endangering your life to do it. He wasn't joking when he said he'd kill you."

She shuddered and rubbed her arms. Suddenly, she was quite cold. "No, I got that. He was serious. I just don't understand any of this. What was my grandfather mixed up in?"

Hawk finished adjusting the tapestry and stood. "I don't know, but I'm going to help you find out."

She felt a rush of relief at those words. Hawk was solid, a source of strength, someone she could depend on, no matter that she'd been taking care of herself for years, only her and no one else. The thought of being in this all on her own was overwhelming and scary as hell. She wasn't sure how much help Hawk would be, but she just didn't have a choice. She'd welcome all the help she could get.

CHAPTER SEVEN

Hawk handed Remy a glass of bourbon and sat down on the chair to her left. It was unsettling to have her here in his space, but his momentary inconvenience was more than offset by the relief he felt having her close and knowing she was safe. Through the glass doors to the balcony a murky thread, the Hudson River, ran through the city, shrouded in darkness, but the sight was a comfort, something old and enduring to soften the weirdness of his day.

Also, there was immense satisfaction that his SEAL instincts made him choose an apartment with no possible angle for a sniper to take aim at him, or his guest. At least, that was true on this side of the river. Less than a handful of snipers could make the shot from the New Jersey side. Always important to note. Although he was a normal citizen when he'd signed on the dotted line, a holdover adherence to training from his Navy days was something he was very thankful for at this particular juncture.

"Do you think Gus might know something?" Hawk asked.

Remy blinked and stared at him, but her eyes were glazed and unfocused and her cheeks were pale. The signs of shock were easy to recognize, and he couldn't fault her for it. He knew just how wrenching it must be for her to realize someone she loved had lied to her for her entire life.

He'd been there.

When he discovered that his much older sister was actually his mother, it had blown his mind. That untold truth had been the catalyst for him joining the military. It was his way of getting away from her and getting back at her at the same time. She'd worried about him every damn day. So had his parents/grandparents, but they'd understood. What they didn't understand was how the fact that his whole life had been a lie had fucked him up inside. In a way he didn't have a clue who he was. It had turned his world upside down.

The fact his mother wouldn't tell him about his father was just the icing on the cake. In life, he'd found that knowing his roots was super important, and once everything he'd ever thought was true was revealed as a lie, it made him feel like his entire life was a lie.

He didn't know if he looked like his grandfather anymore. Maybe he looked more like his father, but since he didn't know who that was, the answer to the question would never be his. It had screwed him up in more ways than one.

The SEALs had helped put his head on right. It brought out a lot of his strengths, and it fed his need for action. But his military service also took a toll on him and, in the end, he was ready to leave. Now, though, he didn't know what he wanted anymore.

The law had a steadying effect on him. It helped him to come to terms with his mother and his grandparents. He had a better relationship with all of them because of it. They weren't close anymore. He just couldn't bring himself to trust them in quite the same way, but at least now he could stand to be in the same room with them. They'd given him some, if not all, of the answers he needed and, in the end, he found he didn't necessarily need the other answers so much anymore.

Well, he hadn't. Now he didn't know. The restlessness was back. The need for action. The desire to be back in the fight. Would working for Callahan Security scratch that itch for him? He still wasn't sure, but he didn't have to make the decision today. The trial run with the current situation with Remy would hopefully provide him with the answers he needed. He'd already emailed Drake and asked for some time off, which had been promptly granted. Now was the ideal time to test the waters and see if it was the right time to go back into the fray. Or if he even wanted to be in that line of work. God, it sucked not feeling like he had a clear direction.

He stared at Remy. She still hadn't answered his question, but the color was coming back in her cheeks from the bourbon. Maybe he should have given her tea.

"Maybe," she said.

"Pardon?"

"Maybe Gus knows something. A few hours ago, I would have said Gus knew my grandfather inside out and backwards but, honestly, I just have no clue."

"It's a tough one." He had the urge to go over, pull Remy onto his lap and tell her everything would be okay. He thought back to when he'd hugged her before and how lust had sharpened as she'd leaned against him. *This wasn't helping.*

"I need answers," she said and then took a sip of her drink.

"I know," he agreed. I know what it's like, believe it or not. If you want my help to find those answers, you have it."

She offered him a thin smile. "I know I haven't been the easiest person to work with, but I sincerely appreciate everything you've done so far. I know you're only doing it because Lacy asked you, but I'm grateful all the same."

Sure, that was the reason. It might have started that way but somewhere in that bookstore today, something in his soul was unleashed and now he was in it no matter what. He knew it like he knew his sixth sense. Remy needed him and he'd be there whether she wanted him to be or not but it would be much easier if she agreed to it.

She continued, "I would love to say something noble like, 'This could be dangerous and I don't want you to get hurt so I'll do it on my own.' But frankly, I have no idea what to do, and I'll take all the help I can get."

Hawk grinned. "Not exactly a ringing endorsement, but I'll take it."

"I didn't mean—"

He waved her off. "No offense taken. I do have some ideas about where we can start. I spoke with Logan again. He'll meet us at Callahan Security in the morning and get the ball rolling on running prints from the key. Maybe they'll have some ideas about whatever is going on at the bottom of the stairs."

"That all sounds great." She tried to cover a yawn, but it was obvious she was exhausted.

It was only a little after eight, but it had been a long day. After locking the shop again, they'd picked up some clothing from her place and then got some Chinese take-out and brought it back to his place. They'd eaten, but Remy had remained silent and pale. He'd finally broken out the bourbon in an attempt to help with the shock. It worked, but now she was falling asleep.

"Why don't we get you settled? You can take a shower

and crawl into bed. It's been a rough day full of shocks and upset. You need some serious sleep." And he needed some time away from Remy. Her presence was screwing with his equilibrium. He needed to focus if he was going to protect her.

She looked like she might argue with him, but then she leaned forward and set her glass on the coffee table. "I think that would be good. I'm exhausted and seem to be in a brain fog."

He stood and gestured for her to proceed him out of the living room and down the hallway. "First door on your right." He grabbed her bag from the front hallway and followed behind her.

She entered the bedroom, but he stayed at the doorway, setting her bag down just inside the door. The room had a queen-size bed with matching nightstands and a dresser. It was large by New York standards and had an en suite bathroom.

"This is really nice," she said in a quiet voice. "I love the cream-colored duvet. It makes the bed look so inviting."

"That's just because you're so tired," he said, "but I'll take the compliment."

She yawned.

He smiled at her. "I won't keep you up. The bathroom is through there, and everything you need should be there, either in the vanity or on the shelves. If you're missing anything, just let me know.

She nodded. "Thanks."

He turned to go.

"Hawk?"

"Yeah?" He faced her again. She walked across the room and stopped directly in front of him. He had the strongest urge to pull her to him and kiss her until the fear in her eyes vanished, replaced by something baser. *Hawkins, don't be an asshole.*

Their gazes locked. "I really mean it. Thanks. I'm not sure I would have gotten through today without your help." She rose on her tiptoes and kissed his cheek, but she stumbled slightly, and he instinctively brought his arms around her and crushed her to his chest. Raw lust sparked through his veins. There was an electric current running between them like nothing he'd experienced before.

He wanted Remy like he hadn't wanted any woman. Those gray eyes held him captive, and the feel of her curves against him was almost too much.

She made a sound in her throat, and the fog of lust lifted. He removed his arms and took a quick step back. "No problem. Glad I could help." Giving her a quick smile, he bade her good night and closed the door.

He walked down the hallway to the living room and picked up his bourbon, downing the remaining alcohol in one big swallow.

Seeing the depth of her vulnerability had kicked every protective instinct he had into overdrive, but the fact that she dropped her tough exterior and gave him a glimpse into her softness had made his heart lurch in his chest just a bit. It had also kicked other things into motion. This was supposed to be a job. If he wasn't careful, he'd end up getting tangled up personally with Remy and that would be all bad.

"Thanks for doing this," Hawk said as he sat down on the same stool he'd vacated a couple of days ago.

"Not a problem." Logan nodded toward Lacy and Remy, who were sitting on the sofa in front of the fire. "She okay?"

He shook his head. "I have no idea. It's a hell of a thing

to find out someone you loved and trusted has been lying to you for your whole life."

"I can't imagine." Logan's phone buzzed, and he glanced at the screen. "That's interesting. The prints didn't have a match in the law enforcement databases, but they did come back in a military one. They belong to one Archer Gray."

Hawk frowned. "Never heard of him. You?"

Logan shook his head. "Apparently, he was in the Army. A Ranger. The file is mostly redacted, so I can't tell you much. Let's see… was born in Europe, country redacted. Jesus, his file is a mess, and a lot of it is missing." Logan scanned his phone silently, a frown pinching his brows. "Okay, he spent the first part of his life in Italy. He grew up all over the world, by the looks of things. The file stops five years ago. I've got nothing on him since then."

"So, you have no idea what he's into?"

Logan shook his head. "I had the tech guys check and check again, but nothing. I even asked Dani to take a look, but she says she can't find anything either. Unless we know where we want her to look, she can't really help."

"Huh. That's weird. Five years is a long time to go dark."

"Agreed."

The elevator doors opened, and Dragan stepped out, followed by Mitch. They strode across the room and took stools on either side of Hawk.

"I hear you're looking for information on Archer Gray," Dragan said. "You don't want to do that."

"What? Why? What do you know?" Hawk asked. Dragan warning him off set off alarm bells. He wasn't known for overreacting.

Dragan studied Hawk for a second. "Archer Gray is a deadly son of a bitch. Nothing good will come from tangling with him."

"I concur," Mitch said and popped a cookie into his mouth from the plate that was on the bar.

"Does someone want to fill us in?" Logan asked.

Mitch swallowed his cookie. "I've only heard rumors about him, but none of them—and I repeat: None. Of. Them—are good. He's an assassin."

Hawk tried to make sense of what they were saying. "So, he's a gun for hire?"

Dragan made a sound. "Not any longer. At one time, he was the best in the business."

"And you know this how?" Hawk needed details. Vague warnings weren't going to work for him.

"Because I used to work with him." Dragan said it so matter of fact that it took a moment for it to sink in.

Hawk blinked. "Um, I…" He had no idea what to say to that.

Logan put a cup of coffee down in front of Hawk. "I think you're gonna need this."

Dragan smiled slightly. "There's no need for detail, but earlier in my…career, I worked for some rather nefarious organizations."

"Nefarious," Mitch sputtered, pointing at Dragan. "You've been hanging out with Logan too much." He turned to Hawk. "After Dragan got out of the SEALs, he worked for serious crime organizations over in Croatia and some other countries in Europe before he saw the error of his ways. He was considered the best at—"

"Problem solving," Dragan said with a sardonic grin. "Let's just say I was proactive, and my bosses liked that."

"So where does Archer Gray come in? I thought you said he was the best."

Dragan nodded as the smile slipped from his face. "Archer and I moved in the same circles. We were…competitors, in a manner of speaking, until I got out of that line of work. Then he rose to the top. Five years ago, he dropped out of sight."

"Well, he's here in New York and he's up to something. I just wish I knew what." And he wished Remy wasn't Gray's focal point. Hawk filled the three men in on the situation at the bookstore. "He said he'd kill us and any cop we brought down there with us."

"Jesus. He's not playing around." Mitch shook his head.

"Logan, pass me that napkin," Dragan said. He pulled a pen out of his pocket and started drawing on the napkin. A minute later, Dragan pointed to the napkin. "Did Archer mention anything about this?"

Hawk looked down at the napkin. Dragan had drawn a key with a skull winking at the bow. "He didn't say a word about it, but how do *you* know about it? That's Remy's logo and she's upset that the locksmith store around the corner started using the same logo as her shop. That's why she called Lacy in the first place. What does this logo have to do with anything?"

Dragan paused. "Back up a minute. You're saying that Remy's book shop uses this logo?"

Hawk nodded. "Yes, her family has used it for almost a hundred years. They used to own a locksmith shop. Now it's a book shop, but they kept the name and the symbol."

Dragan had gone still. "What's the name of Remy's shop?"

"Under Lock and Key Books."

Dragan didn't say anything, but his face went hard. His gaze turned first toward Remy and then back to Hawk. "You need to get her out of town. Far away. She is not safe."

Hawk's gut knotted. "Archer Gray said the same thing." He'd also instructed Remy to drop the legal action against the locksmith. "What the fuck is going on?" Hawk didn't like people telling him Remy was in danger and, for damn sure, didn't like that that they weren't telling him why.

Remy must have sensed something because she asked from across the room, "Are you discussing the shop?"

Hawk hesitated but then nodded. It was her store, and in the end, her problem. He was just along for the ride. "Maybe you should come over here and hear this."

Remy and Lacy walked over. Mitch and Hawk stood and let the women have the stools.

"Dragan was just about to explain something to us. It's something to do with the logo of your shop," Logan said.

Dragan let out a breath. "The key with the winking skull is the symbol of the Lock and Key Society."

Remy frowned. "But it's been our logo for almost a hundred years."

Dragan nodded. "I believe the society has been around that long." He hesitated. "I don't have a lot of information, just some rumors I heard over the years that I've pieced together."

Hawk shrugged. "We'll take anything you have that might help solve the current situation." He tried to remain calm, but his instincts were on blast. Whatever was coming was gonna be all bad.

"Okay," Dragan said, "The Lock and Key Society is…" He stopped speaking and glanced at nothing in particular. "It's hard to describe. Essentially, it's like an old-fashioned gentleman's club, only now it's unisex. It caters to a very select crowd. I'm not sure how they are picked or what they have to do to be admitted. I do know each member possesses a token of some kind that identifies them as a member. They have to present that token before they can enter. Each token is linked to a specific person. However, if someone new shows up with the token, they are admitted and added to the list. The person who no longer has the token is stricken from the list *if* they are still alive. I imagine that most are killed for the token."

Hawk froze. Killed for a token? At his side, Remy made a small sound, and all the color had drained from her cheeks. He swore quietly. "Logan," he said and indicated Remy with a tilt of his head. Logan nodded and quickly brought a glass of water for Remy. Hawk would have preferred something with a bit more kick to remedy the shock, but Remy took the glass and sipped the water.

"Jesus, Dragan," Hawk began, "what kind of club is this?" He couldn't quite get his brain around what Dragan was saying.

"The Society is a place for people to…relax, recuperate, take some downtime without anyone bothering them."

"So, it's a fancy spa hotel thing?" Remy asked in a quiet voice. "Who would kill to go to one of those?"

"No. You misunderstand me. It's more like an extremely luxurious safe house." Dragan studied her for a moment. "Say, for example, the head of a crime family of a certain city wants to hide from the police or some rival family. They can go to a Lock and Key Society location and be completely safe without taking their own security. They can bring their family as well. If they have children, teachers can be brought in so the kids don't miss school. Whatever they want will be brought in to service their needs."

He continued. "Say this person wants to meet with another crime head to sort out their issues. Lock and Key is a place where they can meet where no one else can overhear. If two rivals, criminal or political or whatever, show up, no one is allowed to touch the other. They must obey the house rules. Even non-members can be brought to certain spaces to meet with members. The Lock and Key Society will then provide security and guarantee the member's safety. I assume there's some kind of financial commitment that must be met so that the people in charge can run the society, but I have no details on that."

Hawk cocked his head. "So, if you're looking for a safe place to lie low, you go there."

"If you're a member," Dragan agreed. "Or if you want to hold a sensitive political meeting and want to meet where no one will know, that's the place. It's more discreet than the members' lounge at the United Nations.

It suddenly clicked for Hawk. "Or if you get shot and you need a doctor but can't go to the hospital, you go to a Lock and Key site, and they take care of you?"

Dragan nodded.

"The shoe!" Remy's eyes got big. "This man came into the shop, yelling that he had a shoe and I had to help him. He must have seen the logo on the sign outside. I had no idea what he was talking about, but he had to be looking for the Lock and Key Society. That's what's downstairs."

Hawk didn't say anything. He knew it would take Remy a minute to connect the rest of the dots, but the whole picture was crystal clear to him, and Remy really was in serious danger. A cold, hard ball of fear sat in the pit of his stomach.

"Wait," she turned and looked at Hawk. "That means my grandfather must have, what? Ran the site? He let people in and down the staircase?"

Hawk nodded. "It would make sense." The nightmare for Remy was only beginning. He mentally cursed her grandfather for dragging her into this. At least he should've had the decency to warn her.

"Dragan," he said, "do you think that means Remy's grandfather was also a member?"

"If I had to guess, I'd say there's a possibility he was a member, but almost certainly an employee."

Her eyes widened. "The money! That's where it came from."

Hawk knew she still wasn't getting the full scope of things. He cursed silently again. "Remy," he said quietly, "your grandfather must have been a member. Your shop was tossed twice and his apartment upstairs. People are looking for his token."

Her mouth formed an *O*, then she clamped it shut again, and she closed her eyes. "Shit," she said between clenched teeth. "Wait, why was he the first one to come in? My grandfather died six months ago. Shouldn't someone have wandered in by now?"

It was a good point. "My guess is they must have some way to contact the members when sites close or something happens. The new shop with the same name opened around the block. My guess is he just got mixed up. Being stabbed will do that to you." Hawk didn't say it but he knew from experience.

"Do you think a lot of people will look for my grandfather's token? How many times will my shop get tossed? When will this stop?"

Dragan locked gazes with Hawk. They were thinking the same thing. This wouldn't be over until someone found the token. Remy would be in imminent danger, no matter where she was until the token was found. Hawk's heartbeat ticked up in his chest as adrenaline surged through his veins. Remy was going to need serious protection. It was going to take all his skills to keep her safe but he for damn sure wasn't going to let her out of his sight. Not for a moment if he could avoid it.

Remy looked up at Hawk. "Then I guess we have to find the token."

He blinked. *What? No way!* "Um, Remy, I'm not sure you are understanding this."

"I understand perfectly. My life will always be in danger until that token is found. Running won't make that go away. If these tokens are as precious as Dragan says, then people will stop at nothing to get one. I'm not spending the rest of my life looking over my shoulder, waiting for someone to kill me for something I don't have."

CHAPTER EIGHT

"She's right," Mitch said. "People will come looking for the token, probably already have. They're not going to believe she doesn't have it. It's better that she does have it, and if she wants to give it up, then she can. That should take the pressure off."

Remy cocked her head. They were missing something. Who was she kidding? They were missing nearly everything, but something was niggling at her. What exactly... "Why did no one try and take my grandfather's token until after he died, assuming he had one, of course?"

Hawk nodded. "Good point. Why did no one attack him for his token when he was alive?"

Dragan leaned on the bar. "What makes you think they didn't?"

Remy snorted. "I think I would know if someone attacked my grandfather..." She let out a loud sigh. "Or, at least, I thought I would know." Her body tensed painfully and her heart slammed against her rib cage. "Oh, my god! Do you think that's what happened? That someone attacked him for his token, and that's why he died?"

A wave of nausea rose in her belly. Had she let someone get away with killing her grandfather? The police had said he'd fallen off a ladder and hit his head on the shelving behind him, which then had knocked a bunch of books down on top of him. Did someone make that happen? Her stomach clenched and she fought down rising bile.

Logan immediately set a glass of amber liquid next to her water. "Take a drink. It'll help."

She took the glass and drank half of it. It burned all the way down, but he was right. The warmth spread in her stomach, unknotted it a bit and calmed her queasiness. She set the glass back on the bar. "Thanks." She smiled weakly at him.

Hawk stood beside her. He touched her arm. "Do you want to tell us how your grandfather died?"

She blinked to try to focus. What she really wanted to do was throw herself into Hawk's arms and have him hold her tight. She needed his strength, his calm in the storm that was her life right now but that wasn't going to happen.

She cleared her throat. "Right." Only Lacy knew and, she presumed, Logan but the rest would be in the dark. She explained the situation and then took another sip of the whiskey. It was early in the morning for alcohol, but she didn't really care. It seemed like it was the only thing keeping her steady. That and Hawk's presence. It was reassuring. Solid. Somehow, she knew he wouldn't go off and leave her in the middle of this mess on her own. But could she ask him to continue to help her?

"Was your grandfather buried or cremated?" Mitch asked in a quiet voice.

"Sorry, what?" She'd been so lost in thought she missed what Mitch had said.

Mitch repeated the question.

"Buried," Remy answered. "He picked out a family plot in a little cemetery out in Princeton, New Jersey. My parents are buried there as well. He said if the cemetery was good enough for some of the signers of the Declaration of Independence, then it was good enough for the family. He also used to joke that would be as close as he got to someone famous." She smiled at the memory, but then the smile slipped from her face. "Why do you ask?"

Hawk leaned down slightly. "He's asking because, if you would like to know for sure, you can have your grandfather's body exhumed."

The nausea roared back. There was no way she could dig up her grandfather's body. No way at all. That was just wrong. She shook her head. "No. I don't want to do that. If he was murdered, then he's been through enough violence. Digging him up just seems…so intrusive and wrong."

"Okay. You don't have to do it," Hawk said simply. "To be honest, there are more pressing things at the moment." He hesitated. "I think there are two options." He held her gaze. "We can find a place for you to go somewhere you'll be safe, or we can do our best to keep you safe while we search for the token." He glanced up at Logan and then Mitch. "I'm saying 'we' because I know I can't do this totally on my own."

"Whatever you need," Mitch said.

"Ditto," Logan agreed.

Lacy nodded. "I really liked your grandfather, Remy. He was a good person. I firmly believe that." She rested her hand on Remy's arm and gently squeezed.

Remy gave her a tight smile. She was overwhelmed by the support. Lacy had always been supportive but now Logan's entire family was offering her the help she needed and it was marvelous. The fact that the Callahans were willing to stand by her eased the tightness in her chest. The only snag was Hawk.

She glanced at him. She was drawn to Hawk, and she had to admit that he'd been there for her over the last couple days for no reason other than she needed him to be. That was truly a gift, but the reality was, this whole situation was going to be dangerous. The Callahans were prepared for that. They were a security company after all.

Hawk, on the other hand, was a lawyer and no matter how safe and protected she felt around him, she couldn't ask him to risk his own safety to help her. She'd been glib about it last night, but the scope of danger had increased dramatically with Dragan's explanation. She didn't need a lawyer anymore. She needed a hired gun. She glanced at Dragan. He was a good-looking man, no doubt, but more, he had the experience she needed.

She turned to face Logan and Mitch. "I would like to hire you guys to help me." She glanced at Dragan. "Dragan seems to be familiar with Archer Gray, so maybe he could help."

Mitch shot Logan a glance. Logan gave a tiny shrug. Mitch looked back at her. "We are swamped at the moment. We'll help however we can, but I can't assign Dragan. He's actually heading out of town in the next twenty-four hours."

Dragan spoke up. "I'll poke around some more before then. Maybe I'll turn something up."

Her stomach clenched. She was going to be alone. Risking Hawk's life wasn't something she was willing to do. His law degree was no defense against bullets no matter how secure he made her feel. "Um, is there someone else you can provide?"

"I'm sorry," Mitch said, "we really don't have anyone. Hawk will take care of you, though. He's one of the best. You're in good hands."

She frowned. "One of the best what?"

Mitch frowned. "You didn't tell her?" he asked Hawk.

Hawk shrugged. "Subject never came up."

Heat was rising up her neck and into her cheeks. What

secret had this man kept? She stared at him. Humiliation was imminent. She hated being embarrassed. Moments like these made her want to crawl into a hole and die.

Mitch shook his head. "Hawk is a former Navy SEAL. He was a tier-one operator in most of the hellholes on this earth, and one of the absolute best at it, or so I'm told. We didn't serve together, but I've only heard great things about him. As a matter of fact, we're trying to get him to give up practicing law and come work for us."

She stared at Hawk. The sudden change in him when they were down that stairwell now made sense. As did the way he stepped up to put himself between her and the man with the gun. She could cook an egg on her cheeks at this moment, her humiliation was so complete. "I see. Well then."

Logan cleared his throat. "I'm sure Hawk can help you until you can get this sorted out. We'll start by finding out more about the Lock and Key Society. In the meantime, Remy, if you can make a list where your grandfather might have kept his token, I think that would be very helpful."

Well, no shit that would be helpful. Did he really think she hadn't been wondering that herself? She bit back a retort. She was pissed off because she felt humiliated. She needed to let it go. Her grandfather always told her to hold her tongue instead of lashing out, as was her habit. He was right, of course, but that didn't mean she wasn't still miffed that Hawk hadn't mentioned his past. To be fair, if she had to, they weren't exactly bosom buddies. Until now, he'd just been a man who kept showing up to help when she needed it most. Kind of like Superman or the Avengers.

Shaking her head, she cleared her throat. "I'm at a loss, to be honest. I don't even have a clue *what* it could be. He never seemed attached to any one inanimate object. I would've thought somewhere in the shop or his apartment, but as both of those have been searched, I don't know where to look."

Mitch popped another cookie in his mouth and chewed. Logan snorted and grinned. "Didn't you eat breakfast?"

Mitch swallowed. "That was hours ago. Like, at least two." He turned to Remy. "Do you think he might have had a locker somewhere or a safety deposit box?"

Remy opened her mouth to answer and then shrugged. "Truthfully, I have no idea. I thought I knew my grandfather, but it turns out I didn't know a thing about the man."

Hawk touched her arm. "Why don't we go back to my place, and we can sit down and maybe make a list of things we can do to sort this all out."

He was handling her, and she hated it, but she also knew he was right. Staying there, she was just holding everyone up from working. "Okay, that sounds like a good idea." She gave him a quick smile and then turned away. She was still irritated, but there was no point in yelling at him. It was as much her fault as his. She hadn't taken the time to ask him anything about himself even though he'd been helping her. That thought just made her feel worse. *Way to be selfish.* But she did have a legitimate excuse with what the last forty-eight hours had been like, didn't she?

"Also, I want to talk to Gus. Can you ask him to meet us at my place? He might have some ideas about your grandfather."

"You're right. I'll reach out to him now." She quickly sent a text to Gus. He was one of the few elderly people she knew that loved technology. She usually went to him when she was having any problems, so she knew text was the best way to reach him. He responded immediately and said he could meet them around three if that worked. She relayed the message to Hawk.

"Okay, we can head uptown and maybe grab some lunch on the way if you'd like."

"Actually, I was just about to make something here for everyone," Logan said.

Remy looked at him with disbelief.

"No, he really was. Logan cooks when he's stressed," Mitch supplied. "And I love it," he said, rubbing his belly.

Lacy laughed. "Yes, Logan likes to cook when he needs to think about things. It helps him clear his head."

Logan smiled. "Why don't you two stay? And then you can head uptown after that."

Hawk eyed Remy, but she didn't know what he wanted to do. His face was blank. She gave a small shrug. "Sure, that would be great."

Dragan stood. "I'm going to try and connect with some contacts. I'll let you know what I find out." He strode over to the elevator and hit the button. Everyone else scattered as well, leaving her sitting there with Lacy.

"Are you okay?" her friend asked.

Remy let out a long sigh. "I'm not sure. Finding out that my grandfather had a secret life is kind of mind-blowing. I feel so…betrayed."

"I know all about having a secret life." Lacy's smile was sad.

Remy had always known there was stuff in Lacy's past that was off limits to talk about including her family. She wasn't going to pry but she knew Lacy really did understand what she was going through and for that she was extremely grateful.

Lacy sighed. "What I can tell you is that no matter his actions to the rest of the world, he loved you very much and he was so proud of you. If he didn't tell you about all this, then he had his reasons. Your grandfather didn't do anything without a reason."

"I'd like to think that...the part about him loving me, but it's just so hard to reconcile that with what's been going on. Being involved in some kind of secret society where you need a decoder ring to get it? Seriously?"

Lacy nodded. "I know. My dad was...involved with a lot of shady stuff in his past, too. I finally came to terms with my dad not just being my father, but his own individual as well. I had to see him as Armand, not as Dad, if you see what I mean. As Armand, he did way too many crazy things, but he kept most of it away from me until he didn't have a choice. My guess is your grandfather was doing the same with you. He wanted to keep it all far away from you, so he wasn't going to tell you until it was absolutely necessary."

Remy nodded slowly. "I see what you're saying. As my grandfather, he was the person I thought him to be, but in the rest of his life, he was Remington Tanger, Jr., a man I know nothing about. It doesn't make it any easier, but I can see you're right, and that's how I have to start thinking about him if I'm ever going to get this mess sorted. Don't think 'What would my grandfather do?' but ask, 'What would Remington Tanger do?'" She bit her lip. "That's why Hawk wants to talk to Gus. He's already thinking that way."

"It's easier for him. He wasn't related to your grandfather, and he's trained to think outside the box. He was very successful as a SEAL. I think he had his own team. I know for sure he was their leader, but whether it was in title as well as in deed, I'm not sure. Anyway, you're in good hands with Hawk. The guys all really like and respect him. They've been trying to hire him away from Jameson Drake, and this might just be the thing to make that dream come true. Follow his lead, and you'll be okay." She slipped off the stool. "I'm just going to check on Logan and see if he needs any help. Why don't you go sit by the fire?"

Remy slid off her stool and crossed the room. She

flopped down in an overstuffed chair next to the fire and stared at the flames. Her life had been turned upside down in just a few days. No, that was wrong. It all started when her grandfather died. She thought he'd live forever. Not really, but close enough. She was still trying to get her feet under her when all this happened. Now, she was just…in free fall.

A few hours later, stuffed to the gills and done with being around so many people, Remy was happy to take a cab to the upper west side. Hawk sat next to her in the confined space, and she was suddenly very aware of him.

A former Navy SEAL. That explained so many things. Now she knew why she felt so protected around him. If only she wasn't so damn attracted to him. She'd been avoiding him after last night's run in with Archer Gray. But, damn, it had felt so good to be in his arms. She'd wanted to kiss him. Hell, she'd wanted to take him to bed, but he had the presence of mind to leave the room. At the time, it had smarted a bit. More than a bit, but he'd been right. His presence seemed to wreak havoc on her equilibrium, and she needed to keep her wits about her. She was just a little bit miffed that he could be so calm and solid and damn good looking, as if he wasn't remotely affected by her. *Maybe he wasn't.* That was a definite ego-crushing thought.

"I'm sorry I didn't tell you about my past. It just…never came up. I wasn't hiding it from you. There wasn't really a moment when it seemed like a good time to share."

She let out a small sigh. "It might have been helpful to know. I thought you were just being chivalrous when you stood in front of me with Archer. Who the hell steps in front of a stranger to protect them? I thought you were a bit of a moron for doing it to be honest. But now knowing your history, I understand why you did it. It's what you were trained to do, isn't it?"

He nodded. When his gaze met hers, she couldn't quite tell what he was thinking, but a look had flitted briefly across his features before he shut it down. Regret? Fear? Lust? She had no clue and yet he seemed to be able to read her thoughts so clearly. Did they teach mind-reading in the Navy?

The cab stopped in front of Hawk's building, and they got out. He ushered her inside, nodded to the doorman, and got into the elevator. He hit the button for his floor. "Once Gus is here, I think you might get some answers." Hawk leaned against the back of the lift.

"You think my grandfather told Gus about everything?"

"Gus told me over one of the million cups of tea we drank yesterday that he and Remington had been friends since they were in short pants. My guess is a friendship that lasts that long, there probably aren't many secrets left."

She didn't say anything. It would be good if Gus knew something and could tell them what the hell was going on, but at the same time, she didn't want him to know. A flare of jealousy reared in her chest at the thought that her grandfather trusted someone else more than he'd trusted her.

"It wasn't about trust," Hawk said in a quiet voice, as though sensing the path of her thoughts. "Your grandfather's relationship with Gus was that of contemporaries going through life together. He was responsible for you. Your safety would be paramount to him. He didn't want you in any danger."

"How do you know?" she demanded.

"Because I know what it's like to be responsible for people's safety, and I wouldn't have told them jack shit if I thought for one moment it would put them in greater danger." He moved forward as the elevator stopped on his floor.

Remy grimaced. It was essentially what Lacy had said. She'd been kept in the dark so he could protect her. But she wasn't protected now. Now she was in deep shit, so it all had backfired. *Thanks, Gramps.*

CHAPTER NINE

The elevator door opened, and as Hawk stepped out into the hallway, every hair stood up on his arms. A tingling at the base of his spine came at the same time as his gut knotted.

"Shit." He turned to Remy, arms outstretched to push her away. "Get back!"

"What?" she said as her eyebrows drew down in confusion.

He was about to shove her back into the elevator when a door opened behind him, followed by an enraged shout.

He grabbed her arm. "Run!" He sprinted toward the stairs, dragging her along behind him. He moved so quickly, she couldn't get her footing and stumbled. He darted a look over his shoulder in the direction of his apartment. Two men were storming down the hallway. His door was standing wide open.

"Move!" he roared.

Remy recovered her footing and they made a mad dash for the stairwell.

He hit the door and pulled her through before letting it slam behind them. "Go down!"

They rushed down the stairs two at a time to the floor below. Remy had turned at the landing to continue down the stairs, but he grabbed her arm and pulled her through the door to the hallway.

"Why did we stop going down?" she demanded as she ran after him toward the elevator.

He hit the button repeatedly, even though he knew logically the elevator was already called. "We'll never outrun them going down the stairs."

When the elevator door opened, he practically threw her inside and then pushed her to the wall while he hit the lobby button and then held the close door button. The stairwell door clanged open. "Come on, come on," he begged the elevator doors. Slowly, they slid closed. He caught a glimpse of the men just before the doors shut.

"It was a gamble," he said, "but those guys look young and in good shape. From their neck tats, I would guess they are Asian gang members, but I can't be sure. There was no way we would have made it to the bottom of the stairs before they caught us. They'd start jumping the stairs, and we'd be done for before we hit the tenth floor. Twenty-one floors is a lot of stairs to go down at breakneck speed without... breaking your neck," he finished. "Especially in winter coats and boots."

The doors opened, and he popped his head out to check the surroundings. The coast was clear, or at least no Asian gang members appeared to be in the lobby. He seized her hand and jerked her out of the car. "Do exactly as I say when I say it. I know your tendency is to argue with me and question everything, but don't. We aren't out of the woods yet, and I have no interest in either of us dying today. Understand?"

She narrowed her eyes at him but gave him a curt nod.

Well, she could be furious and outraged all she wanted, but later. After they evaded this threat and came out of this situation alive. If she kept questioning and fighting him, they'd be dead within the hour.

They approached the counter where the doorman sat. "Pierre. How are you today?" Hawk asked in a jovial voice.

"I'm well, Mr. Hawkins. And you?"

"Fine, Pierre. Did you see any Asian men go through the lobby? They have neck and hand tattoos."

Pierre frowned. "No, sir. It's been fairly quiet for a Sunday. No visitors. Only residents."

"Okay, thanks Pierre." He turned away from the counter but then turned back immediately. "Pierre, is anyone using the car at the moment?"

"No. Like I said, it's been a quiet day. Mrs. Lovelace and Mrs. Clements both said it was too cold today, so I think they are staying in."

"Great. Do you think we could use it?"

"Sure. Just let me call Ernie." He picked up the phone and spoke quietly into it. Then he hung up. "Ernie will bring the car around in about ten minutes."

Hawk weighed the options. Chances were good the Asian men had come in through the garage. If they went down there, then they were more likely to confront them. On the other hand, standing in the lobby for ten minutes wasn't the smartest move either. They needed to be out of there. "You know what? Tell Ernie we'll meet him in the back alley. If he can be there in five minutes, there's a hundred-dollar tip in it for him and you."

Pierre blinked but made no comment. He just picked up the phone and made another call. As he hung up, he said, "Ernie will be in the back alley in five minutes sir."

Hawk pulled out his wallet and took out a few hundred-dollar bills. He put the wallet back and stuffed the bills in his pocket. He then offered his hand to Pierre with a hundred in it. The men shook hands, and the hundred disappeared. "Can you have Dominick walk us out the back way please?"

"Of course." Pierre nodded to a large man in a suit in the corner.

"Thanks, Pierre."

"Of course, sir."

"What the hell is going on?" Remy muttered. "What kind of building is this?"

Hawk didn't answer, just walked toward a large man standing near a hallway. "We're going to the alley, Dominick."

The large man nodded and started leading the way.

"We may encounter some difficulties. I would like you to be prepared."

Dominick glanced over his shoulder at them, but just nodded. He opened a door to a hallway and held it open for them to pass through. He closed it behind them and then pulled a Glock out of an under-arm holster. He resumed the lead and held the gun along his thigh.

Remy's eyes were the size of golf balls. She grabbed his hand and squeezed it. He squeezed back. He'd explain later. Now they had to be on their toes.

When they arrived at the back door of the building, Dominick spoke quietly, directing his words toward a discreet earbud. He turned. "The alley is clear. Ernie is waiting."

"Thanks, Dominick." He handed the man a hundred. "Do me a favor, stay in the alley until we hit the street just in case someone decides to block it."

"Certainly, Mr. Hawkins." His voice was soft. It belied the strength of the man who possessed it.

Dominick opened the door. The door of the Rolls Royce

was only inches from the door of the building. They were in the car in seconds and being whisked down the alley and out onto the street.

"Where would you like to go, Mr. Hawkins?" Ernie asked. His white hair was neat under his black chauffeur cap, but his blue eyes sparkled in the rearview mirror.

"Um, give me a minute, Ernie. Just drive around. Make sure we aren't being followed."

"Of course, sir."

Hawk turned to Remy. "Call Gus and see where he is. We need to reroute him." He thought for a moment. Where would be a safe place to meet? O'Shea's. The owner was former SAS and a friend. "Ernie, take us to O'Shea's in Hell's Kitchen."

Ernie nodded.

"Hi, Gus," Remy said. "Can you meet us at"—she glanced at Hawk—"O'Shea's in Hell's Kitchen?" There was silence for a moment. Then, "I'm not sure." She turned to Hawk and relayed the address Gus had recited.

"Yes," was all he said.

He settled into the cushy seat and closed his eyes for a second, blocking out what little traffic noise filtered into the elegant car. He needed to take stock and see what his inner antenna was saying. The tingling in his spine had stopped, and his hair was no longer standing on end. His stomach knots eased slightly. He and Remy were not being followed. They were fine…for the moment.

He released a breath and opened his eyes. Remy was staring at him.

"I'll explain when we get to O'Shea's."

Her eyes narrowed. "It had better be one hell of an explanation," she murmured.

Ten minutes later, they emerged from the Rolls right in front of the door to O'Shea's Irish Pub. Hawk got out and thanked Ernie once more as he held the door open for them. "I really appreciate it, Ernie."

"Of course, sir." He straightened his uniform and nodded with a sober expression on his face. "But I have to say, this has been a lot more fun than driving the ladies around on their shopping trips. Been awhile since I had the old girl doing anything more than a sedate pace."

Hawk laughed.

Ernie's eyes twinkled. "Let me know if you need a ride back or anywhere else, Mr. Hawkins."

He clapped Ernie on the shoulder and offered his hand with the hundred tucked into it. They shook, and Ernie nodded his appreciation.

"I'll call if I need anything, Ernie."

Hawk turned and opened the door to the pub for Remy. They entered and found a booth at the back. Hawk ushered Remy into the side facing the door, then crowded in after her.

A waitress came by immediately, and Hawk ordered a beer. Remy asked for a cup of tea. After the waitress left, Remy shifted her back against the corner of the booth and pinned her gaze on Hawk.

He let out a long breath. "So, what do you want to know?"

She frowned at him. "I can see you're a man of many secrets. First, you're an ex-Navy SEAL, and now you have superpowers. And you live in some kind of crazy-ass building." She leaned forward. "Probably not fair to ask, but I want to know it all."

His gut churned. He really didn't want to get into the weird feelings thing, but it looked like he was going to have to. He wasn't sure why, but he trusted her to keep her mouth shut about it, so it wasn't that. He was more worried that she would become dependent on it, and that thought vaulted his heart rate into the stratosphere. He'd quit the SEALs because he didn't want that kind of responsibility anymore.

He opened his mouth to speak when the waitress arrived with their drinks. Out of the corner of his eye, he caught the wave of a hand. Connor O'Shea was standing behind the bar. When he nodded at him, Hawk nodded back. "I've got to go talk to Connor for a moment. I'll be right back."

Remy scowled but didn't say anything.

He moved out of the booth and walked up to the bar.

"Hawk, good to see ya, mate." Connor offered his hand.

"Connor," Hawk said and shook the other man's hand. He tilted his head toward the end of the bar. Connor cocked an eyebrow but let go of Hawk's hand and moved down to the end of the bar where the wait staff stood to get drinks.

"Siobhan, why don't you go check on table twelve and see if they want some food or something." Connor's words held a distinct Irish lilt as he spoke with the waitress.

The young, blond waitress looked at her boss and then at Hawk and nodded.

Hawk slid into her spot and leaned over the bar. "I'm in a bit of trouble. Can we use your upstairs room for a couple of nights?"

Connor nodded. "Of course. What kind of trouble are we talkin'?"

Hawk cocked his head. "Have you ever heard of the Lock and Key Society?"

"Feck me," Connor mumbled. "You know better than to get involved with that lot."

Hawk shrugged. "I had no fucking clue who they were. Innocent bystander and all." Connor snorted and a grim smile pulled Hawk's lips tight. "There's a lot of weird shit going on, and I don't have much in the way of details, but there were two Asian males with what I'm pretty sure were gang tattoos at my place just now. The woman I'm with had her store tossed twice, after which we met Archer Gray. Someone is looking for something, and they seemed willing to kill for it."

Connor made a sound at the back of his throat when Hawk mentioned Gray. "Jesus! What a cluster. Yeah, you can stay as long as you need. Do you need some hardware?"

Hawk nodded. "Yeah, that would be good."

"I'll leave ya a bag in the room upstairs. It'll have what you need. Keep your head down, and I'll see what I can find out for ya. I know a few people who know a bit about the L&K Society. I'll see what's what."

"I can't thank you enough, brother."

The man snorted. "You've done more for me over the years. No worries, mate. Go drink your beer with your lady friend and relax. I got your back on this one." Connor walked back down the bar and started pouring another beer.

Hawk made his way back to the booth. Connor O'Shea was one of the good guys. They'd met in Iraq when they were both after the same terrorist group. He'd been surprised at Connor's accent since the SAS was a British special forces group, but Connor explained his dad was British and his mom was Irish. He'd grown up in both countries, but the Irish accent had stuck.

Hawk slid into the booth and got comfortable. Remy sipped her tea and waited for him to speak.

"Sorry about that." He tipped his head toward Connor. "I made arrangements for us to stay here tonight."

"Here?"

"Upstairs. I thought about a hotel, but too many eyes and ears. If people really are on the lookout for you, then someone will have contacts at the hotels. We might get away with it for a night or two, but most likely we'd get found out pretty quick. No one will find us here."

She shrugged. "Okay. You were going to explain a few things."

Hawk took a sip of his beer and swallowed. "I'm not exactly sure—"

"How did you know there was trouble at your place before those guys shouted at us?"

Hawk dragged his finger through the condensation on his glass, avoiding her gaze. "When I was in the SEALs, I had to live on instinct a lot of the time. I sort of developed a sixth sense that tells me when there's immediate danger. When I stepped off the elevator, I knew there was trouble."

She nodded slowly. "I bet that kept you alive more times than you can count."

"Yeah."

"That's a big burden to carry." She took another sip of tea.

"How do you mean?"

She shrugged. "Lacy said you were responsible for your own team. I would imagine you relied on that instinct to keep everyone alive. That's a lot of responsibility. A lot of pressure."

He sat back stunned. In all the years, no one else had ever put that together. Not one person. Remy was smart, but more than that, she was observant. Her mind was quick. He liked that about her.

He cleared his throat. "Yeah, to be honest, it was one of the reasons I got out. I needed a break. It's difficult to rely on something you can't really explain all the time."

"The fear that it would suddenly not work one day would be enough to drive anyone over the edge."

He stared at her. Was *she* reading *his* mind now?

She took a sip of her tea and sighed. "I'm kind of an anxious person. I would be constantly living in fear of losing my touch. I think you're probably a bit like me."

He relaxed against the banquette. "That's it exactly."

She touched his hand. "Thank you for all of your help. I know I'm putting you in a bad place. If I had other options, I would… But I just…"

"No, I'm okay. I want to help you." He smiled at her, and she smiled back.

He liked the way her eyes crinkled slightly at the corners when she smiled. He also liked the way her lips looked. Definitely made for kissing. He let that thought go. This wasn't the time or place for those types of thoughts.

Remy removed her hand, and he immediately missed her touch.

"So how did you end up in a building like that? I didn't even know buildings in New York City had cars, let alone armed security."

"After I left the SEALs and started law school, I was still a bit…high strung. It took me a long time to come back down to normal. I was always very careful, very security conscious. I wouldn't say I had PTSD, but probably pretty close." He'd never admitted that to anyone before. "I was a bit on edge. Not seeing danger everywhere but making sure it wasn't there.

"Anyway, I burned through law school as quickly as possible. Knowing my military background made Jameson Drake offer me a job even before graduation. I had a lot of job opportunities and a few firms chasing me."

"You must have gone to a good school. I graduated from Columbia and the top people share some of that experience. But I decided pretty quickly that studying law wasn't for me."

"Harvard." He shrugged. "Drake has connections there. He told them to keep an eye out for the best and the brightest students so he could have the first crack at hiring them." It sounded like he was tooting his own horn, but facts were facts. "In my case, it worked. He offered me a large signing bonus and helped me get into that building. He understood that I needed a place where I knew I would be completely safe and could relax. He vouched for me. I had to pay more than I could afford, but I worked my ass off and earned enough in bonuses to make it work."

"Huh. Are there a lot of buildings like that in the city?" She drank the last of her tea and refilled her cup from the small pot on the table.

"I don't know about *a lot*, but if you stop and think about it, it makes sense. There's a lot of money in New York, not to mention very important businesspeople from all over the world. There must be a few buildings like mine that offer security services as well as a car."

"I guess. The Lock and Key Society is a bit like that, isn't it? Secure location for whatever you need, no questions asked."

Hawk took a sip of beer. "My building isn't quite like that, it's a safe analogy. Security is good in my building. Or used to be. I'm not sure how those men got in. I'm guessing through the garage but that would mean someone had to let them into the garage in the first place. You can't access the garage unless you live in the building. The security guard at the entrance has to physically identify you, and there's someone at the entry gate twenty-four hours a day."

"Do you think they bribed the guard?" she asked.

He shook his head. "No. I know Jeff. He's a good guy. He's also ex-Secret Service like Ernie."

"Ernie is ex-Secret Service? But he's old."

Hawk laughed. "Now. He wasn't always. Neither was Jeff. They worked together in the bad old days. Both men are above reproach. Good people. They can't be bought off. They do this so they can still serve in a way. A lot of VIPs reside in my building. Those two keep an eye out better than any security system."

"But the guys got in so maybe not?"

Hawk frowned. "No. My guess is that someone in the building, a tenant, brought them into the garage in the trunk of their car. Someone who may or may not be a part of the Lock and Key Society."

"Maybe. Or it could be someone with Asian gang affiliations," she suggested.

He narrowed his eyes for a second. "That makes more sense. Most of the people in my building are older. We don't have very many young people, and none would seem to be related to an Asian gang, but we have a few elderly gentlemen that I have often wondered about."

She leaned forward again and propped her elbow on the table and her cheek on her palm. "What made you wonder about them?"

He paused. Did he admit the truth? Why not? He'd admitted everything else. "My gut. I just got a vibe off them. I'm pretty sure they are stone-cold killers, just dressed nicely with excellent manners. They're older so they posed no threat to me, at least I didn't think so, but now, I can see that they could have gang ties."

"Old men with gang ties?"

"Asian gangs aren't like the street gangs you're thinking about. They do have that aspect to them, but the upper echelon is usually very successful businesspeople in their own right. They run legit businesses to cover their other stuff. The Triads out of Hong Kong are famous for it."

"So, there are elderly Asian men in your building that you think could possibly have helped these men get in?"

"There are, but at this point, I'm only speculating. It could have been anyone really. Who knows? I think, though, that this is a lesson for us. We can't trust very many people. Unless we know them very well, I think we just keep our heads down and don't say anything."

The TV that was above the bar suddenly blared out a harsh, grating voice. Austin Davis. He was being interviewed by some talk show host. He set Hawk's teeth on edge.

"I can't stand him," Remy said, nodding toward the TV.

"Me either. He's the worst kind of asshole. Smart enough to know better but mean enough to not give a shit. He's a master at manipulating people for his own gain. He's greedy about everything. He's the type of guy who isn't content to just win. He wants all the marbles."

"Hey, Remy," Gus called out as he walked across the room.

Hawk looked at the older gentleman and smiled, offering him a greeting. As he watched the man get settled across from Remy in the booth, he tapped into his sixth sense and waited to see if it pinged. Nothing. Gus seemed to be a nice elderly gentleman with no ulterior motives. Hawk wanted to believe that. Wanted to trust his gut, but at the same time, he needed to make sure that Remy was safe, so his plan was to give Gus only minimum information. Besides, if the old man knew too much, it might put him in danger. They might come after Gus and kill him if he couldn't provide them with the location of the token. And once again, Hawk was in the position of worrying that someone would die if his instinct failed. That was a sobering thought.

CHAPTER TEN

"Thanks for meeting us, Gus," Remy said. She studied the older man's face. He looked tired. He'd aged since her grandfather had passed away, but so had she in a way. Somehow, Gus had seemed to shrink into himself a bit. Never a robust man, now he seemed physically smaller. He'd helped her out at the store a few times like he used to help her grandfather. Kept him going, or so he said. But in light of everything she'd learned today, she wondered.

"How are your kids and grandkids, Gus?" she asked. It had been a while since he'd talked about them.

He smiled. "They're doing well." He turned to Hawk. "They're all out in California. I see them a couple times a year."

Remy tipped her chin toward Gus. "I keep telling him to move out there with them. New York in the winter is too damn cold. His family lives in San Diego. He could be warm all year round."

Gus laughed. "Can you see me in San Diego all year? I've been a New Yorker all my life, and I'm not gonna stop now."

She glanced at her grandfather's best friend. She'd always

thought Gus had stayed because her grandfather was here. The two of them were almost closer than brothers. They were family. Their wives had been close like that, too. Now, Gus was the last man standing. It made her sad to think about that. It must make him sad as well. Maybe it was time to push him to go, especially now.

Hawk waved over the waitress.

"What can I get you?" the blond Siobhan said when she came to the table.

Hawk finished his beer and said, "I'll have another. Gus?"

"I think I'll have a scotch."

"Well, if you two are both partaking, I guess I will have a dry martini." Remy grinned at Gus.

"And maybe bring us a couple of menus," Hawk added.

Remy glanced at him and winked. That was probably a smart idea. She wasn't the least bit hungry, but if she was going to indulge in a martini, then food would be a must.

"So, I walked by the store. It's closed." Gus frowned.

Remy let out a long breath. "I know. It's going to be closed for a while, Gus. I haven't gotten it back together yet."

"You should've called. I would've worked on it today. We could've had it back in order and had it opened tomorrow."

She shook her head. The waitress showed up with their drinks, and Gus raised his glass. "Since we're in an Irish pub, *sláinte!*" They all sipped their drinks.

Remy set hers on a napkin, then cleared her throat. "Actually, Gus, that's why I want to talk to you. It's going to be a while before I can open the store because it seems Gramps had something that a lot of people want. I have a feeling the shop might be broken into again once I set it to rights. Gramps's apartment was searched as well. It's a mess, but neither of them seems worth putting in order until I know what's really going on." She studied Gus's face. "Do you know what they're looking for?"

Gus's gaze skittered away from hers, and he took a large gulp from his drink.

Hawk leaned on the table. "Gus, people tried to hurt Remy today. They're going to continue to chase her down until we can figure out what exactly they're looking for."

Gus gasped and he darted his gaze toward Remy. "Are you okay? Your grandfather would never forgive me if anything happened to you. He'd want me to watch out for you. You come stay with me. I'll keep an eye on you and make sure you're okay."

She smiled and touched his arm. "That's kind of you, Gus, but I'm okay. I'll be better if you can tell us what you know." She was trying to be gentle with the elderly gentleman. He was a good man and a family friend from before she'd been born, but at this moment, she wanted to shake him until his teeth rattled. He knew something, and she needed to know it. Now.

"I… That is, I'm not sure…"

"Tell us what you know, Gus, and start at the beginning," Hawk advised. "We know about the hidden door."

Gus's shoulders immediately sagged, although she couldn't tell if it was from relief or something else.

"You know about that then?" he asked.

Hawk nodded. "But what do you know about it?"

Gus took another sip of his drink and swallowed. "I don't know a whole lot other than it's some sort of club. Your grandfather would never tell me details. Just that it was his job to let people in. I asked if he was like a bouncer, but he just laughed and said the club was his key to success. Then he'd laugh some more like that was a big joke. I never understood it."

Remy's own shoulders sagged. She was hoping for more. "Is there nothing else you can tell me?"

Gus thought for a second. "I know that it's been around

a long, long time. I remember Remington and I as little kids, hiding in the aisles back when his dad ran it as a locksmith shop. We'd frequently see your great-grandfather let people down those stairs."

Remy blinked. "My great-grandfather? Are you sure?"

"Yes. Remy and I used to wonder what was down there, but we were too afraid to ask. We weren't supposed to know anything about it." He gazed off across the bar, and his eyes went out of focus. "I remember when we were older and your great-grandfather was ill, Remy came over to our place. Millie was alive then. He looked like he'd seen a ghost. I remember asking him what was wrong, but he wouldn't say. He just said he found out what the mystery was, and it wasn't good. I think he and his father had words about it. He never did tell me anything else."

Remy took a sip of her martini. So, this whole thing had been in her family for generations. They'd all been a part of something not so nice. That didn't make her feel good about her heritage. She was Remington Maxwell Tanger the Fourth, and it looked like the Second and the First had both been involved in something shady. Maybe it was a good thing her father had died, or he probably would have been involved in this mess, too. All this made her wonder about the first Remington Maxwell Tanger. How did he get involved in the first place?

Hawk asked in a quiet voice, "Gus, do you think Remy came to accept this whole thing?"

Gus bobbed his head back and forth. "Yes and no. I think he accepted it, but I don't think he loved letting all of those suspicious people into the basement. He never really revealed the purpose, or even that it was part of a society, but he was philosophical about it. He said he didn't have a choice, so he might as well make the best of it. That was his nature, you know. Lemonade from lemons and all that. He had to go to meetings occasionally, although he never said as much. But I knew when they traveled internationally, it had something to do with the secret. He and Clissy would make a big vacation out of it. Paris, London, Hong Kong. They made it into an adventure."

"I remember some of those trips," Remy said. "They seemed to have a lot of fun."

Gus nodded. "They even brought me and Millie along a few times. We did have a lot of fun. Remy used to say to me that he had to do whatever it was so he might as well enjoy himself and spend the money it made him. Your grandfather was very generous to me and Millie. He made sure we had everything we ever needed, and then some. He even paid for some of Millie's medical expenses."

She patted his arm again. Gus was lifting a heavy weight off her shoulders. Her grandfather was a good man. He made the best out of the circumstances and made sure to take care of friends and family. Who could ask for more than that? She let out a breath she didn't even realize she'd been holding and took a sip of her drink. *Here's to you, Grandpa.*

Hawk offered each one of them a menu and then studied it himself. A few minutes later, the waitress was back, and they placed their orders.

"So, Gus, did you ever see some of the people that went down the staircase?" Hawk said in a relaxed voice.

Gus looked around the room and then down at the table. "Er, well, I wasn't supposed to but, yes, I saw some of them. Shady, every single one, if you ask me. Some of them looked all crazy with long hair and tattoos. Some were in business suits and looked like they could be the President. It really was a mishmash of people, but they all had a certain look about them. Shady. Mark my words."

A thought struck Remy. "Would you recognize any of

them if you saw them again?" Hawk shot her a look, but she ignored it. "If you saw their picture."

Gus thought about it for a minute. "Maybe. I saw one in the newspaper one time. It was years ago now. He was a guy in a business suit. He had gone down the staircase, and then a couple of weeks later, he was in the New York Times. He was some visiting dignitary from…France, I think. Do you have pictures you want me to look at?"

"No," Hawk said quickly. "It was just curiosity."

Remy gazed intently at him, but Hawk gave her a slight shake of his head. He turned back to Gus. "So, since the store has been broken into and the apartment upstairs, do you know what people might be looking for? We assume it has to do with 'the club,' as you call it."

"I expect they're looking for the thing." Gus finished his drink.

"What thing?" Remy stared at the man. What was this now?

"Your grandfather had one of the trinkets. He said he had to have one because of his position. He didn't tell me what it was, and he never showed me, but he had one."

Remy was back to wanting to throttle him. "What is the trinket you're talking about, Gus?"

Gus sighed. "In order to get down the staircase, people had to show your gramps something, a trinket of some sort. That was their ticket in. If they didn't have one, then your grandfather wouldn't let them go down."

"And you never saw one of these 'trinkets'?" Hawk tapped a finger on his beer glass.

"Nope." Gus shook his head. "Like I said, Remy would just say it was the key to his success and then laugh about it."

Their dinner arrived, and they dug in. Remy noticed Hawk kept the conversation light while they ate. He asked Gus questions about family and his career. Just get-to-know you stuff. It was nice to see Gus the focus of attention. Remy surmised that it didn't happen often these days since the older gentleman lit up when answering Hawk's questions.

Finally, Hawk brought the conversation around to Remy's grandfather. "So, do you have any idea where Remy hid his 'trinket'?"

Gus shook his head. "No, but I have often wondered. I used to think he kept it in the shop, and I asked him one day, but he just smiled and shook his head. He wouldn't tell me anything about it."

Remy set down her knife and fork. "Well, we know it's not in the shop or the apartment. Both have been thoroughly searched."

"Gus," Hawk said, "is there anything else Remy used to do on a regular basis? Any place he used to hang out or go all the time?"

The elderly gentleman frowned. "Not that I can think of. He went to the shop and his apartment. He came to my place, but I'm pretty sure he didn't store the thing there. He would've told me. I know he was always slightly worried about it. He wouldn't keep it anywhere where it would put anyone else's life in danger."

"Another dead end." Remy rubbed her temples. This whole thing was just getting out of control. She needed something solid she could sink her teeth into. Something that would help her sort out this mess so she didn't have to spend the rest of her days looking over her shoulder. She frowned. How did that work? If someone could be killed and their token taken, then how come people weren't dying all the time? How come no one had ever gone after her grandfather before? She really wanted to ask Hawk what he thought, but now wasn't the moment. Gus didn't need to know anything else about this whole thing. She was already worried about him as it was.

"He used to go for a walk every single day, rain or shine. Said it kept the wheels greased." Gus ate the final bite of his shepherd's pie.

Hawk placed his cutlery across his empty plate. "Did he always take the same route?"

Gus nodded and swallowed. "Always. It was about a forty-five-minute loop." Gus told them the street names and mapped out the route with a pen on a napkin.

"Thanks." Hawk smiled as the waitress approached.

She took their empty plates and asked about dessert, but everyone was full. Remy was overstuffed, if truth be told. She was a stress eater, and this situation was seriously stressing her out.

Hawk asked for the check. Then he turned to Gus. "I know you want to help, Gus, and Remy appreciates that."

"I do," she agreed and put her hand on Gus's arm, "but, Gus, this is getting dangerous. The people who are after whatever it is that Gramps had mean business." She hesitated. "I think there's a possibility they killed him for it." There, she'd said it out loud to Gus. That made it more real than anything else, and Hawk wasn't the only one who trusted his instincts. She knew it in her bones. Her grandfather was murdered. She'd thought something was off when she'd been told what happened, but she'd dismissed it. He was elderly. He shouldn't have been on a ladder. Her Gramps was as sure-footed as a goat. He didn't fall, at least not by himself. He had been pushed.

Gus closed his eyes for a second and then laid his hand over hers. When he looked at her, she could have sworn he'd aged twenty years in that minute.

"I've been thinking the same thing. I didn't want to frighten you, but God help me, I think someone murdered your grandfather." Tears trickled down his face. "I've been trying to figure out who would have wanted him dead, but no one in his life was angry with him. None of our friends. He had no enemies. He was well-liked and respected. He lived a normal life except for that staircase and the club below. That's what killed him. I just know it, but I have no idea what to do about it."

Remy swallowed the lump building in her throat and squeezed Gus's arm. "I'm going to look into it, Gus." She looked at Hawk. "That is, *we* are going to figure it out." There was no way she could do this without Hawk. She needed him to not only keep her safe, but she also needed his quiet strength to draw from. She turned back to her grandfather's best friend. "But we need you to be safe. It might be best if you went to California for a while. Just until we get this sorted out."

"But—"

"Gus," Hawk said in a serious tone, "Remy and I couldn't live with it if something happened to you. It won't take them long to figure out you were the only constant in Remy's life. Then they'll come looking for you. They'll probably want to search your place. It's too dangerous for you to stay here."

"But I can help you search," Gus protested.

Hawk shook his head. "You could, but it's a huge risk to your safety." He pointed to Remy. "You are her defacto grandfather now. The only family she has left. If anything happens to you, she is all alone. I know you don't want that, Gus."

The old man's shoulder sagged, as though defeated. "No, you're right." He turned to Remy. "Your grandfather would never forgive me."

She smiled at him through her tears and then gave him a big hug. "We'll keep you updated as we can, okay?"

He nodded. "Okay, pipsqueak."

She giggled. He hadn't called her that in years. It lifted her spirits immensely.

Gus used his napkin to wipe his face. "I'll call my kids and tell them the good news. They've been after me to come visit since Remy died. I have to find a flight. Today's Sunday. Maybe I could find one for Wednesday or Thursday."

Remy shot Hawk a look. Gus couldn't wait that long. No way. He'd be in trouble by then.

"Why don't you let me take care of that?" Hawk said as he picked up his cell off the table. "I think we can get you out tonight."

"Tonight! But I have to pack and clean out the fridge and —and—get ready."

Hawk stood up and put his cell to his ear as he walked away from the table.

"Gus, I know this is sudden, but I have to know that you're okay. I just need you to go as soon as possible. Hawk wasn't wrong. I really won't forgive myself if something happens to you."

"I know. I'm just so…frustrated that I can't do more to help. Your grandfather was my best friend for ninety years. The fact that I can't help him is driving me crazy."

"You are helping him by being safe. You can always call me if you think of anything important."

"Okay." He let out a sigh. "That sounds like a good plan. These old bones could use a dose of sunshine, and an even bigger dose of my grandchildren and great-grandchildren."

She smiled. Gus was always a glass half full kind of guy. He was already cheering himself up. *Thank God.* Now they just needed to get him packed and safely to the airport.

Hawk came back to the table. "Gus, a friend of mine named Ernie is going to pick you up here and take you home to pack, and then he's going to take you to the airport. My assistant booked you on a night flight to San Diego. It leaves at eight p.m. It's going to be a long haul, but you'll be in the sunshine before you know it. Don't worry about your place.

I'll have the fridge cleaned for you. I assume there's a spare key to your place at the shop?"

"Yes, in the can under the counter."

"Okay then, you're good to go." Hawk smiled.

Gus stood up. He offered a hand to Hawk. "You take good care of her now. I'll come after you if I hear anything different."

Hawk nodded. "Understood, sir. I will do my best."

"See that you do."

Remy didn't know whether she should be pissed off or should laugh. The two men talking about her like she wasn't there was annoying but also charming. She decided instead to stand up and give Gus a big hug. "Thanks for this, Gus. Stay in touch and let us know when you get there. Call if you think of anything."

"I will. You take care, pipsqueak." He gave her a smile before he shrugged into his coat. Hawk walked him to the door.

Remy sat back down and watched them go. She said a prayer that Gus made it safely to San Diego and that no one bothered him out there. She looked down at the old, scarred tabletop. It was time to figure out the next step, but she had no fucking clue what that was. All she knew was she was in a desperate place, and people wanted her dead.

CHAPTER ELEVEN

H awk returned to the table and sat down. "How are you holding up?"

She'd moved to the other side of the booth after Gus left. Hawk had a straight- on view of her face as she blew out a sigh between puffed cheeks. "I really don't know, to be honest. I'm all over the place. I can't seem to wrap my head around any of it. My grandfather lied to me my entire life, and yet everyone else thinks he was a good man. He supposedly didn't have a choice, but he used the money he made from the club or society or whatever it's called to enjoy life. Does that make him a good person or a bad one?"

"I think that makes him human." Hawk leaned back. "I stopped trying to sort out good from bad a long time ago. The world is shades of gray. There's nothing black or white about it. Worrying about whether your grandfather was a good man doesn't matter. What's important is that he was good to you. And what matters more right now is that we find his token."

Remy rubbed her face. "Yeah, I know, but I can't seem to come up with any ideas about that either." She dropped her hands onto the table. "What time is it? It feels like it should be midnight."

"A little after five."

"Jesus. I feel like I could sleep for a week."

Hawk nodded. He knew what that felt like. Being on edge, adrenaline pumping at random times, no real relaxation because even when there was an opportunity to lay down and rest, the mind just kept on chugging. He'd spent too many days, weeks, months like that when he was in the SEALs. When the crash came, it was usually brutal.

The one thing that usually worked to bring him down enough to sleep was sex. There were always women, fellow soldiers, who were in the same boat. Everyone knew the score. It was just sex. A physical release that allowed the body to shut down and sleep.

The idea of having sex with Remy was so damn appealing he was struggling not to grab her hand and pull her up the stairs. Fuck, he was turning into some kind of Neanderthal around this woman. All he wanted to do was protect her and bed her, but not necessarily in that order. He mentally gathered the tethers of his control, ordering himself to get his shit together.

"Why don't I get the key to the room upstairs, and you can go up and get settled? I know you don't have any clothes so I will go buy some for you while you rest up."

"I couldn't let you do that."

He snorted. Maybe it was because he was lusting after her and he couldn't have her, or maybe it was because he was tired and frustrated. But whatever it was, he was done being nice. She needed to understand the gravity of the situation.

"We went over this before; you need do what I say and stop questioning me. These are not normal times. I've been trying to cushion things for you because you've been through a lot, but the reality is we can't go back to your place or mine to get what we need. People will be watching. Those guys didn't want to chat with you. I'm guessing they wanted you dead. Your grandfather has a token, and they want it. You are just in the way."

She paled out at his words. A sudden wrench in his gut startled him, but she was overdue for a reality check.

Ignoring the churn in his stomach, he continued, "I'm pretty sure I can run out and get toiletries and clothes for us without being seen, but I won't let you risk the trip. So, what I'm telling you is you need to get your ass upstairs where I know you'll be safe because Connor over there is a former Special Forces guy who's not going to let anything happen to you. I will get what we need and be back quickly."

She frowned. "Listen I—"

"Enough." He rapped his knuckles on the table making sure he had her complete attention. "You need to do what I tell you because you want to stay alive. Get over being pissed off at my tone. No more coddling, do you understand? It's too dangerous."

She reared back like he'd slapped her. Maybe he'd gone too far, but he needed her to understand her precarious situation. It didn't hurt if she was angry at him because that would create distance between them and, right now, if he was going to keep her alive, he needed space to keep a clear mind.

"Fine," she said through clenched teeth.

They stood up, and Hawk threw enough money on the table to cover the bill and leave a hefty tip for Siobhan. When he walked over to the end of the bar, Connor shuffled over and handed him the keys. "Let me know if ya need anything."

"Will do." Hawk went through the door to the stairwell, making sure Remy was behind him. At the top of the stairs, he turned right. He put the key in the lock of the first door on the left. He opened the door and moved out of the way so Remy could enter.

She glowered at him as she walked into the room, but then she gasped. He entered quickly to make sure nothing was wrong. His sixth sense hadn't triggered, but he needed to be sure. Remy stood there staring. "I thought it would be......I guess I don't know what I expected. Certainly not this."

Hawk looked around the room. A large king-size bed made out of mahogany with matching bedside tables dominated the space. The comforter was white with splashes of big, colorful flowers. The floor was wide planks that shone with a high gloss that was partially covered by a rug that also had flowers on it. The wallpaper was cream with gray swirls. There was a desk and chair across from the dresser, and an armchair in the corner by the window. The space looked like a high-end hotel room, which suited Hawk fine. The duffel bag on the desk was of more interest to him than anything else.

"There's a bathroom over there." He pointed to the door in the corner.

Her eyes narrowed. "You've stayed here before."

He nodded. "A few times." He didn't bother to mention it was because he and Connor had gotten shit-faced together, and there was no way he could manage to get home on his own. He walked over to the desk, opened the duffle bag, and pulled out a Glock. He checked the magazine, and weighed the weapon in the palm of his hand, then tucked it into the waistband of his jeans underneath his blue sweater. Then he grabbed a pad of paper and pen from the top of the desk. "Write down your sizes. Please," he added as an afterthought. He'd been abrupt with her, which is what she needed, but regret flowed like a river in him.

The lightness in her expression evaporated. He wasn't

sure if it was the gun or the fact that her current situation was starting to sink in, but she took the pad and pen and started writing. A minute later, she handed both back to him. "I'm going to take a long hot shower and then sleep."

He nodded. "See you when I get back. Lock the door when I go. I have the key. If you need anything, call down to the pub and ask for Connor."

She stood in the middle of the room with her arms crossed over her chest. "Fine."

He turned and went out the door, closing it behind him. Maybe pissed off wasn't better. She looked just as cute when she was angry as she did when she was smiling, and neither one was going to help him stay focused.

Two hours later, bags in his left hand to keep his right free, he arrived back at the bar. Shopping had been a nightmare. He had no idea what she liked, and then got annoyed at himself for even worrying about it in the first place. He finally gave up and picked out stuff that looked comfortable and outdoorsy and hoped she might find them acceptable. The underwear thing had been more complicated. He'd never bought women's underwear before. He'd never given thought to the many styles and cuts, instead focusing on getting a woman out of them. He bought her several pairs in each style and color. He hoped that at least one of them would be usable. Men's styles were so much easier. Boxers, briefs, or boxer-briefs. Or commando. Too many options for women for sure.

He unlocked the door and moved quietly into the room, assuming Remy would be asleep. Instead, she was sitting in the armchair in the corner next to the window. Her hair was down and curling over her shoulders. She was wearing a big, white fuzzy robe and had curled her legs beneath her. It would be the picture of comfort if it hadn't been for the tension in her face and the fear in her big, gray eyes.

"Don't worry. No one can see me from outside. I have the blinds down."

"I see that. Do you need anything from downstairs?"

She shook her head. "Connor brought me a kettle, a mug, and some tea bags a little while ago, and I'm still stuffed from before."

He nodded. "I'll get some water bottles then, and we should be good for the night."

"He brought some of those as well." She gestured to the dresser where four bottles stood.

"Then I guess we're good." He wanted a bourbon, preferably the whole bottle, but a shot would do. He shook the bags in her direction. "These are for you." He didn't bother to justify his purchases. She was just going to have to live with it.

"Thank you."

He nodded as he set the clothing down beside the dresser. He then pulled the gun out from his waistband and put it on the bedside table closest to the door. He would take that side. If she wasn't comfortable sharing a bed, then she could take the floor or the chair. He was wrung out, and things were only going to get worse from here, so he needed sleep.

He went over to the duffel bag and rummaged through it. A smile, the first in hours, lifted his lips. Connor had come through for sure. The bag still contained three guns and plenty of ammo. He took another nine-millimeter pistol out, walked over to the bed, and put it under the pillow on his side.

He glanced over at her. He was willing to bet she didn't get any sleep. "Too wound up to sleep?"

She nodded. "No thanks to you."

He bit his lips to keep from apologizing. "You needed to hear the truth. Life sucks at the moment. But the other truth that you have to carry with you is one my family taught me. 'This too shall pass.' And it will. There's no telling what the outcome will be, but you won't always be here in this moment."

She cocked her head. "I don't know if that's profound or ridiculous. I could be dead by tomorrow."

"True," he agreed, "but you won't be sitting here, worrying about everything then, will you?"

She burst out laughing. "That's one way to look at it." She shook her head. "I'm so fucking tired I can't see straight, but I can't seem to unwind enough to sleep. How did you do it?"

"What?"

"When you were in the military, how did you manage to sleep?"

"Ah, well, we were sort of trained to just shut down. There are some breathing exercises that we did. They helped."

"Breathing exercises." She snorted. "I'm not sure breathing exercises are going to help."

"Don't knock 'em 'til you try them. They really do help to you relax."

She stood up and moved over to the bags. "Did you get me some pajamas?"

He grimaced. "Shit."

She started laughing again. "Remind me to make sure you're not in charge of shopping anymore. Did you at least get me a toothbrush and some toothpaste?"

"In the CVS bag."

She reached down, pulled out a plastic bag, and disappeared into the bathroom, closing the door behind her. He sat down on the bed and flopped back on the mattress. Pajamas. Shit. Didn't even occur to him. He didn't use them, so it just wasn't on his radar. He rubbed his eyes with the heels of his palms. He was tired, too. Breathing exercises. They wouldn't help much tonight sleeping next to Remy.

He heard the bathroom door open, so he sat up. "There's a bag with T-shirts in it. Grab one of those. You can sleep in it."

She nodded and then rummaged around in the bags. She pulled out the T-shirt and the underwear bag and disappeared again back into the bathroom.

Great. Now he was going to picture her in the underwear he bought. He flopped back on the bed and folded his hands over his chest. There wasn't much they could do tonight other than brainstorm about where her grandfather might have left his token, but that wasn't going to help her sleep.

The bathroom door opened again, but he didn't sit up this time. "There's a brush and some hair ties and other stuff in the CVS bag. And some snacks in the other one if you're hungry."

"I saw that, thanks."

He let out a long breath and sat up. "Do—' He temporarily lost the ability to speak. Remy stood just outside the bathroom door dressed in a black T-shirt that barely skimmed her thighs. His gaze locked with hers. "Um, that is, uh, do you want to…?"

"Do some breathing exercises?" she asked in an innocent voice, but there was a smile on her lips and a wicked gleam in her eyes as she crossed the floor to stand in front of him.

"Remy," he growled. It was a warning. This was not a good idea.

"Hawk," she responded and cocked an eyebrow. "Do you know what I usually do when I'm wound up and can't sleep?"

He ground his teeth but he couldn't stop himself from asking, "What?" She was directly in front of him now.

"Well, I'll give you a hint. It involves toys, the sort my mother wouldn't approve of."

Jesus. He closed his eyes briefly. He did not need the image of Remy using sex toys in his head. He opened his eyes again. "Shit, Remy, this isn't a smart move."

She put her hand on his chest. "No, you're right. It's probably not, but I could be dead tomorrow, so I'm not as concerned about it as I might be."

"You won't be dead tomorrow. I won't let that happen." He needed her to know he would do everything in his power to keep her safe.

"Possibly," she conceded, "but I still need to sleep, and this seems like way more fun than breathing exercises." She leaned down and kissed him.

He stayed perfectly still. His soldier's brain argued this was a bad move, but the rest of him ignored the logic. He tried one more time. "Remy this is dangerous. I need to be able to keep a clear head. Having sex—"

"Shut up." She kissed him harder then.

Fuck it. He stood up, and his heart rate climbed as she molded her curves to him. He'd wanted her from the first moment he'd seen her in the shop. He deepened the kiss as she wrapped her arms around his neck. He pulled her closer, bringing her hips to his while cupping her ass. She felt so damn good pressed against him. So right.

He broke from her mouth and trailed butterfly kisses down her jaw to the hollow of her neck.

"Hawk," she moaned as she wound her fingers through his hair.

The sound of his name on her lips was enough to push him over the edge. A wave of fierce possessiveness washed over him as he claimed her mouth again in a fiery kiss. She returned his fierceness, and their tongues fought as they slid over one another.

He cupped her breast and ran his thumb over the soft fabric covering her nipple. She moaned and reached for the bottom of his sweater. He broke the kiss and reached over his head and pulled his sweater off with one hand, then dropped it on the floor. He immediately reached for her again and held her firmly against the length of him. He didn't want any space between them. She was amazing and strong and fierce, and that was the biggest turn-on of all.

He ran his hand down her ribs and then under the T-shirt. He fingered her belly and then traced his way back up to her breasts where he lightly flicked them over her nipple before he pinched hard. Remy moaned as she ran her hands down his chest and across his belly, stopping only to tug on his belt buckle.

He grasped her hands. "Not yet," he said in between kisses and then reached back under her T-shirt. She broke away from him and pulled the T-shirt off over her head. Dropping it on the floor, she stepped back into his embrace. He was speechless once again. She had on a smoky gray pair of thong underwear that he'd bought for her. He smiled. He'd been right. They matched her eyes perfectly.

"What are you smiling at?"

"My shopping prowess."

She snorted. "That's not the prowess you should be worried about at this moment."

Hawk chuckled and then dipped his head to draw her nipple into his mouth. He sucked hard and she gasped. When he swirled his tongue around the hard bud, she gasped. She stroked her hands from his hair down his back. Then she brought them around front to his buckle once again. When she touched the waistband, he took a quick breath. He was throbbing with need.

He moved his head to her other nipple and nipped at it playfully. She sunk her fingers into his hair again and brought his mouth back to hers. Her mouth was demanding again as her hands ran down his back, pulling him closer.

He dropped down onto the bed and brought her with him. She straddled him and undid his belt and then the button on his jeans. He set her aside and lifted his butt to pull off his pants, then dropped them on the floor. When he rested flat once again, she crawled back onto his lap, lowering herself so her hot center rubbed against his hard cock. He groaned. He wasn't going to last if she kept that up.

He quickly flipped her onto her back on the bed and positioned himself over her. Slowly, he lowered himself onto her. As he kissed her, he ran his fingers down her hip. She was so incredibly beautiful. He lowered his mouth to one nipple, then the other. She arched beneath him, whispering his name.

Slowly, he left a trail of kisses down her stomach to her thong. He'd been dreaming of her, of this. Now, with her in his arms, the dreams didn't come close to reality. Her skin was so soft. Her eyes had turned the color of storm clouds. She looked like a siren beneath him, and her song was enough to drive him mad. He ran his tongue over her hip and along the top of her thong. When she moaned, his dick throbbed harder.

He trailed his fingers over the skin his tongue had just traveled, and then when he reached the middle of her belly, he dipped his fingers lower.

"Oh, Hawk," she breathed.

The sound of his name on her lips touched something deep inside him. It resonated in him in a way that was inde-scribable. She was his. No matter what. *She was his.* He went back and ran his tongue over a nipple once again, then moved lower. He tugged her thong and brought it down over her hips. She kicked it off and dropped it on the floor.

He kissed her belly again and then her pelvic bones. Then, as he hovered his mouth over her center, he blew softly. She whispered his name again, straining her hips to reach him. He dropped a kiss on her core.

Breath sizzled between her lips and she fisted her fingers in his hair as he slid his hands under her hips to bring her to his mouth. He used his tongue to tease and suckle her.

He took her to the brink, then eased back. The sounds she made had him smiling all the while. She was under his spell, and he was hers to command.

She pleaded, "Don't tease me."

He swirled the tip of his tongue over her clit as he eased his fingers past her entrance. He set a slow, steady rhythm that made her buck her hips.

"Oh, god. Faster," she demanded.

"You're very bossy," he said but yielded to her demands. She yelled his name as she arched beneath him, her channel undulating on his fingers as she crashed over the edge. He felt powerful and possessive of her. It made no sense, but he was beyond caring. She was amazing and incredible.

She was his.

Remy lay panting on the bed, Hawk beside her. This man had taken her so far beyond anything she'd imagined, she couldn't process it. His caress was magnificent and his body hard and unyielding—she loved it. It didn't hurt that she also adored his wit and his smile made her heart thrum faster.

She turned on her side and leaned against him, running her hand down his chest. He was lying on his back. She brought her mouth down to his and claimed it with a harshness she didn't know she possessed. She climbed on top of him. Maybe it was the craziness of the situation, but she wanted Hawk like she'd never wanted another man. She wanted *him*. Inside her. Now.

She broke their kiss. Their gazes locked as she reached down to rub him through his shorts. He swore when her hand first stroked him. He was hard as rock. Power surged through her. He was hard for *her*. She eased her fingers under the waistband as he kissed her neck. She started to tug them down, and he lifted his hips to help her pull them off.

She kissed him hard again, her tongue stroking his, but then broke off the kiss. "I want to feel you inside me," she stated boldly.

He made her feel bold. In control. The rest of her life was totally out of her control at this moment, but she could control this. Him. And she loved it. His eyes were a deep blue, glassy and filled with desire.

She rained kisses down his jaw and ran her hands across his chest. She sucked on his nipple, then blew on it. She did the same with the other and grinned as he groaned. She loved that she had the power to drive him crazy with her touch. It was intoxicating.

She shifted her weight until she straddled his hips. As she slowly rubbed her core across his cock, he flexed against her.

He reached for her, but she shook her head. "Not yet." She pushed his hands down onto the bed. "I'll let you know when you can touch me."

"Remy," he growled. She loved the way his voice, when it rumbled through his chest, sent shivers down her spine, and caused heat to bloom between her legs. God, she was so ready for him. She raised her hips and moved over his cock. She lowered herself down onto him. First, she just let the tip enter her. Teasing him, she pulled back.

He swore. "Remy, fuck," he growled again.

Smiling, she started lowering herself again. This time, she took in more of him. She wanted to tease him longer but couldn't. She needed him now. He reached out and grabbed her hips. She didn't deny him. Instead, she rode him, picking up the pace. The feel of him inside her, filling her up, was exquisite.

Her breath puffed out in small, sharp gasps. She was going to come. She said his name and urged him on, her hips rushing to meet his rhythm, her fingernails raking across his chest as he thrusted up into her. Nothing had ever felt this good, this right. She was teetering on the brink and had to bite her lip to keep from screaming.

He thrusted deep inside her, and she crashed over the edge, euphoria filling her every cell. Hawk followed, and her body kept squeezing him as wave after wave washed over her.

She collapsed against his chest, sweaty and out of breath. Neither of them could move. She wanted to stay there forever, or until the madness was over. If only that were a possibility.

CHAPTER TWELVE

R emy crawled out of bed and went into the bathroom. She quietly locked the door and then turned on the shower. She leaned against the door while she waited for the water to get hot. Sleeping with Hawk was not smart. Okay, the sleeping part was fine, but the sex part was a mistake.

Oh, it had provided her with the much-needed release that allowed her to sleep like the dead, but as soon as she woke up, fear had slammed into her like a fist. She'd just turned her nightmare ordeal into…what was worse than a nightmare? She needed Hawk. Needed his help, but that was it. She didn't need a man in her life. They complicated things.

Panic set in. Her limbs trembled, her heart raced erratically, and she'd have better luck drawing a deep breath underwater. Yes, Hawk was easy to talk to and there was no doubt they were compatible in bed. She'd never enjoyed sex so much in her life.

But.

But she needed this mess sorted so she could move on with her life. She was by herself now. When her grandfather passed away, she realized she was truly on her own. That meant she couldn't afford to make a mistake with who she let in. There was no one there to help her pick up the pieces if something went wrong. Her grandfather had helped her after Drew but now there would be no help. Her life would be better…safer…if she stayed single.

She got into the shower and groaned aloud when the hot spray hit her aching muscles. With all the cleaning and running and lack of sleep, her body felt like she was ninety. She let the heat work its magic while she shampooed her hair.

Besides, she continued her train of thought, weren't one-night stands what men really wanted? All the dates she'd gone on in the last year seemed to be that way, so much so she'd stopped going. She massaged her scalp harder, working up a lather, physically and emotionally. She didn't want a one-night stand. She wanted more but only with someone who wouldn't break her heart and leave her alone. Hawk was not that person. Sure, he was helping her now but when this mystery was sorted, he'd be gone and she'd be alone again.

No, sex with Hawk had been a bad idea that seemed like a great idea when she'd been in the moment. Now she had to get over it.

There was a more pressing question than why the hell had she slept with Hawk. What did she want to do with her life? Now that she knew where the money came from, she had to decide if she wanted to spend any of it. Was it blood money? Who the fuck was she kidding? She was going to spend it, and it was blood money. Her family's blood, by the sounds of things. And their sweat and tears. Four generations of her family were all locked up in this. She was going to take that money and run.

She rinsed her hair and then massaged in conditioner. But where to go? Where could she run that they'd never find her? The Lock and Key Society was a global organization. There was no safe corner of the earth until they had this figured out. As Hawk had pointed out, maybe she'd always be perceived as a threat. *Great.* She may never be truly safe. She might always have to travel with security.

Hawk would keep her safe if they traveled. She could picture them sightseeing all over Europe. Discovering little shops together and great hole-in-the-wall restaurants all the while he would make sure she was okay.

Stop! Getting attached to Hawk was not an option. He was helping her now, but once this was done, it wasn't like he was going to stick around. He was thinking about getting back into the personal security game, about joining Callahan Security. Hadn't he said this was sort of a trial run for him? Once this adventure was over, he'd want to move on to other adventures, and quite possibly other women. Seriously, what did she know about him?

She finished rinsing her hair and then turned off the spray. After grabbing a towel, she patted her skin to dry off.

Nope, the smart play was to keep it more professional from now on. Sex with the man had been amazing, but it would only interfere with things in the long run. She'd end up being the one to get hurt. Keeping Hawk at a distance from now on was going to suck, but it was better to rip the band-aid off now before it got too sticky and dirty and ending up hurting her more than it helped.

She got dressed in a pair of jeans and a blue sweater. Hawk had good taste in clothes. Just because she wanted to cool things off didn't mean she didn't want to look her best. She pulled her wet hair into a bun and secured it in place. Then she put on a bit of mascara and eyeliner that Hawk had so kindly purchased. Instead of thinking it was because Hawk thought she looked so bad, Remy would instead consider them a gift for scaring her to death. She tried to downplay the dark circles under her eyes, but she hadn't found concealer or foundation among the other toiletries. At this rate, she could be mistaken for a raccoon.

Finally, she stepped back and studied at herself in the mirror. Not great, but it would have to do. She opened the door and walked into the room.

Hawk was on the phone. "She just entered the room. Let me put you on speaker." He hit a button on the screen and set the phone down on the bed. "Go ahead, Dragan."

"Hi, Remy. How are you holding up?" Dragan's voice came through the phone.

"Hanging in there," she replied. "Do you have some news?"

"Yes and no. I still can't get much in the way of details about the Lock and Key Society functions, but I did find out a bit more about your family."

She plopped onto the edge of the bed. She wasn't sure she could take hearing too much more, but she gamely braced herself. "Go ahead."

"According to my sources, the Lock and Key Society started sometime around nineteen-ten to nineteen-twenty. Your family was one of the founding families. At the beginning, there were only a few locations, New York, Philadelphia, Washington D.C. Over time, they expanded across the world. As a founding member, your—I guess it would be great-grandfather—had voting rights. This is where it gets a bit vague. I don't know what that means. I'm not sure what they vote on. I don't know how many founding members there were. The token is handed down through the family line, which is the way for every token, but the founding members have some sort of special token. I'm not sure what it is, and I don't know if it does anything special."

Remy closed her eyes for a second. *Great.* She came from

a family of criminals. She opened her eyes when Hawk touched her shoulder.

He handed her a cup of tea. "Dragan, did you manage to find out anything about Remy's grandfather's death?"

"Not much. I'm getting all of this from someone that I knew from my bad old days." His chuckle was meant to lighten the mood. It didn't. "He knows Archer Gray as well. He wasn't keen to talk, but I, uh, persuaded him. So, I have no idea how much of it is true." He paused. "I did hear there's a rumor your grandfather was murdered. Apparently, that's a big deal because it's a big no-no. As a founding family member, he's supposed to be untouchable."

Remy took a sip of tea. She let the warm liquid warm her frozen heart. "Dragan, I have a couple of questions. First, do you know, or did anyone say, why my great-grandfather wanted to start this…organization? I mean, was he in the mob or anything?"

"I don't know about having mob ties, but I can hazard a guess as to why they started it."

"Why?" she asked and braced herself for the answer.

"Prohibition. The US government made it illegal to produce, import, transport, or sell alcohol around the time it was founded. There were all kinds of underground clubs that sprang up because of it. My guess is this was one of those and then became…something else over time."

"That makes sense," Remy said. She'd read all about prohibition years ago, but Dragan was right. There were all kinds of underground clubs and groups that worked to provide alcohol to those who wanted it.

"You said you had another question?" Dragan asked.

"Um, yeah. You said that no one was allowed to…" She was having a hard time saying the word 'murder'. "That my grandfather was supposed to be untouchable because he was part of the founding families. Does that mean I'm supposed to be untouchable, too?"

There was a long silence on the other end of the phone. "Honestly?"

She glanced at Hawk, whose gaze was trained on her face. "Please, just tell me."

"I'm gonna reiterate that this is all hearsay. I could have it all wrong."

"That's fine," Hawk said. "Just spit it out, Dragan. She needs to hear this."

She shot Hawk a grateful look. He understood her need for information.

"Okay. My understanding is that under normal circumstances, your grandfather would have brought you into the fold before he died. Introduced you to everyone as his successor. Once that happened, you would be the member of the founding family on the board. He would cease to have protection after that, and it would switch to you.

"Because that didn't happen..." Dragan paused again. "Because that didn't happen, your grandfather's token is up for grabs. Anyone who finds it gets to be on the board."

"Shit." Remy damn near dropped her mug of tea. "That means..." She cleared her throat. "That means it's open season on me. No wonder everyone is in a mad rush to find the token. It sounds like it's the holy grail of tokens."

"Dragan, any chance you can delay your trip?" Hawk asked. "I think I might need some help with this."

"I wish I could. I'm on my way to Italy. I'll make it as quick a trip as possible, but I have to go. You'll be fine. Call Gage or Mitch if you need backup. Hell, call Logan in a pinch. He's a damn fine shot."

Remy's stomach rolled. Shooting? Jesus, would people be shooting at her? Did she need to wear body armor? This was getting seriously out of control.

"There's one more thing," Dragan said. "One of the reasons there's such a push to find the token is, apparently, there's a board meeting the day after tomorrow. It's going to happen behind the scenes at some big shindig at a museum or something. It's a charity thing that they're using for cover. Whoever has the token will be recognized as the new board member then."

"That doesn't give us much time." Hawk ran a hand through his hair.

"What if no one finds the token? Then what happens?"

Dragan coughed. "My understanding is that the board seat remains empty until the next meeting, which could be a couple of months out."

"That's not good." Hawk let out a long breath.

"Why?" Remy was totally confused. "Why isn't it good?"

Hawk drummed his fingers on the desk. "Because it means it will be a free-for-all until the seat is filled. If someone finds the token after the first meeting, they have to keep their mouth shut about it and stay hidden until the next board meeting. Otherwise, someone else will try to take it from them, most likely killing them in the process. People will assume you have it."

Remy couldn't get her brain around it. How could this token thing be so important? "What makes this Lock and Key Society so fucking important that people are willing to kill to be admitted?"

There was only silence and then some muffled sounds coming from the phone. Dragan said, "I have to run."

"Dragan, one more quick question." Remy was surprised her voice sounded even. She was shaking on the inside. "What stops people from killing the token holders? I mean, the regular token holders, not the board members. Why aren't they dropping like flies if all you have to do is possess the token to be a member?"

"I think they do get killed, but I think more often the token is just stolen. I would imagine someone steals it, and then someone else steals it back. But the real answer to your question is secrecy. No one ever admits to being a member of the society and having a token. Only members of the society are allowed through the doors so everyone on the inside has a token. The board members are a separate group but either way, it is forbidden to talk about the society."

"Then why did this guy talk to you?" she asked. "Is he a member?"

There was another long pause. "Let's just say I can be persuasive."

She frowned. She opened her mouth to ask another question, but Hawk shook his head at her.

"Thanks, Dragan. This is all good information. Good luck in Italy. Let me know when you hit town again."

"Will do. Be safe." And then Dragan was gone.

"Why didn't you let me ask him about his source? It would be nice to know how much of this is true."

"Because he was trying to protect you from the truth."

"What truth?" she demanded.

"Dragan found someone with an ax to grind with Archer Gray and had some knowledge of the society. Dragan probably threatened to kill him. Or do him grievous bodily harm. It would have taken a lot to get the words flowing."

Remy's stomach rolled as nausea struck in full force. "You mean he hurt someone to find out the stuff he told us?"

"He did what was necessary." Hawk's arms were crossed over his chest. "Sometimes life isn't so pretty. To answer your other question, it's just a guess, but from what Dragan has said and Gus's observations, I think the Lock and Key Society is a safe haven. Meaning, if you have a token, you're protected once you're there. No one can kill you or arrest you. No one can do anything to you that you don't want to happen. You can meet whoever you want in total secrecy. Think of it like the ultimate luxury hotel. My theory is they can bring you whatever you want. Make anything happen for you. Take care of every need imaginable."

"Still, a good high-end hotel will do most of that." Remy still didn't get it.

"Maybe, but you're thinking along strictly legal lines. With the society anything goes. Anything. If you were a bad guy, where would you want to spend your time? Somewhere you know you will be safe, no questions asked. Somewhere your every wish is granted. Somewhere you can let your guard down and say or do whatever the hell you want. They can't do that at high-end hotels." His face hardened. He wasn't going to spell it out any further for her, but she got the message.

She nodded. Her family helped the worst of the worst do whatever they wanted. Revulsion clawed its way up her throat, freezing her from the inside out.

This was a world she wanted no part of.

She met Hawk's gaze. He was a trained killer. She'd forgotten that, but looking at him now, there was no mistaking it. And as much as she might wish it wasn't so, his skill was probably the only thing that was going to keep her alive over the next couple of days.

CHAPTER THIRTEEN

Hawk kept his arms crossed over his chest because if he didn't, he'd reach out and pull Remy to him. He wanted her safe in the circle of his arms, but his training forced him to be realistic. Having sex with her had been a major mistake. When he most needed a clear head and laser focus, he'd clouded the line. Emotions, including lust, were a big distraction, and they weren't ever helpful.

That was one of the reasons he was glad that, as a SEAL, he'd never had a wife back home for him to return to after a mission. He'd witnessed his team struggle to leave their lives in the US behind. To not think about their wives and kids when it came time to missing anniversaries and birthdays. It was drilled into them that they needed to disengage with life at home, once they got on the airplane that was taking them to their next assignment. Hell, they'd even had to leave wedding rings and family pictures in their gear lockers.

He never wanted to have to struggle like that. Thanks to his fucked up parental situation, he never thought about all those things. He didn't have anyone to really miss, and that made him fucking good at his job. Like scary fucking good. But it also made him lonely.

Now he needed to be his old self. The calm, focused, cold-as-ice asshole who would get the job done. Emotion would just cost him, and Remy was too dear of a price. He swallowed. "We need to start seriously thinking about where your grandfather could have hidden his token."

"We don't even know what it is. How can we look for it?" Remy huffed out a breath. "Plus, everyone has beaten us to the two places I thought he would hide something. Do you think they missed it?"

Hawk rested his ass on the desk. "It's a possibility, but not likely. I think your grandfather was a smart man. It sounds like he didn't need to show his token regularly. Only for board meetings. He didn't have to have it when he let people use the stairs because at most he would have to walk them down. He wasn't always going in, so it wouldn't have to be in the shop or his apartment. No, I think he put it somewhere he could retrieve it when he needed it but kept it out of reach in case such a situation arose."

Remy set her mug on the table next to the bed. "Why do you think he didn't introduce me to the board?"

Hawk didn't want to answer that. "I have no idea. He must have had his reasons." He didn't know Remy Jr. so he didn't want to comment on the man's integrity, but Dragan had said that Remy Jr. would have lost his protection the moment he introduced Remy to the board. Was the old man that selfish? Was it because he had already lost his son and daughter-in-law, so he was super careful with his grand-daughter? Keep her out of it as long as possible? Who the fuck knew? And it was pointless trying to figure it out. He'd leave those machinations up to Remy. Now, his prime responsibility was to create a plan of action for them to find the token before it was too late.

"What if someone else finds the token?" Remy asked. "What happens to me?"

Hawk frowned. "I'm not following you."

"Well, what if we just wait until someone else claims the token and becomes a board member? Then the danger is over, and I don't have to worry anymore. Maybe that's what we need to do. Just lie low until the meeting is over and the new board member is put in place."

"Remy." He didn't know how to point this out to her, so he was just going to be blunt. "If you don't claim the token and the seat on the board, then you're a loose end. You heard Dragan. No one talks about this society. Do you think they'll just leave you alone? Logically, it would make a whole hell of a lot more sense to kill you. Then the threat of exposure is over." He hated even voicing that thought but he had to make it clear to her.

"Also, with you still alive, there's always the threat that you'll take the token back. Dragan didn't say anything about stealing the token. Your grandfather was supposed to be untouchable because he was on the board. No one is supposed to be allowed to kill him, but who knows if they're allowed to steal the token and then claim a seat on the board.

She blinked owlishly at him.

He continued with his brutal assessment. "You have a target on your back. The only way to get that mitigated is to find that token and claim your seat on the board. Then you'll be as safe as possible."

She stared at him. "As safe as possible. You didn't stop at safe. I'll never really be safe again, will I?"

With every rebellious fiber of his body, he wanted to tell her that it would all be fine. That she could go back to her normal life. But, logically, he didn't believe she ever could. To be truthful, he thought what she once considered normal was fading in her rearview mirror. Suddenly, he had a deeper understanding of the decision that her grandfather had wres-tled with.

He shrugged. "I don't know."

It was a lame answer, but he didn't think she could take any more truth. Her eyes were huge, and she was blinking back tears by the looks of things. Her hands were shaking, and she was struggling to draw a normal breath. He desper-ately wanted to comfort her, but he wasn't going to lie. He just wouldn't do that.

"We need to go over everything you know about your grandfather. Who were his friends besides Gus? Where did he go on a regular basis? What hobbies did he have?"

She let out a long breath and cleared her throat. "I could use more tea and possibly some food."

She had her hand on her stomach like it was bothering her, but if she wanted food, he'd dig some up for her. She needed to keep her strength up. Besides, he was starving.

"I'll go downstairs and rustle up something. Do you have any preferences?"

She shook her head.

"Okay, I'll be back. Don't open the door to anyone but me, okay?"

"Sure."

When he stepped out the door to the landing, only then did it occur to him that she probably said she wanted food because she really wanted time alone. He started down the stairs. This was a lot to take in. He didn't blame her one bit, but if they didn't figure out something soon, life was going to get a whole lot more complicated.

He walked out of the back stairs and into the bar area. The bar was still closed, but the smell of food hit his nose. He pushed open the kitchen door. Connor stood over the grill, making eggs and bacon. "Did you save any of that for us? I could eat the ass out of skunk."

Connor turned around and gave him an appraising look. "I bet you could at that." He smiled. "I'll make you some breakfast. Bacon and eggs, okay?"

Hawk nodded. "Sounds good."

"There's coffee in the pot over there." He gestured with his chin.

"Thanks."

"You look like you could use it. Was it a rough one then?"

Hawk tried to suppress a grin. "It was…fine." It was a hell of a lot better than fine, but at this moment in time, he wasn't going to discuss it. He needed to bury it. Put it in a box and seal the lid up tight. Maybe wrap it in chains to get through this and keep Remy alive. He poured himself coffee and found a stool tucked under a prep counter. He pulled it out and sat down.

"I checked around a bit about what you were askin'. No one wants to talk about it. They're all afraid, but I did hear that there's a lot of people wantin' a chance to speak with your lady friend. She's got somethin' they all want."

"Fuck." Hawk shook his head. "That's the problem. She doesn't have it. We need to fucking find it before someone kills her over it."

"So, it's like that, is it?" Connor flipped the bacon. "I can help ya keep her safe, but you gotta know the list is long, and it's growin' by the day. I hear there's three different groups lookin' for her. I presented myself as number four, just so you know."

"Do you know who the groups are?"

"There are the Asian gang guys you mentioned yesterday and some Euro-trash gangsters. The third group is a mystery."

"Terrific." Hawk rubbed his face with both hands. "How am I supposed to keep her safe and find the token?"

"That's what they're after then, a token of some sort." Connor put the bacon on two plates and then started frying some eggs.

"I don't know what it is to be honest. Her grandfather didn't say a damn thing about it to anyone."

"Those are the rules from what I understand. Does make it hard, though."

"Yeah." Hawk took a sip of coffee.

"You're welcome to stay here as long as ya need, but to be clear, with this kind of firepower comin' at us, I might need to call in some reinforcements. The thing is, they're gonna cost money."

Hawk nodded. "I'll pay. Just tell me how much." He took another sip of coffee and swallowed. "I do wonder, though, if you call in reinforcements, will that trigger something? Will people suddenly pay attention and wonder why these extra hired guns are around? The last thing I need is for any of the three groups to find out we're here."

Connor frowned at him. "Are you sayin' you think my people don't know how to be discreet?"

"No, brother. I'm saying how do you know none of them are members of the Lock and Key Society?"

"Huh. I gotta admit, I'd not thought of that, and it's not like they'd tell me, would they? They aren't allowed." Connor slid the fried eggs onto the plates beside the bacon. "Let me have a think on it, and I'll get back to ya." He handed Hawk some cutlery and then the two plates. "I'll bring you more coffee and tea in a few minutes."

"Thanks, Connor. I really appreciate it."

"It's only breakfast." Conner grinned at him.

"You know what I mean."

"I do, and you're welcome. Now take those up to your lady friend before they get cold."

Hawk went back up the stairs and banged lightly on the

door with his foot. "It's me. My hands are full. Open the door please."

The door swung open, and a much calmer looking Remy stood there. He cocked an eyebrow but all she said was "breathing exercises" and gave him a quick smile.

He entered, then handed her a plate along with some cutlery. She took a seat in the armchair across the room, and set the plate on the arm of the chair. Hawk closed the door and went and leaned his butt on the desk. He'd eaten standing up more times than he could count, and not just in the military. He lived alone. A lot of times he ate leftovers out of the carton while standing on his balcony. It was habit.

Remy didn't touch her food. Instead, she played with what looked like a piece of cloth in her lap. "I think we need to walk the neighborhood like my grandfather."

He stopped chewing. "That's—"

"I know what you're going to say, but it's the only place I can think of as to where his token could be."

Hawk finished chewing. "I was going to say that's a good idea."

"Oh." She blinked and ran the cloth through her hands one more time.

"What's that in your hands?"

She glanced down. "It's a handkerchief. My mother gave it to me the last time I...we were together. I fell off my bike and scraped my knee. She picked me up and gave me this to dry my tears. She told me to keep it when I tried to give it back to her. She said just in case I had any mishaps and she wasn't there to wipe my tears, then I would have this to use and to remind me that she loved me." She stopped talking.

"How old were you when you lost them?"

"Eight."

Jesus. His heart hurt at the thought of a very young Remy losing her parents. He understood the pain to an extent. He'd been much older, but it was much the same thing. He had this insane urge to go over and pull her out of the chair and into his arms. To tell her she wouldn't be alone ever again. He blinked. What kind of ridiculous thought was that? *Shit.* The lack of sleep and close proximity must be getting to him. He cleared his throat. "Back to the idea of walking around the neighborhood."

She nodded as she put the cloth back into her pocket and then picked up a piece of bacon. "I know the route. I've walked it with him a few times. I know Gus also gave us the street names, but I know most of the shopkeepers he was friendly with. Maybe if we talk to them, we can figure it out."

Hawk swallowed. "I think it's a good idea, but I think I should go alone. You can tell me the names of the shopkeepers, and I'll talk to them."

She stopped eating again. "No. That's just not going to work." She put up a hand like a traffic cop to fend off the argument he started to make. "I know these people. They will talk to me. Do you think if my grandfather left his token with any of them they would just give it to you? A total stranger?"

Fuck. She had a point. "I just don't want you out there risking your life unnecessarily."

"Yeah, me too, but this is necessary."

She was ready to continue arguing with him. The set of her jaw was a dead giveaway, but she was right. He would save his energy. He had a feeling there would be more arguments in their future, and he would need to pick his battles carefully.

"Okay, I get it. We'll go, but I need to find you a disguise of some sort first. I'll have to go out and get a new jacket and maybe a hat for both of us."

She nodded. "That sounds like a good idea. Once we

have that, we can go." She dug into her food enthusiastically now. "I think we should start a few blocks down from the store," she said as she chewed on her bacon. "He wasn't close to too many people on the street where the shop is. The stores around him have all changed hands too many times. But two blocks down, he had more friends. We should start there."

Hawk finished his meal and put his plate down on the desk. He was going to have to see if Connor was free. He didn't want to do this alone. Just then, there was a knock at the door.

Hawk reached over and opened it. "Just the man I wanted to see."

Connor walked in with coffee and tea. "Ya just love me for my coffee," he said as he handed Hawk a mug. He walked over to Remy and handed her the tea.

"Thank you," she said with a smile. "Breakfast was excellent."

"Thank you, my darlin'."

Hawk frowned. Why the hell was she smiling so big at Connor? He took a big gulp of coffee and promptly burnt his tongue. "Jesus," he mumbled and put the mug down next to his empty plate. "Connor, you have any big plans for today?"

"Mondays are usually pretty quiet. What do ya need?"

"We need to go back to her shop and do a walk of the neighborhood. I could use another set of eyes and ears. Hell, another set of guns if it comes to it."

"I'm your man. When do you want to go?"

Hawk glanced at his watch. "I need an hour or so. I have to get new jackets and hats."

"Perfect. I'll get things sorted downstairs and be ready to head out in an hour." He collected their plates and left.

Hawk straightened. "I'll go grab us some new coats and hats."

"You don't want to finish your coffee?"

He met her gaze. "I want to get this done, the sooner the better." He grabbed the gun from the nightstand and tucked it in the waistband of his jeans at the small of his back and then pulled his sweater down over it.

Remy sat and sipped her tea and he'd thought he'd seen a hurt look flit across her features but it was gone too fast for him to be sure. He hadn't meant to hurt her if that was the case but being near her was killing his concentration.

"I'll be back shortly."

He pulled on his jacket and headed out, closing the door behind him. What he hadn't said was he wanted this over because she was a serious distraction. He wasn't much for relationships, but he'd sure as hell would like to have sex with her again, and he couldn't do that as long as he was trying to keep her safe. So, for now, it was hands off, but that was easier said than done so keeping her at a distance from him was the easiest way to guarantee he didn't grab on to her and make her yell his name like she'd done last night. Just the thought of that made his cock jump. This favor for Lacy had turned into a nightmare in more ways than one.

CHAPTER FOURTEEN

I f she wasn't so worried about getting killed, Remy would have put on her jacket and gone back to her shop on her own. Jesus, what a friggin' thought that was. How had her life gone off the rails so damn quickly?

She flexed her head from one side to the other, trying to release the painful tension. The mess her grandfather left her in wasn't the only source of her discomfort. Hawk announcing that he didn't want to waste one minute drinking coffee with her had pierced her like the thorn of a cactus. He wanted this sorted. Well, no shit. She did, too, but taking a moment to drink coffee wasn't going to change things.

She took a sip of tea and tried to calm herself. The sex had been great but she didn't want a relationship. So why did the pang in her chest at that thought make her need to grind her teeth? She was being stupid. *Grow up*. She could think about relationships later when she knew she was going to live longer than forty-eight hours. Even entertaining the thought of a relationship with the man was plain old stupid. Hawk had just made it very clear that he was not interested in anything long term.

She set her mug down and closed her eyes for a minute. Her current situation was responsible for turning her into a ninny. Stress and uncertainty were creating havoc with her emotions. Hawk was the only strong, true thing in her life at the moment. Maybe that's why she wanted to cling to him. He was her anchor, and she was currently being caught up in a major storm. It made sense that she was falling for him. She was desperate.

But it really was time to grow up and get her head on straight. She was approaching her mid-thirties. She'd never needed anyone to take care of her. She'd stood on her own two feet for ages. *Time to stop being so wishy-washy.* She opened her eyes as she picked up her phone and glanced at the screen. Gus sent a text late last night to let her know he'd made it to San Diego safely. *Thank God.* She didn't have it in her to deal with any more loss.

She pulled up the notes feature on her phone and started making a list of names of people from the neighborhood that her grandfather spoke to on a regular basis.

They should start with Abdul at the bodega three blocks down from the bookshop. He and her grandfather played chess together on Saturday afternoons when Emily was working at the shop.

Then it would be Madam Zalinski. Thinking of the woman brought a smile to her face just as the door opened.

She tensed, then relaxed as she spied Connor.

His face was ice-cold as he bit out, "You have to move."

"What? What's goin' on?"

"A group of Asian gang members just came in downstairs. They could be here because I put out the word I'm interested in finding that token, but I don't want to take any chances."

Remy pulled on her shoes. "Did you tell Hawk?"

"Yes. He's gonna meet ya at the back door. Leave your coat. He's got a new one for ya." She grabbed her phone and tucked it in her back pocket. She took her gloves from her old jacket pocket and then rounded the bed.

Connor stepped back into the hallway. "Okay, come with me." He shot her a glance. "You're gonna be fine. Your man is excellent at taking care of people. He saved my bacon twice." Then he winked. "Although I won't admit that to him. Can't have his ego getting too big, can we?"

She nodded and tried not to freak the hell out. How the fuck had the gang members found them? Or was it Connor they were there to see?

They went down a different staircase at the other end of the hallway. The stairs terminated at a large metal door with three massive deadbolts on it.

"Do you have a lot of trouble here?" she asked in a quiet voice.

Connor grinned. "No, and there's a good reason." He pointed at the locks. "No need to make it easy."

She tried to return his smile but just couldn't manage it. Her hands started to shake so she jammed them into her jeans' pockets, finding comfort in having her handkerchief there, like a security blanket. Cold seeped through the door, and suddenly her sweater didn't seem nearly as warm as it had upstairs.

"Okay," Connor said, looking up from his phone. "Hawk is outside." He put his phone in his pocket, pulled a gun from his waistband, and started undoing the locks. The clunks and clinks were loud in the silence, unnerving Remy further.

She knew she shouldn't be shocked by the gun, but she was. Connor and Hawk had discussed weapons earlier, and she had seen Hawk stash a gun at the small of his back. But the idea of needing firearms to protect was surreal. When had her life devolved into hanging out with gun-toting men?

Connor opened the door to Hawk standing just outside on a small landing. He was wearing a black Canada Goose jacket with a black skull cap. He nodded at Connor and then handed her a matching black jacket from the same brand. "This should keep you warm enough."

She pulled it on, and then he gave her a scarf, which she tucked around her chin. He pulled a blond wig out of the bag. "It's not great, but it should provide enough cover."

She stared at him. "Seriously?"

"Yeah. We don't have much time." He turned to Connor. "Are you sure you're going to be okay on your own?"

"I called some mates. They'll be here in under three minutes, according to the last text"

Hawk nodded grimly.

Remy had the wig in her hands and was turning it to get it situated right on her head. She pulled it down over her bun and tried to straighten it as best she could.

"Don't worry about how it looks." Hawk pulled a navy beanie with a pompom on the end out of the bag and pulled it down over the wig until it covered her ears. "There." He stared at her for a second but didn't say anything else.

"How do I look?

Connor grinned. "I'd never recognize ya. You look cute, but I like ya better as a brunette." He winked at her, and she found herself smiling back.

"You ready?" Hawk snarled.

"Yeah," she said as she zipped up her jacket and pulled on her gloves. She turned and gave Connor a quick kiss on the cheek. "Thanks for your help. Please be safe."

"Don't worry about me, luv. I'm hard to kill, just like a cockroach." He winked again.

After Remy stepped onto the stoop, Hawk nodded to

Connor, who then closed the door. They heard the locks click in place. Hawk started down the outside stairs, and she followed him. She had to jog to keep up as he moved across the small space and then checked the back alley. It was clear.

"Stay close. We're gonna go out to the end of the alley and turn left. There's a car waiting for us at the end of the block."

"Ernie?"

"No. Just some random Uber driver."

They made their way to the car and got in.

"Do you know where we're going?" she asked Hawk.

He nodded but nodded at the driver and then shook his head slightly. He wanted her to stop talking. She let out a sigh. Fine... The silent treatment. That worked for her.

Twenty minutes later, they pulled to the curb a few blocks from her bookshop. Hawk climbed out and checked the street, and then helped her out of the car. He slammed the door, and she started walking to the bodega, which was a few stores down.

"Where are you going?" Hawk asked.

She pointed. "Abdul runs the store on the corner. He and my grandfather played chess together in the summer." When she walked into the store, Abdul wasn't behind the cash register, but his great-granddaughter, Maysoun.

"Hi, Maysoun," she said with a wave.

The woman smiled. "Hi, Remy. How are you? I almost didn't recognize you with your blond hair."

She reached up and touched the wig. She'd forgotten about the hair. So much for being unrecognizable. Then again, she was the one to say hello first. "Right, I thought I would try something new. How are you doing?"

"I'm good. I like the blond." She smiled and then shivered. "It's cold out there, huh?"

Remy nodded. "I keep thinking winter will be over soon, but it doesn't seem to want to end."

"I hear that." She was wearing a long navy sweater over a white shirt. "Can I help you find something?"

"Actually, I was looking for Abdul."

Maysoun frowned. "He's not here."

"Do you know when he'll be back?"

"Not until April or May. He hates the cold. He went home to the Middle East for the winter. He left back at the beginning of October."

"Oh, I didn't realize." *Strike one.* There was no way Gramps would've given his token to someone who wasn't around all the time. It needed to be accessible.

"We were all sad to hear about your grandfather. My great-grandfather will miss him very much."

"Thanks, Maysoun." She gave the other woman a smile. "Tell your family I said hello. See you in the spring when it's much warmer." She gave the young girl a wave and left the shop with Hawk at her heels.

Back out on the sidewalk, heading south, she turned to Hawk and said, "We can scratch that one. The token would need to be somewhere that Gramps could get it when he needed it. Abdul being out of town for months on end makes it unlikely he would be in charge of it."

"Agreed." Hawk's gaze darted about their surroundings.

Remy wasn't sure if that made her feel safer or more freaked out. She decided not to dwell on it. Let him do whatever it was that he was supposed to do to keep her alive, and she'd just concentrate on finding the token.

They walked down another two blocks and then turned onto West 75th Street. "Do you know where we're headed?" Hawk asked. He still didn't look at her but kept his gaze sweeping the streets.

"Yes, the second stop is right up here." She pointed, and Hawk followed her direction to the store front.

"We're going to see a psychic?" He shot her a glance then.

She nodded. "Madam Zalenski. Maria is her first name. She knew both of my grandparents. She'd invite Gramps in for tea when he was walking past if she didn't have a client." Remy walked over and glanced in the window. It was a huge plate glass affair with *Psychic Readings* stenciled in bold red lettering. Across the inside of the window hung strings of gold beads of varying lengths that had different symbols mixed in among the beads.

"Maria has been here for donkey's years, as my grand-mother used to say. I remember looking for my sign in among all the gold beads." She pointed. "There, see that symbol? It's mine, I'm a Virgo." She pointed to the gold charm attached to one of the bead strings.

Hawk stood mute beside her. He seemed to be using the window's reflection to see what was going on around them.

Maria Zalenski waved at them. Remy moved around Hawk and opened the door. "Maria, it's so good to see you."

"Remy," the older woman said, as she came forward and gave Remy a warm hug. "It's so good to see you, too." She touched the blond hair and cocked an eyebrow. "A wig?" She narrowed her eyes slightly but didn't say anything else.

Two for two. Apparently, the wig wasn't fooling people when they were up close. Remy let out a sigh as she marveled at how the older woman hadn't seemed to age a day since they'd first met when Remy was about twelve. Maria's long white hair still curled around her cherubic face. Her brown eyes danced with laughter more often than not, and she exuded an air of warmth and pure joy of life.

"Come, sit for a minute," Maria said as she moved back toward the chairs in the corner of the room. There was a table covered with a black tablecloth between two chairs, and her tarot cards and crystal ball were there in the center, as they'd always been.

Once seated, she turned to Remy. "Who did you bring with you today?" She nodded toward Hawk.

"Um, this is Hawk. He's a friend of mine."

Maria studied Hawk for a full minute. Hawk held her gaze with seemingly no issue and then went back to looking out the window when Maria turned back to face Remy. "He's more than a friend."

Remy didn't quite know what to say to that. "Um…"

"You're in some kind of trouble." The older lady studied Remy. "You're in danger. He's here to keep you safe." She stared over Remy's left shoulder. "I'm not sure he can," she mumbled and then grabbed her tarot cards. She quickly shuffled the deck and then cut them. She drew out three cards, none of which meant anything to Remy.

"There is much change coming for you, dear," Maria said. "Some of it is good. Some, not so much. You will have to come to terms with things before you can move on."

Remy wasn't sure what she should say to that, if anything.

Maria looked at the cards again. "You have discovered that your grandfather kept secrets." She lifted troubled eyes.

Their gazes met. A chill went down Remy's spine. "You know, don't you? You know about—"

Maria held up her hands. "Don't tell me. I don't know the details, and I told your grandfather I wanted no part in it. Nothing good can come from it *for me*. For you, it will be different."

"What do you know?" Remy demanded.

Maria shook her head. "I don't know anything. Only that your grandfather struggled with his secrets. And now those secrets are very dangerous to you. You must be very careful."

Maria glanced at Hawk. "He will do his best to keep you

safe. His best is very good, but there might be…someone who wants what you have. Several people. It will not be easy." She turned and faced Hawk. "You have the gift," she said.

He kept his face blank.

"I see you don't like to talk about it, but it's there. It's very strong in you. You need to trust it. Your gift will not fail you. Only you can fail it."

Hawk stared at her and then checked the window one more time. He turned back to Maria. "You have the token."

She cocked her head and gave a little shrug. *Maybe or maybe not.* It seemed to say.

Remy wanted to scream. These two were playing some kind of game that she didn't understand, and she wanted answers.

"It's a key," Hawk said suddenly.

"What? Why do you think that?" Remy demanded.

Hawk was still staring at Maria. Then suddenly he turned and reached above his head to pull something down from a gold beaded string. He held it up for Remy to see. It was an old-fashioned key with a winking skull as the bow of the key.

"Son of a bitch," she said. "How did you know?"

Maria smiled. "Because he has a gift." The smile slid off her face. "But now you must go. It's a very dangerous time. Be very careful and trust no one." She stood and gripped Remy's hands with surprising strength, drawing her to her feet. She gave Remy a big hug, her arms tight around Remy's shoulders. Then she stepped back. "Except him." She pointed to Hawk. "You can trust him."

Hawk had pocketed the key. He nodded to Maria and opened the door. He ushered Remy out and closed it tight behind him. "We need to move," he said in clipped tones.

"How did you know it was a key?"

"We can't talk about this now. Now we have to move." He grabbed her hand and tugged her along the street. He turned right at the end of the block, and they headed south. A couple of blocks later, they were at the 72nd Street subway station.

"We're going to catch an express train downtown." Hawk's gaze skimmed the crowd before he led her down the steps into the station. They scanned their metro cards and then took the escalators down to the tracks. Standing on the platform, waiting for the train, was nerve-racking for Remy. Hawk's head was on a constant swivel. It was driving her nuts.

Finally, she gave in and asked, "Are you sensing anything?"

He shot her a cold look, and she immediately regretted her words. They'd talked about how hard it was for him when people depended on his talent. She knew it would be difficult for him to be in this situation, and she didn't want him to be uncomfortable but, shit, her life was on the line, and he was as tense as a bow string. The least he could do was tell her if she was in danger.

"There's…something." He didn't elaborate.

She knew asking him anything else would be pointless. As her belly rolled, she almost regretted asking him in the first place.

The train arrived, and they hopped on with a small group of what looked like college kids. Two of them had backpacks and the third had a scruffy beard and a tattered beanie. He smelled skunky, like pot. Oh, for the carefree days of university when her biggest worry had been what grade she got in the geology class she had to take as her single science credit.

The car was half empty, not surprising since it was midday on a Monday. A few businessmen in suits sat at the other end of the car, and the college kids sat chatting in the middle of the car. Hawk directed her to sit next to the end door. He stood in front of her and held on to the pole.

"Are we—" She stopped when he shot her a look.

Essentially, he was telling her to keep her mouth shut and do as he said. She got the message. Now wasn't the time. Still, she had so many questions, and questions were good because they kept her from thinking about whatever threat was lurking.

The doors opened at Times Square, and more people got on. The train started moving again. The next stop was 34th Street. It was farther south than they needed to go. They should have gotten off at Times Square. She nudged Hawk's shoe. He just shook his head slightly.

They stayed on the train until 14th Street where he hustled her off the train and out to the street. "I think we're being followed."

"What? How? Who?" She tried to turn around to see who was behind them, but he grabbed her arm and propelled her forward. "Take your phone out of your pocket and give it to me."

She did what she was told as he kept her walking north. He pulled her into a small deli. "Stand here," he said and then took her cell phone back out of his pocket. He asked the guy at the counter for a paper clip or a sharp knife.

The guy looked around and came back with a small safety pin. "Will this do?"

Hawk nodded and thanked the man. Then he used the safety pin to pop the sim card out of her phone. He broke the sim card in two and dropped it in the garbage can. He put her phone back in his pocket and pulled out his own, repeating the procedure.

"Now," he said. "We're going to hightail it out of here and see if we can find a cab to take us uptown again. We're going to keep going in circles until I know we're not being followed."

A million questions ran around her head, but there was

no point in asking them. His focus was on keeping them safe, not on indulging her curiosity. He dragged her out onto the street once more, and they walked north for a few more blocks. Then, by some miracle, they managed to hail a cab. Hawk gave the driver an address on West 45th Street but told him to take a nice circuitous route. The guy started to ask questions, but Hawk just said, "Drive like you're trying to lose a tail, and I'll give you a hundred bucks over the cost of the fare." The driver stopped asking questions and did as he was told.

Twenty-five nauseating minutes later, they pulled up in front of Callahan Security. "Shit," she said. "We're not going back to Connor's?"

Without a word, Hawk paid the cabbie and hustled her across the sidewalk and through the doors. The elevator ride to the top floor was silent and tense. When they stepped off, Mitch, Logan, and another man, who was obviously their relative, were waiting for them.

"Any trouble getting here?" Mitch asked.

Before Hawk could answer, Logan pointed to the man standing to his left. "This is our brother Gage, by the way."

She nodded to Gage. "Nice to meet you," she murmured.

"You look like you could use a cup of tea, or maybe something stronger," Logan suggested.

"Tea would be great."

He smiled and ushered her over to the seating area by the fireplace. "Why don't you sit down and relax a bit?"

She nodded her thanks and peeled off her jacket and gloves, then discarded the hat and wig. Logan took it all and placed it on a bar stool and then walked behind the bar to make her tea.

Mitch and Gage sat on the sofa, and Hawk took a seat on the chair across from her. He pulled off his hat and jacket. "To answer your question, I think we might've been followed for a bit, but I ditched the sim cards on our phones, and then we rode around for a while in a cab, so I think we lost them."

"Do you know who it was?"

"A group made up to look like college kids."

Remy stared at him. "You mean those guys on the train?"

He nodded. "They weren't as young as they looked. The one without the backpack had a gun under his jacket. The two with the backpacks were speaking in Moroccan Arabic. It's got a very specific accent. I couldn't make it all out, but they were trying to figure out if we found the token or not. I think we lost them when I got rid of our phone sims and we hopped in the cab."

"You think someone hacked your phones and followed you that way?" Gage asked.

"Yeah. Makes the most sense." Hawk stretched his legs out in front of him. "The only thing we have going for us at this point in time is that they don't know if we have the token. And when I say 'they,' I'm talking about all the people after the token. The thing is, we don't know who *they* are."

"You said the Asian men turned up at your friend's bar. Do you think they followed you two there?"

Hawk shook his head. "Connor did some poking around for us. He said the rumor is that there are three groups looking for the token. He put it out that he's part of a fourth group. He thought it might get him more information. I haven't had a chance to call and see what happened."

"Give me a minute, and I'll arrange for burner phones for you." Mitch stood and went over to the bar area where he made a phone call.

Remy leaned back in her chair. It had been a long day, full of emotion. No, that wasn't true. It should have been full of emotion, but all she felt was numbness. Like all of this was a dream.

"Let me see the key," she said. She'd suddenly realized she hadn't actually held it in her hand.

Hawk hesitated but reached into his pocket and pulled out the key. He leaned forward, and she did the same, then he dropped the old-fashioned gold key into her hand. It was heavier than she thought. The skull in the head of the key winked at her as if it knew all the secrets. It probably did. If only skulls could talk. Had her great-grandfather made this? She suspected he had. What the hell had he been thinking, getting involved in all of this?

She snorted to herself. He'd probably been thinking *I want a drink*. It all started during prohibition, so that was the logical thought. The question now was, when did it turn into something different, something more sinister?

Another man entered the bar area and handed Mitch some phones. "Thanks, Gunnar."

"Um Mitch," the man held up a file. Mitch raised an eyebrow. Gunnar leaned in and said something in a quiet voice but shot a look in her direction.

Her stomach cramped. Something in that look shot cold fear through her heart.

Mitch said something and Gunnar nodded and left again.

"Here's a phone for each of you." Mitch held a phone out to her and Hawk. She tucked the key into her pocket and took the phone. She couldn't think of anyone that she needed to contact, so she put the phone down on the coffee table in front of her. "What?" she asked.

Mitch hesitated.

"You might as well tell me," she said trying to sound much braver than she felt.

He nodded. "I asked Gunnar to look into your grandfather. I thought any information we can get might help us with the society. Gunnar uncovered something…about your parents' death."

She went cold and then hot. Her breath caught in her throat but her heart kept pounding like it was trying to escape her chest. She couldn't speak.

Hawk moved forward in his chair. "What did he find?"

"I'm so sorry, Remy, but your parents didn't die in a car accident. Well, they were in a car accident but the medical examiner's report says they were shot before their car went off the road. They were dead before they ended up in the ravine."

All the air left her lungs in a whoosh. She couldn't breathe. Her parents were murdered. *Murdered.* Just like her grandfather. She was sure of that now too.

Suddenly, Hawk was beside her. "Breathe."

She blinked and slowly turned to look at him. The edges of her vision were getting fuzzy.

He gently pushed her head between her knees. "Take deep breaths."

Finally, her lungs began to work again. A few seconds later, she sat up again. "Thanks." She gave him a weak smile. "It's just such a shock."

He nodded and went back to his chair.

Remy looked at Mitch. "Tell me the rest of it." She knew there was more.

Mitch frowned. "It looks like your grandfather covered up what happened as best he could. I guess he didn't want you to know the truth. He was trying to protect you. It was only because Gunnar found the original autopsy report that we found out. I would imagine the society helped him hide your parents' real cause of death." Mitch shook his head. "I am really so sorry, Remy."

She nodded. Speaking wasn't an option at the moment. She was so angry, betrayed and hurt that her grandfather had lied to her but she was livid that her parents had been murdered. The society had to be the reason. It had to be. The key burned a hole in her soul as if she'd been branded by it.

She reached for the handkerchief her mother had given her. It was all so unfair.

CHAPTER FIFTEEN

Hawk's phone rang. He excused himself, stood up and moved over to the corner of the room before answering it. "Connor, how'd it go? Everything okay?"

"Yeah, it's fine. The Asian boys and I had a right old chat. You were correct. They are part of the Triads. They didn't say which one. Their leader wants a token, but this one, in particular. He needs the protection it offers as a board member. He's willing to use all his power to get it. He would happily pay me for it if I find it but they were very clear that if I stuck my nose in, and didn't sell it to them, they'd be happy to chop it and several other body parts off."

Hawk had leaned forward in his chair. "What did you tell them?"

"I told them I'd happily back off *if* they had the token, but until then, it was up for grabs. They got a bit nasty, but my mates and I handled it. A few of their number will be spending the night in hospital, I reckon."

Hawk grinned. "They should've known better than to attack you at your own place."

"The cheek!" he said and chuckled. "Anyway, it's all clear

if you want to come back. They're not watching the place so far as I can tell."

"Ah…" He glanced at Mitch. "We found somewhere else to stay for tonight at least." When Mitch nodded, Hawk continued, "Thanks for your help, though. I hope we didn't bring too much trouble to your door."

"It'll blow over, I expect. Once this business is sorted, they'll forget I ever existed. Hard to imagine, I know," he joked.

Hawk smiled. "Thanks again, brother. I might need some help tomorrow night. Will you be around?"

"I'm always a phone call away for you, my friend." He chortled as he hung up.

Hawk leaned back again. His gut had unfurled only slightly at the news that the Triads didn't actually know he and Remy had been there. It was a close one. He had known the moment Connor told him the Asian men had entered the bar. He didn't know any specifics, but he knew there was danger. His senses had told him, and he'd already been on his way back from getting their jackets when Connor called him.

He glanced at Remy. She'd paled again. His heart broke for her. She kept getting pounded by all her family secrets. Wave after wave. She had to be crushed, not to mention exhausted. God knew, he was.

"So, what is the next step?" Gage asked in a quiet voice.

Gage was right. Decisions had to be made. There wasn't a whole lot of time to let her process everything before making them. Hawk tried to catch Remy's gaze. "I think that's up to Remy."

She looked up at him. "Sorry, what?"

"The next step. It's up to you. I know there's a lot going on in your head right now, but we need to make some decisions. What do you want to do now that you have the key?"

She looked at him. "How did you know it's the key?

When we were with Maria, how did you know that it was specifically this key?"

Fuck. He'd been hoping she wouldn't ask that. He felt the weight of all three Callahan's stares on him. He hated talking about this stuff. It made him feel...fucking ridiculous. He cleared his throat. "Gus said that your grandfather used to say the club was the *key* to his success. That just stuck with me.

"When we looked in the window of the shop, you pointed out all the different charms mixed in with the gold beads. I got to thinking as you and Maria were talking. Your grandfather walked every day. He would need to be able to access wherever it was at any time, but he would also want to know it was still safe. What if it was like the logo on your shop? In plain sight, but only relevant to those in the know? I decided that made sense. And where else to put it but in a window where he could see it every time he walked by? I was betting on him having a key to Maria's shop just in case.

"Then I just let my eyes wander over all those charms in the window. When I saw the key, I just... I knew."

He stopped talking. He had nothing else to say. It was all true, just not maybe the whole truth. He had known the minute he saw the key. As soon as he saw it, his sixth sense had pinged, and along with Gus's retelling of her grandfather calling it the 'key to his success.' He'd actually contemplated leaving it there and not telling Remy he'd found it, but no need to share that thought either.

"So"—he locked gazes with Remy—"now that you have the key, what do you want to do with it?"

She let out a breath. "I'm not sure. I don't think I have much of a choice. Do you?"

"You do, actually," Logan said as he placed a tray of pita chips and spinach dip down on the coffee table. "From my understanding, you have several different options."

She arched a brow. "Explain please."

"One, you can keep the key and assume your family's seat on the board. We have no idea what that means, but it does seem to come with money from what you've said. Two, you can turn the key over to Archer Gray and let him do whatever he wants with it, which would hopefully keep you out of harm's way, or three, you could turn it over to one of these groups of people who are looking for it in exchange for keeping you safe."

Remy's gaze locked with Hawk's again. His stomach knotted. Logan was presenting everything in a rosy light, like it would all be easy, but there were no guarantees.

Hawk told her, "There are some serious disadvantages to each, which I think you need to consider."

"Such as?" she asked.

"If you give it to another interested party in exchange for protection, you would only have their word that they would follow through on their end of the deal. They may take the key and then kill you anyway."

She glanced at Logan. He nodded. "Hawk is not wrong."

Hawk went on. "You can give it to Archer Gray but, again, you have no guarantee that whoever he gives it to won't come back and kill you just to be sure that your family's claim on the key is completely destroyed."

"Again," Logan said, "he is not wrong."

Hawk leaned forward. "The last option, where you become a board member means you will be caught up in whatever this society entails, just like the rest of your family. There is no guarantee you'll be safe that way either, although, theoretically, once you have your seat on the board, you are supposed to be untouchable, if Dragan's source is to be believed. I'm not sure that's true."

Remy chewed her bottom lip as she looked about the room. Logan handed her another cup of tea.

Remy accepted the tea and took a small sip. "Well, I guess I'm damned if I do or damned if I don't. I'll have to think about it. If I do decide to give it to someone, how do we make that happen?"

Hawk's breath froze in his chest. Was she really thinking of giving it away? He viewed that as a far more dangerous scenario. Keeping it at least afforded her some protection. She could run her shop like her grandfather had done, and hopefully no one would be the wiser. Giving it away meant she'd be looking over her shoulder all her life. Did she not see that?

He cleared his throat. "I think, if you want to do that, we'd have to come up with some sort of plan for the handoff. It would involve a lot of security and would be dangerous."

"The board meeting is at some event tomorrow night, yes?" Gage asked.

Hawk nodded. "Some charity event at a museum. How many of those could there be on a Wednesday night in New York City?" The whole idea seemed ludicrous to him, but then again, the whole idea of the Lock and Key Society was beyond his comprehension. It was just too scary to contemplate.

"You'd be surprised," Logan chimed in, "but if I had to guess, I would suggest it's the one at the Gotham Art Museum. Tomorrow night, they are celebrating their major donors by having a massive dinner in one of the atriums."

Gage said, "That would seem to me to be the safest place for you to hand the key off to another party if you wish to do so. Security will be onsite. People are less likely to whip out guns in that kind of a setting, especially since it might kill their chances of actually becoming part of the society."

Remy frowned. "How do you mean?"

"Well," Gage continued, "secrecy is one of the mainstays of the society. From what we've gathered, I would bet there are serious consequences for anyone who talks about it. So, to pull out a gun at a major social function in New York City would be like turning a spotlight on it. Whoever did that would never be allowed to join. That's all supposition, but it fits with what we've learned so far."

Hawk nodded. "Gage is right. Secrecy is the key—if you'll pardon the pun—to the society. Doing something that brings it into the public eye is likely to be a death knell for whoever does it. Doing an exchange at the event makes the most sense. Even if you decide to join the society, doing it at the event will be the smartest way."

"Why not just go back to the shop and go down the stairs if I want to join the society?" Remy speculated. "It's my shop. I can just go down the stairs and bang on the door, show them the key, and be admitted."

"Not to scare you," Mitch started, "but chances are good you would be dead before you hit the sidewalk in front of your shop. Or any other Lock and Key Society location in New York City. At this point, they all must be under surveillance. Anyone who wants the key is just waiting for you to show up at a site so they can steal it from you. Hawk's right; killing you would be the most expedient method of making sure you're no longer a threat."

Remy made no sound. She slowly picked up her mug of tea. Her hand shook slightly. Hawk's gut twisted. He wanted to tell her they could run away together and he would keep her safe. It wasn't logical. Hell, it wasn't even doable, but she looked so vulnerable, so lost in the big chair, that he'd promise her the moon to make her feel better.

"So regardless," she said, "we're going to have to find a way into that party."

"I guess so," Hawk agreed.

"Well…" She looked up at him. "I'm going to need a

party dress. You'll probably need a tux." She turned to the brothers. "Any chance you all could attend?"

Mitch grinned. "Oh, I think that can be arranged." He turned to his brother. "Right, Logan?"

Logan shrugged. "I'll make some calls."

"Until then," Gage said as he stood, "I think you've made the right choice to stay here. We have a lot of security features in place. We can lock this building down and make it a fortress. You should be safe here until you have to leave for the party. We can start on those plans later today."

"You good with that?" Hawk asked.

She nodded, but his gut told him something was off. There was something she wasn't saying, something that she wasn't sharing. He didn't like it. Not one bit.

"Remy, maybe we can chat for a second," he said.

She gave him a slight smile but stood. "I think if it's okay with you, I'll go lie down in one of the bedrooms."

"Sure," Logan said. "Let me show you the way."

Hawk watched her walk out of the room with Logan. He understood her need for some peace and quiet. She'd just been told that one of the fundamentals of her entire life was a lie. It was going to take some adjusting but his senses were in overdrive, warning him that things weren't neutral. There was danger in the offing, more than the party tomorrow night. Closer than that. He didn't like that he couldn't see Remy. He wanted his gaze on her at all times. That was truly the only way he'd believe that she was safe. He needed to see it with his own two eyes.

"Hawk," Mitch said, "come on over here for a second." He and Gage stood next to the bar. Hawk walked over and stood next to Mitch, who said, "We're going to need to get you some firepower. And a tux." Mitch grinned. "Firepower is easy. The tux might be more complicated. Why don't you tell me what you like in both, and we'll get started."

Hawk listened with half an ear as the brothers discussed which guns might be the easiest to bring into the event. His mind was stuck on Remy. His gut was telling him to storm the bedroom and see what the hell was going on. But was that because something was up or because he didn't like to see her in such turmoil? Was he reacting to unseen danger or was he reacting to seeing her suffering? Fuck if he could figure it out.

CHAPTER SIXTEEN

Remy sat on the bed but knew she couldn't stay there. She couldn't breathe. Suddenly she was claustrophobic and craving wide open spaces. Hadn't Logan said there was a rooftop garden? Surely that would be safe enough. It didn't matter. She needed to be outside on her own. All of the pitying looks she was getting from Lacy and others were just too much to bear.

Anxiety riddled Remy as she tiptoed down the hallway to the staircase. God, her life was a mess…everything she'd believed about her family was false, she was falling for a man she had no business falling for, she was relying on the kindness of people whom, except for Lacy, were essentially strangers.

Holding her breath, she quietly climbed to the roof. She figured that chances were good, once she opened the door, they would know she was up there but she didn't care. She just needed to breathe.

She pushed open the door and stepped outside. The cold air stole the breath from her lungs. She'd forgotten how frigid it was outside. Her coat was downstairs and she wasn't going back for it.

There was outdoor furniture in the corner of the roof set on top of some turf. There were sofas, chairs, and tables. She bet it was really attractive in summer, with plants around and twinkling fairy lights. It would be lovely.

But the flowers were all dead this deep in winter, and the beds empty. That's exactly what she felt like. Empty.

She moved to stand in the corner by the furniture and look over the roof tops. Pulling the handkerchief from her pocket, she pressed it against her cheeks and almost broke down. Gunnar's revelations had been wrenching, and she felt as if she was losing her parents all over again. Her whole world had shifted and she couldn't seem to figure out which way was up. Crushing the cloth in her hand, she rubbed her arms. The cold was seeping into her bones, but her heart was already icy.

Remy let out a long sigh and became aware of a sound behind her. They found her already. "I know I shouldn't be up here but—"

"You're right. You shouldn't be up here," a heavily accented voice said.

She whirled around but it was too late, a man wearing a large khaki-colored parka appeared in front of her. He was tall and vaguely familiar. She reared back tried to scream, but the man clamped a hand over her mouth and spun her around. He held her against him, one hand over her mouth and his arm squeezing her neck.

"Make a sound, and I'll throw you over the side." He pushed her against the edge she'd been leaning on.

She froze. Her lungs wouldn't work. Her knees weakened, and she struggled to remain standing. The hand pressed over her mouth and nose cut off her oxygen. She couldn't breathe!

Her heart slammed against her ribs as she tried to pry off the attacker's hand. How could this be happening? She clawed at the hand, but she couldn't seem to break the man's hold.

Another man appeared at her side. He was young looking. It hit her suddenly that he'd been one of the "students" on the subway. *Shit,* the Moroccans.

"Now," he said, "you're going to give us the key."

"Let her go," a voice growled. Hawk was standing a few feet behind the sofa. He had a large black gun with the deadly barrel pointed at the man holding her hostage.

Thank you, God. Hawk was with her. She was not alone. Suddenly, Mitch and Gage came into view, followed closely by Gunnar.

"Stay back or I'll throw her over." Her captor started dragging her along the wall to the opposite corner. Her joy at seeing Hawk turned to dust. She didn't feel the outside cold any longer only the block of ice crowding her chest.

The guy increased the pressure of his arm over her mouth, "Back off," he demanded.

"Let her go," Hawk repeated.

"No. One of you has the key. Hand it over and then I'll let her go."

Hawk's hand didn't waver. He was so calm, so focused. She stared at him, but he wouldn't meet her gaze. She was struggling to breathe through the guy's meaty hand. They were at the far corner now. The roof was attached to the one next to it. This must have been how they got up here in the first place.

"Give me the key or she dies." Her vision was dimming and if she didn't catch a breath soon, she was sure to pass out. Her mind raced, seeking a way out of the mess she'd gotten herself into.

"Then I'll kill you," Hawk said matter of fact.

What? Was he being serious?

"You'll try, but my friend over there will shoot you first." The other man who had appeared was now aiming a gun at Hawk.

Mitch snarled, "And then we'll kill him. Stalemate, motherfucker."

No. No. NO. This was all wrong. Hawk couldn't get hurt. The Callahans couldn't. That wasn't right. She couldn't deal with something happening to any of them, but she was certain she couldn't survive it if Hawk died because of her. She'd rather forfeit her own life than have that happen.

The younger of the two Moroccans swept his gun from Hawk to Mitch and back.

The stout guy said to Hawk, "You should do as he says if you want to live. If you want her to live."

Hawk just stared at the two men.

Remy's vision was shrinking. Blackness was closing in.

"Give me the key, and we let you both live." The man holding her let go of her nose and mouth.

Her head swam as she sucked in as much oxygen as she could. Suddenly, she was upside down. The man had hefted her over the side of the building. She was staring at the street six stories below.

She couldn't make a sound. Her vocal cords wouldn't work. She flailed around.

"Give him the key, Remy." Hawk's voice had gone hard. "Now, Remy." There was an urgency in his tone as well as fear. It was the fear that sank into and freed her brain from the fog of terror. If Hawk was scared, then it was bad.

"Pull me up and I'll give you the key," she rasped.

Rough hands jerked her back onto the relative safety of the roof. She opened her hands to brace on the side of the building and her mother's handkerchief fell. The wind blew at that moment and took the piece of cloth, making it swirl and float. Almost like it was dancing. *Goodbye Mom.*

He put her on her feet but wrapped an arm around her neck and placed his hand over her mouth and nose again.

"Give me the key."

The other man still aimed his gun at Hawk. She would do anything to save Hawk, but she was having a hard time making her body function properly. Finally, she managed to pull the key out of her pocket. She held it up.

The guy with the gun took it from her hand. "Thank you." Lack of oxygen must be making her loopy, because Remy almost laughed at his politeness. She was going to pass out.

"Let her breathe," Hawk demanded.

The pressure on her mouth let up a bit, and she managed to suck in some much-needed oxygen.

"I'm going to take her with me to that roof. I'll let her go when we're at the door. If you move, I will have my friend here shoot her anyway." The guy with the gun and the key went first. Once he was on the other roof, her captor lifted her up and she was on her belly on the wall. She swung her legs over and stood up on the other roof. He followed her and then grabbed her in the chokehold again. They moved to the access door to the building and then suddenly, violently, pushed her forward. She fell flat on the roof just barely catching herself with her hands.

In an instant Hawk was beside her helping her up. "Are you okay?" He helped her to a sitting position.

She shook her head. It would be a long time before she was okay. She looked up at him. "I lost the key. My family's legacy and I lost it." The key had cost her her entire family. She wanted it back. A deep-seated rage blew through her. She'd lost too much to the society. She wanted to claim what was hers. She had nothing left to lose.

"Jesus Christ, Remy, you could have been killed and you're worried about the key. What the hell are you doing up here? Fuck!"

She shrank away from his anger. "I'm sorry, but I really needed some air. I was feeling claustrophobic. I never imagined they would come onto the roof."

"You risked everyone's lives for some air." He shook his head and then helped her up. He walked with her to the wall and then helped her over. Mitch took her arm and brought her back inside and down the stairs.

"We owe you an apology. It never occurred to us that you would go out on the roof. We should have had someone with you. We got there as soon as we realized."

She shook her head. Her teeth were chattering. "M-m-y-y f-fault. S-stupid."

They stood beside the bar and Lacy came over and put a blanket around her shoulders, giving her a hug in the process. "I'll make you some tea." She disappeared into the kitchen.

Hawk came in and stared at her. She desperately wanted him to take her into his arms. To make her feel safe.

Instead, he turned to Logan, who was sitting on a stool, watching Hawk approach "Logan, we need a plan B."

Logan nodded. "Come down to my office." The two men went out the back hallway and presumably down the stairs.

Remy was left standing in the room all on her own. Her knees gave out, and she ended up in a puddle on the floor. Her whole body shook and bile choked her. She thought she might vomit. She burst into tears. What the hell had she just done?

CHAPTER SEVENTEEN

"Are you alright?" Logan asked as Hawk paced back and forth in Logan's office.

"No, I'm not fucking alright. Jesus Christ, she risked her life for what? Getting some air? And then the key was fuckin' taken, which now she wants back. Unbelievable!" He ran a hand through his hair.

Logan leaned back in his chair. "Are you upset because she lost the key or because she risked her life?"

"Both. Neither. I don't fucking know."

He grinned. "Oh, I've been there. Women. Nothing can screw you up more."

"What? What are you talking about?" Hawk demanded as he scowled at Logan.

"Nothing. So, what are you thinking? Now that the key is gone, what's the game plan?"

He went back to pacing. "I don't know. She wants the key back. I guess we have to try and get it before the board meeting tomorrow night."

"That's going to be tough."

Mitch walked into the office and sank down into one of

the guest chairs.

Hawk plopped down next to him. The brown leather chair was soft and comfortable. It matched the color of Logan's desk. The office was done in shades of brown and Hawk found it comforting somehow.

Logan cleared his throat. "First, we owe you an apology. The roof should have been secured. Obviously, they couldn't get in from there. You need a passcode. Remy would have frozen to death out there if we didn't have cameras and alarms. But we should have anticipated her going out there and had someone in place."

Hawk shook his head. "You couldn't have known. It's not your fault. What's done is done. We need to move forward." He needed to punch something. But he couldn't blame this on anyone but himself. It wasn't the Callahans' fault. It was his and it had almost cost Remy her life. He let out a long breath and turned to Mitch. "Remy wants the key back. It was the Moroccans on the roof."

Logan asked, "Do we know who the Moroccans are? These 'student' looking guys aren't the mastermind behind getting the key."

"We do, and you're right," Mitch said. "These guys are just henchmen. I had one of our techs run some fingerprints from where the asshole who was holding Remy had left on the building's railing. His name was Farouk Haidar. He is a known associate of one Asad Najeddine."

Logan froze for a second. "Shit."

"Fuck," Mitch agreed.

"What am I missing?" Hawk asked. "I guess I've been out of the game too long. I don't know any of the players."

Logan explained, "Najeddine is a fixer for the royal family in Morocco. We've had a few run-ins with him. Not us exactly, but our people. He's a nasty piece of work."

"Fucking wonderful." Hawk scrubbed his hands through his hair, hanging his head.

"Getting the key back from him is going to be damn near impossible," Logan said.

Mitch nodded. "It's going to have to be the museum event. That's going to be the only time he'll have the key with him."

"What intel do you have on him?" Hawk asked. "Can we figure out how he's going to carry the key?"

Mitch got up and went over to a mini fridge in the corner and pulled out a bottle of water. He offered one to Hawk, who nodded even though he truly wanted a double shot of something more potent. Mitch tossed the bottle to Hawk, then grabbed a second one for himself. "What are you thinking?"

Hawk twisted the cap off. "I think that other than Remy, who doesn't know any better, everyone else will carry the key in some kind of special way. They'll want it to be hard to steal because they are going to be at the event and they know chances are good someone else will, at least, attempt to take it off them."

Logan folded his hands together. "I see where you're going with this. It's not like he can bring fifteen guys to protect him. It's a social event, and no one is allowed to call attention to the Lock and Key Society. I think that's why Gray decided to hold it there. If the board members, including whoever will take the newest seat on the board, can't hold a meeting without attracting attention, then they don't deserve to be on the board. Sort of like running the gauntlet."

"Makes sense." Mitch took a swig of his water. "I imagine he's also thinking it might keep the violence to a minimum. If they did it at one of the other locations, no doubt there would be bloodshed. Hard to do that at the museum without the world hearing about it."

Hawk opened his bottle. "So back to my original question. Do you have any intel on him so can we figure out what he's going to do with the key to keep it safe?"

Logan tapped his blotter with a pencil. "What would be the safest method of carrying the key so no one else can steal it while at this party?"

Hawk snorted. "I know what the safest would be, and if he's doing that, he can keep the damn key. I'm not getting it."

Mitch started to laugh. "Me either."

Logan's eyes narrowed. "You don't mean…" He curled his upper lip. "Well, if he does shove it up his ass, he's going to have to dig it out again at some point. He has to show it to get inside the meeting."

Hawk smiled. "Still not touching it." Then he set down his water bottle and rubbed his face with both hands. "Realistically, I don't think he's going to do that. I think he'll carry it in some kind of case that probably locks through biometrics."

Mitch nodded. "Yeah, that seems the most reasonable. Let me do some digging. We might be able to find out if he's used such a thing in the past." He stood up.

"Do you mind if I come along?" Hawk asked. "I'd rather be doing something than staring at the walls."

"Come on," Mitch waved at him. "I'll show you the brains of the operation."

Hawk got up, grabbed his water, and followed Mitch out the door. The last thing he wanted to do was go upstairs and see Remy. He was still so angry at her for taking such a huge risk. Beyond that, he was furious at himself for not stopping her before she went up there. He had known something was off but hadn't trusted his instincts. *Always a mistake.* She just threw him off his game so much that sometimes he wasn't sure which way was up.

They arrived on the fourth floor and got off the elevator. A huge steel panel without any doorknob or any other way to open it, barred their progress. There was a biometric scanner beside it, not unlike the setup down the stairs at Remy's shop. Mitch put his hand on the screen and then his eye to the retinal scanner to the right of the door. A few seconds later, the door slid open a couple of inches. Mitch used his fingers to push the door to the side, and they walked into a small antechamber.

"You guys take this stuff seriously," Hawk commented.

"You have no idea." Mitch waited until the door they'd entered through closed again, and then he punched in a code on the keypad next to the door ahead of him. Once again, he had to do a retinal scan, only this time, it was his left eye. Again, a few seconds later, the second steel door slid open, and this time they were in a large room.

The open room appeared to occupy almost the whole floor but it was hard to tell because there were no windows. Instead, banks of computers and oversize monitors lined the walls. There were five people looking at screens. He only recognized a couple of the men who were down at one end. Gunnar and Dex. The third guy he recognized but couldn't recall his name. He nodded to the guys and they nodded back. Gage and Dani were staring at a screen on the far side of the room. Mitch walked in their direction, and Hawk followed.

"Hey," Mitch said as he grabbed a nearby chair. He wheeled it over and offered it to Hawk. He took another one, and the two men sat down. "Got anything yet?"

Gage nodded. "Hey, Hawk."

Dani looked up, too. "Hi, Hawk."

"Hey, Dani. How are you?"

She nodded but went back to staring at her screen.

"Don't mind her. She's working on something," Gage said with a smile.

Hawk had no idea what she was hacking, but her fingers were moving in a blur on the keyboard, and her eyes remained glued to the screen. "Do you want to move so we can talk?" he asked.

"Nah. She'll just tune us out. No need to move." Gage rolled over to another computer and brought up a picture on the screen. "This is what we think Najeddine will carry the key in."

The picture was of a man dressed in a suit walking across the tarmac at what looked to be a private airfield, carrying a small case in one hand. Gage blew up the image of the case so they could see it better. It was black, about four by six inches and about two inches wide. There appeared to be a screen of some kind inset on one side.

"Is that some sort of biometric wallet?" Hawk asked.

Gage nodded. "We think so, yes. But it's not just fingerprints. It's an iris scanner."

"Shit," breathed Mitch. "They aren't playing."

"Yeah," his brother agreed. "We think he's going to use this because the man in this picture is one of the members of the Moroccan royal family, and he and Najeddine are tight. It's also perfect for the situation, small enough to tuck inside his jacket pocket. Not obvious. But also hard as hell to break into.

"When you think about it, it's the perfect choice. Let's say Najeddine goes to the party, but the wallet gets stolen there somehow. Only he can open it, so the key is his, and so is the spot on the board even though he may not be in direct possession of it when the key itself enters the room."

Hawk cocked his head. "But how does he get into the room in that scenario?"

"Good question. Not sure but he must have some kind of plan."

"And so do you, I'm guessing, when it comes to dealing with the wallet."

Gage grinned. "We have a few ideas. Once Dani finishes up here, then we'll firm up the plan. I have Alex working on something as well."

Mitch snorted. "Why am I not surprised that my girlfriend is involved in something nefarious?"

"You would be disappointed if she wasn't," his brother said.

"True," Mitch agreed and then stood up. "It's just gone three. I'm late for a meeting. I'll catch up with you guys later. Hawk, you okay to stay here?"

Hawk nodded. "I'm good."

Mitch turned and walked out.

"Hawk, we've got this under control. If you're up for it, I think it would be a good idea for you to go down to the gun vault and choose what you want for tomorrow night. It's in the basement along with a gun range. You can practice. You can also hit the gym if you want. It's on the third floor."

"How do you have space for a gun range in the basement," Hawk asked as he stood.

"We own a few of the buildings on the right side of this one but not the left. We pushed through a couple of basements to create the space we wanted."

"Smart." Hawk was impressed. They'd thought of everything."

"Gunnar," Gage called. "Can you take Hawk down to the basement and get him set up?"

"Sure." Gunnar stood up and flicked his dark hair out of his eyes. "Happy to."

"Thanks," Hawk said. "I think I'll take you up on the

gym as well. That sounds good. I'll check back with you later."

Gage nodded, and Hawk followed Gunnar to the gun vault. Half an hour after that, he was in the gym. Working out soothed his jangled nerves. It also put him in a meditative state, something he needed. Remy was throwing him off his game. He was normally so even-keeled, so in control. Around her, he was all over the map. If whatever Gage was cooking up was going to work, he needed to keep a level head, something he hadn't been very much of in the last twenty-four hours.

Three hours later, he got out of the shower and pulled on the clothes that one of Callahans' employees had collected from Connor. He'd rescued his stuff from the bag that had been left in the living area. He left the bedroom he'd taken and walked back out to find everyone gathered around the bar.

Remy was sitting on a barstool, drinking a glass of white wine with Lacy on one side of her and Alex on the other. Her hair was up in a bun, and she had on the gray sweater he'd bought her. It did bring out her eyes as he thought it would, but she looked pale and sad. He didn't know whether to be mad as hell at her for risking her life or to just be thankful that she was still alive. He decided he didn't have to choose at the moment.

He went over and sat down on the opposite end of the sofa from Gage. "Did you get it sorted?"

Gage nodded. "Yeah. We'll go over it when everyone is here. Logan is cooking."

Hawk leaned forward and grabbed a piece of cheese and a couple of crackers off the charcuterie board on the coffee table. "How does he do all this and still get any work done?"

"This is how Logan relaxes. He cooks like we work out. It

gives him the same sense of Zen and accomplishment. It's how he stays balanced."

Mitch came over, grabbed some olives and cheese, and flopped into the armchair on Gage's left. "I hear we're good to go."

Gage nodded. "We have the makings of a plan, but there's still a lot to do." He munched on a cracker. "How did your meeting go?"

Mitch shook his head. "Dragan is on his way back. There's more going on than anyone is saying, and I don't like it."

Gage let out a sigh.

Hawk remained silent. He knew if he said that he wanted to join them here at Callahan Security, they would tell him what was going on and ask his opinion about it. That's who they were. But he wasn't ready to commit yet. He couldn't quite put his finger on why.

He knew he wasn't going back to working for Drake. That decision he'd already made. He glanced over at Remy. The rest of it was up in the air.

CHAPTER EIGHTEEN

Remy walked over and collapsed into the armchair next to the fire once again. Dinner had been amazing. The leg of lamb was divine and the lemon potatoes were so satisfying, of course, she'd eaten too much. But that had been her strategy to avoid having to talk to Hawk.

She settled into the chair and tried to suck the warmth of the fire into her bones. Her insides hadn't unfrozen since earlier when the man had put his hand over her nose and mouth. Strike that, her cheeks were on fire with embarrassment over her fucking stupid action. She could have claimed it was a mistake, but it was more than that. She'd risked everything, including Hawk's life because she was claustrophobic. She could have just done yoga, but no. Not her. Hawk had told her to do what he'd said, when he said it, and she'd ignored his instructions. Stupid.

She glanced at him as he'd entered the room. Somewhere over the past few days, he'd become important to her and the fact that she'd jeopardized him was unforgivable.

Gage and Mitch pulled up some bar stools at either end

of the sofa while Lacy sat down on the sofa nearest to Remy. Alex sat next to Lacy, and Dani sat in the far corner.

"We need to talk out a plan," Lacy explained. "We think we can get the key back and get you to the meeting, but it's going to take some doing." She reached out and squeezed her friend's shoulder. "You okay?"

Remy nodded. "I can't thank you enough, Lacy. You, Logan, all of his brothers…it's just so overwhelming, what you all are doing for me." She swallowed the lump building in her throat. "It means the world to me to know that you have my back. I've felt so alone since Gramps died."

Lacy squeezed her arm and gave her a sympathetic smile. "You don't have to feel alone. We've been besties since college. You'll always have me—"

"And me," Alex chimed in. "Once you're part of the pack, we won't let you go. It's like being in a gang." She grinned and Remy couldn't help but smile.

Hawk sat down across from her. The weight of his gaze heightened her discomfort and chagrin. She tried to swallow the guilt she was feeling, but it was like a pill stuck in her throat. No matter what she did, she couldn't seem to dislodge it.

Logan placed a plate of cookies on the coffee table and then claimed the bar stool closest to her. "Just in case someone needs a little bit of sugar to get them through." He winked.

"Don't mind if I do," Mitch said, reaching for a cookie.

Alex playfully batted his hand away. "You just ate five of those."

"I'm a growing boy." He grinned.

"You'll be growing in the wrong direction," Gage said as he plunked down on the floor next to Dani's feet.

Mitch took his cookie and sat on the bar stool. "Not me, bro. I have the metabolism of a teenager."

"Yes, and it's so damned annoying," Alex agreed.

Gage started, "We think we've figured out how to get the key back, at least in theory. We know Asad Najeddine has it, or at least his people stole it, so it follows that he has it. We're reasonably sure he's going to use a biometric wallet to carry the key in." He went on to explain how that worked. "What we need to do is get the wallet from Najeddine to Remy so she can be at the meeting."

Remy listened with a growing sense of panic gnawing at her belly. "How are we supposed to open it if it needs a fingerprint and a retinal scan?" That seemed impossible to her.

Dani piped up. "It's not a retinal scanner. It's an iris scanner, which is completely different. If it was a retinal scanner, we'd have to carve out his eyeball to open the wallet, and the eyeball would have to be fresh. Anything more than about five hours, and the scanner would be able to tell it was dead."

"Oh, well, so glad we don't have to do that," Remy said with a snort. "Seriously? Carve out an eyeball?"

Dani grinned. "No eyeball carving necessary. An iris scanner uses mathematical pattern recognition techniques to identify and verify the patterns of the user's eye. So, all we needed was the data of the patterns in Najeddine's eyes."

"How in the hell did you get that?" Remy asked. This was seriously fucked up. Way more intense than she thought possible. Iris scanners?

"I borrowed them from the TSA." Dani grinned again.

"You hacked transportation security? For real?" Remy demanded.

Dani nodded.

Remy put a hand to her belly. "I'm going to be ill."

"Don't worry about it. It's not as hard as it sounds, and they had no idea I was even in their system."

Sweat broke out across Remy's body, and she swiped a hand across her forehead. *This just couldn't be happening.*

Gage confirmed, "So, now all we have to do is get the biometric wallet and his fingerprints, and we're good to go."

"Is that all?" Remy murmured. This was getting too dangerous. Too crazy.

Alex asked, "You couldn't get the fingerprints from the TSA?"

"Well, I could've, but I tried to minimize my time in the system. I don't want to go back in because it could trigger their security, and then they'll take a deeper look around and possibly see my intrusion. No need to take the risk. Fingerprints are easy."

"True, they shouldn't be too difficult," Alex agreed.

Remy's head was starting to spin. "How will you get his fingerprints? You're not going to cut off his fingers, are you?"

"Nah. We'll get his champagne glass. It's a social event. They'll serve drinks. We'll just get his glass and then lift the print," Alex said in a matter-of-fact tone. "I bought a biometric wallet and have been practicing with it all day. The fingerprint will be easy. Once we have the iris scan uploaded on something with a great quality screen, we should be fine."

"The hardest part of this is going to be stealing the biometric wallet from Najeddine," Mitch said and then popped the last bit of cookie into his mouth.

"Agreed." Alex frowned. "It's going to require a couple of different distractions because he's going to be prepared for people to try and steal it."

Remy's stomach rolled, and her heart rate kicked up. Even her palms were sweating now. "I—I don't think we should do this."

"You don't want the key back?" Dani asked.

"I… I do, but—" Her voice faltered, and she found herself sucking in oxygen. She was starting to hyperventilate.

Hawk got up, crossed in front of the fireplace, and pushed Remy's head between her knees. "Just breathe. You're going to be fine."

She sat like that for a moment and then, magically, the world stopped swirling. "I'm okay," she mumbled. Other than being completely mortified. As she straightened, Hawk studied her for a moment. He must have thought she was fine because he returned to his side of the room and sat down. She was anything but fine.

Logan appeared at her elbow with a mug of tea. "Careful," he said. It's got a bit of a kick," and he winked at her.

She took a sip of tea. It was laced with rum, and it immediately warmed her belly. Her body started to relax. "Sorry," she croaked.

"You don't have to apologize." Lacy reached out and touched her friend's arm once again. "It's a lot to take in. You've been through the wringer in the last week. And we sometimes forget that not everyone is used to bending the rules a little bit when necessary." She winked. "You should have seen Logan hyperventilate in the beginning. He was always running around in a panic. Now he's just used to it. He cooks a lot to get rid of his stress. It's been hard on my waistline but my tastebuds enjoy it immensely."

Remy appreciated her friend's attempt to keep it light but she needed to own up to her mistake. These people were sticking their necks out for her and she had been stupid. "It's just…I was an idiot today and took a risk that I shouldn't have. I guess I didn't really care about the danger to myself. I'm so used to not relying on anyone but myself. It's always been only me so, in a sense, it doesn't matter if something happens to me."

She quickly held up her hand. "Not that I want something bad to happen, just that…it's only me that it affects. But…" She glanced over and met Hawk's gaze for the first time since the whole mess that afternoon. "I put Hawk's life in danger. That was truly selfish and stupid of me. Unforgiveable." She looked away. "And now you all are talking about getting iris scans and fingerprints... It's all so dangerous. I can't ask you to do any of this. I couldn't stand it if something happened to any of you. It would break me. I just can't have you risking yourselves for me."

The room was silent for a beat. Then Hawk said in a quiet voice, "Remy, we're all doing this because you're in trouble. You are...fearless and brave and sassy and smart, but you wouldn't last a minute out there on your own. You're not trained for this type of thing. We are. All of us, in our own way, are trained for exactly this type of thing. If something happened to you and we didn't help you, none of *us* could live with that. You need the type of help that the people in this room are skilled at providing. Just accept what we're offering and say thank you because we're going to help you whether you want it or not. Our consciences wouldn't let us do otherwise."

Remy swallowed the lump building in her throat. She wanted to crawl into Hawk's lap and throw her arms around his neck. That was probably the nicest thing anyone had ever said to her. It wasn't praise or compliments; it was an admission that she still had family of a sort. That she mattered. That was what going to get the handkerchief had been about: still mattering to someone or something.

"I—I don't know what to say," she murmured.

"What Hawk said is all true. Just say 'thanks' and stop worrying. We're gonna get you through this." Gage sent her a smile.

She nodded and took a rather large sip of the spiked tea.

Lacy smiled at Remy then turned to Alex. "So, we can get the iris scan and the prints, but Alex, how do you see it working to get the biometric wallet?"

"It's going to be tricky," she said. "I think some of it will have to be determined onsite. We just don't have enough intel yet, but I think we're all gonna need to be there. I'll steal the wallet, but Lacy, you and Dani are going to have to work the magic on it.

"Piece of cake," Dani said.

Gage piped up. "Mitch, you and Logan and I are going to have to keep our eyes open and give the women updates on the room. Hawk, you're gonna hang with Remy to keep her safe. If someone thinks she still has the key, they might take a run at her."

Hawk nodded. "I think that sounds like a good plan. Is Dragan back yet?"

Mitch shook his head. "Soon. What are you thinking?"

"He might be the way into the room. Chances are excellent that Archer Gray isn't going to want to let everyone into the room. He's going to let the board members in and whoever can show him the key. Dragan might make it easier for us to get entry. Nothing like your top frenemy showing up at the door to pique your interest."

"It's a thought," Gage agreed. "If he's back, we'll do it."

Remy sighed. "How do you think these people who are after the key know about it? I thought this society or club or whatever was supposed to be a secret."

"It is a secret. Ninety-nine percent of the world knows nothing about it," Hawk pointed out. "Your great-grandfather helped found it, and you knew nothing about it. So, it's a secret, but there are always rumors. Little hints of its existence here and there. Dragan managed to dig up information on it. Connor had heard of it. No one but the members know the details, and few outsiders know of its existence. So to answer your question, I think the people after the key are some of the very few who know of the society's existence or, more likely, are already members."

Logan cocked his head. "You think they want Remy's key specifically so they can be on the board and be involved in wielding the power of the society."

Hawk nodded. "I think people are ambitious. Why settle for just being a member when you can be on the board?"

"Makes sense, I guess." Remy leaned forward and put her empty mug on the coffee table. "That means they have a much better chance of getting in the door than I do unless it truly is just a board meeting."

"True," Gage agreed. "We're all going to have to be extra careful on this one. There are still a lot of unknowns and anything can happen."

Remy's stomach rolled. *No truer words.* Six months ago, she'd been working as a librarian and her grandfather was still alive. Now she was involved with a secret society and people wanted her dead. Life could change on a dime.

"I can't thank you guys enough. Seriously, you are… saving my life, and I truly appreciate it. Logan, please draw up an invoice so I can pay you for your services. My grandfather left me more money than I know what to do with. I would like to put it to good use. Saving my ass seems like a good use of the funds."

Logan grinned. "I'll work something up."

"You know what we're going to need?" Lacy said.

"What?" Remy frowned.

"Gowns and tuxedos. If we're all going to go, we all need the appropriate attire." A slow smile crossed her face. "I think we'll have to do some shopping."

Remy's heart lightened. "That sounds like fun. I need some fun. We'll have to go tomorrow first thing."

"You're not going anywhere," Hawk growled.

She shot him a glance and was about to argue, but the reality of the situation made her stop. He was right. She couldn't risk her life and the lives of those around her because she wanted to cheer herself up. For all she knew, the Asian gang and the other group Connor mentioned were still looking for her. They didn't know she no longer had the token.

She turned to Lacy. "I guess you will have to pick something out for me."

"Nonsense. I will have a selection of gowns and shoes brought over. We'll try them all on and see what we can come up with."

Remy shot her friend a grateful look. "That sounds like a lot of fun."

"Great. I will arrange it." She winked at Remy. "In the meantime, maybe you can make a list of what you need in terms of makeup and anything else so we can be prepared for tomorrow." Lacy glanced at her watch. "I've got a conference call at eight that I need to prepare for. Why don't you text me the list in the morning, and we'll go from there."

Remy nodded and tried to stifle a yawn. The rum in her tea made her head fuzzy. That, and the endless, emotional day. "I think I might crash. I'm exhausted."

Everyone started moving. "Alex, let's talk through what you're thinking for tomorrow," Mitch said.

Gage got off the floor. "I'd like to be there for that, too. Dani, you want to join us?"

She nodded.

Lacy and Logan started toward the elevator. "We'll be in Lacy's office if anyone needs us," Logan called over his shoulder as they headed out of the room.

"We'll be in Mitch's," Alex responded as she and the whole group headed toward the back hallway to go down the stairs.

Remy looked across at Hawk. "I'm going to go to my room."

He nodded.

She started out of the room and then stopped. She turned back to him. "I…I want to apologize for risking your life earlier. I know you think what I did was stupid, and you're right it was but I…just…It was just such a shock. I wasn't thinking clearly."

Hawk stood and walked toward the bar. "I get it. Being lied to on a fundamental level is difficult to absorb and process but, Remy, you need to think of your safety."

"That's just it. Safety doesn't seem so important when your whole life is tied up in lies."

"I know. You'll eventually come to terms with it, but you need to be more cautious."

She sighed. "I know you think you know what I mean but, honestly, until you've been through it, I don't know, it just changes how you see the world. Safety just doesn't seem so important."

He walked behind the bar and poured himself a bourbon. He raised the bottle, but she shook her head. He picked up his glass and added a lot of ice. "When I was eighteen, just after high school graduation, my older sister told me that she was, in fact, my mother. The people who I'd grown up calling 'Mom' and 'Dad' were actually my grandparents." He took a swig of his drink and swallowed. "So, I know what it's like to have your whole life based on a lie."

Her heart lurched. "Oh, my God. That must've been so painful." She couldn't imagine the betrayal he must have felt. She drew in a breath. Her pain was a fraction of what he must have felt. "I'm so, so sorry." The scope of her words covered condolences, and another sincere apology.

He shrugged. "I also know what you mean about safety. I immediately joined the Navy after finding out. I had no interest in being around the people who had lied to me for all those years. It took a while, but then I made it through BUDS training and became a SEAL. I didn't care about my safety. As far as I was concerned, I didn't have anyone back home. I could do my job and take more risks than the others because my death would cause the least amount of pain. I made sure to not have any connections anywhere. My death would matter the least." He locked gazes with her. "So, I fucking get it."

He did get it. He understood what she was saying. She shouldn't be surprised. Hawk had seemed to understand just about everything she was going through before she even realized she was going through it.

He rattled the ice cubes in his glass then put it down on the counter. "But the truth is, that's just a defense mechanism. Push everyone and everything away because then no one can hurt you again. I understand that all too well. Trust me, eventually you will come to accept that your grandfather had reasons for doing what he did. You may not agree with them, but you just have to go with the fact that those decisions were made with your best interests at heart."

"Are you in contact with your family?" she asked in a quiet voice.

He nodded. "We're not close like we used to be, but I stay in touch."

The pressure in her chest eased a bit. The thought of Hawk alone bothered her. It was nice to know his family was still part of his life. She'd give almost anything to have her family back.

"Thanks for…setting me straight. I get what you're saying. I'll try to take it one day at a time." She gave a small shrug. "I think I'm going to head to bed." She turned and walked to the room she was staying in, closing the door behind her.

She got what Hawk was saying, but it *was* different for her. She had no family left. There were friends, but she knew there was no one who would be devastated to lose her. She suddenly realized that she should communicate that thought to Alex and Mitch. If there were risks to take, she should take them. She had the least to lose.

She walked back over and pulled open the door only to find Hawk blocking her doorway. He seemed to fill up the whole space. Was he always this big?

"No. You shouldn't volunteer to take the most risk," he growled.

CHAPTER NINETEEN

"Jesus, how did you know—" She broke off.

Hawk crossed his arms over his chest. "Like I said, I've been there. You're thinking my situation is different because I still have family, but you don't. You're not thinking clearly."

She narrowed her eyes at him. "I understand you've been in a similar situation, and perhaps you have an understanding of things, but don't tell me what I'm thinking."

He snorted. "Remy, you're easy to read. It's not a mystery what you're thinking. And you're wrong. People would be really upset if anything happened to you." He wanted to tell her he'd be so angry with her that he'd never forgive her or himself, but that thought was too raw, too much to share.

"Gus," he said instead. "Gus needs you. All the people that come to your shop need you. I'm sure you have lots of friends. The point is, don't take stupid risks because you think you're on your own or that you have the least to lose."

A look flashed over her face but was gone too fast for him to be sure it was disappointment. What would she be disappointed about? That he didn't say he would be upset? Hell, he'd be gutted, but sharing that piece of information would be distracting. For both of them.

"As I said, I will consider what you said. Now, if you'll excuse me." She gestured at him to move.

He refused to budge. She'd just go downstairs and tell them she didn't want them to risk anything for her—to let her take the risk. She didn't get that it was much less risky if she let the Callahans handle things. She was still too caught up in the emotion of it and the Callahans are professionals at what they do. Her common sense was gone for the moment. Well, he was just going to have to stand there and keep her from shooting off her mouth. It was a sexy mouth, and he didn't want anything to happen to it.

"Hawk, please, I'd like to leave the room."

"No." He stood there blocking the doorway.

"Seriously. I need to get out."

"And do what?" He cocked an eyebrow at her.

She frowned at him. "Fine," she huffed. "Please close the door. I want to get some sleep." She turned away and walked toward the en suite bathroom. Hawk stepped inside, closed the door, and went back to leaning against it with his arms folded over his chest. Did she really think he'd fall for that?

She whirled around, and a small sound of surprise escaped her lips. "Are you going to stay here all night?"

"If that's what it takes." His gaze traveled over her curves, the memory of last night still fresh in his mind.

Her cheeks turned a dull red. She was remembering it, too. Glad he wasn't the only one. He grinned. He couldn't help it. She'd yelled his name when she came, and it had sounded like music to his ears. If he had to spend the night making her yell his name over and over again to stop her from doing something stupid, he was game. He just needed to make sure it wouldn't interfere with his ability to protect her.

Fat chance. It was way too late for that. He knew it in his bones. Remy had gotten under his skin, and now he wanted her in his life. No matter what.

"I'm going to get ready for bed." She turned on her heel and went into the bathroom, closing the door behind her. He ran a hand over his scalp and sighed. This was going to be a long fucking night. He wasn't leaving her by herself. He had a primal need to make sure she was safe, which meant making sure she wouldn't volunteer to do something stupid.

He rubbed his face with both hands. He hadn't talked to his family since Christmas. He'd sent them all gifts he thought they would enjoy, apologizing for not being able to get away. In truth, he had worked but he didn't have to. He could have taken a few days off if he wanted to, but he just didn't like to be back in that house. It made him remember all the times he had been so happy there. He mourned it every time he went home. He just wouldn't be happy that way again, not there anyway.

He understood perfectly why they'd lied. He came from a small town in Kentucky where everybody gossiped. A pregnant sixteen-year old would get labeled as some kind of no-good white trash, and her life would be over as far as the town thought. Her parents tried to protect her from a situation there was no coming back from. He got it. That didn't mean he had to like it or want to be a part of it.

Maybe he should go down and tell Mitch and Gage that Remy was in a bit of a tailspin and not to listen to her when she came to them to volunteer for something dangerous. The whole thing was going to be dangerous enough without her trying to steal the biometric wallet or break into the meeting room.

The bathroom door opened, and Remy came out wearing a black lace thong and nothing else. *Fuck.* Every lick of spit in his mouth dried up. She looked so damn hot; it was hard to remember he wasn't supposed to touch her. It was fine to joke about spending the night in bed with her but, in reality, it was a shitty idea. The type of idea that led to him making poor decisions in the heat of battle. The type of idea that led to him having blue balls.

She walked over and stood in front of him. "Since you're going to spend the night here, you might as well make yourself useful." She ran her hands over his chest.

He gritted his teeth. Jesus, he was hard already. How the hell was he supposed to turn her down? "Remy"—his voice shook with desire—"you need sleep, and us being involved… It's just not smart." He had no idea what he was doing after her situation was settled. None. He wanted to be able to travel across the world and not have a thought about anyone being left behind. *Didn't he?*

"I don't want to be involved, Hawk. I want to have sex. I want to sleep curled up in your arms where I feel safe, and more than anything right now, I want to feel safe."

His heart lurched. It was possible he wanted her safe more than she did. Remy secure in his arms was the only thing that would make the knots in his gut unfurl. He could relax then knowing she was out of danger and she was his. God, this was killing him.

"Honey, I need to have a clear head to protect you. We broke all the rules last night but there can't be a repeat performance." His heart couldn't take it. Too bad his body had other ideas.

She cocked an eyebrow and ran her hand over his erection. "I want you to make my knees weak and my insides melt. I want to feel you and yell your name. Are you game?"

It was stupid and dangerous and he needed her probably more than she needed him at the moment. *Fuck!* He moved so fast that she let out a small squeak as he pushed her against the door. "You bet your ass I am." He had one hand on either side of her head. "Are you sure about this?"

When she nodded, he glanced at her parted lips and swore. Then he swooped down and claimed her mouth. She opened wider to let him in, and their tongues moved over each other. She tasted like toothpaste. He moved one hand up to hold her head while he deepened the kiss. He wanted to touch and taste every fucking inch of this woman.

She wrapped her arms around his neck and brought her body in full contact with his. He cupped her ass and pulled her hips against his rock-hard erection. His body was already aching, knowing where this kiss was leading.

He dragged his lips down her neck. She let out a moan and tugged on his sweater. He leaned away from her and pulled his sweater over his head with one hand. He dropped it on the floor and immediately reclaimed her mouth.

Her fingertips trailed down his chest and then she started to undo his jeans. Before she could unfasten, he moved away from her and ran his gaze over her smooth skin noticing a star-shaped mole on her rib cage for the first time. She was beautiful standing there in the underwear he bought her. He dipped his head and circled one of her nipples with his tongue. He kept his hands on her ass and squeezed. She moaned as he sank his teeth gently into her skin.

"Hawk, that feels so fucking good."

She was struggling with his belt buckle, but he brushed them off again. He grabbed both her wrists and held them in one hand above her head. He claimed her mouth again, their tongues tangling, the throbbing in his cock growing more insistent. He kissed her from neck to nipples, the hard buds just waiting for his tongue. When he nipped the other one with his teeth, she sucked in her breath. She tried to squirm out of his grasp, but he held her fast. "If you keep trying to get your hands free, I'll stop what I'm doing," he whispered against her flesh.

She groaned. "But that's so unfair. I want to touch you."

He turned her around to face the door, but kept her hands pinned. He kissed her neck as he rubbed his hard-on against her lush ass.

"Hawk," she whispered, her breath ragged now.

He reached around and rubbed her folds through the fabric of her thong.

"Yes," she moaned. Her hips bucked, pushing back hard against his aching dick.

He moved aside the fabric of her thong and found her clit. She was so wet. With a finger, he rubbed her clit faster and faster until her hips were rocking hard. Then he drove his fingers inside of her and she called out his name as she came.

He turned her back around and let go of her hands. She reached for him, but he stepped back. "It's better if we don't. I... need to keep a clear head, and when I'm around you like this... it's...difficult." That was all he was willing to admit. Remy was beautiful all flushed from her orgasm, and she was his. Only his.

"Hawk. Tomorrow when it counts, I know you'll be clearheaded. Tonight, I need you with me."

He ground his teeth. His desire for her was so great he felt it in the very marrow of his bones, but his head—his head was screaming at him to stop. Be responsible.

She pushed her thong down over her hips, "I need this. I need you. My life is so messed up right now. I just want peace that only you can give me. You make me... feel. I've been numb for a long time and somehow with you, I feel alive again. And safe. Please Hawk."

She had him at "I need you." He kissed her, a deep and sexy kiss, putting his whole body against hers, trapping her bare ass against the door. The feel of her skin against his sparked an insane throbbing inside him. He had a hard time keeping himself in check. When he touched her hot center, her hips bucked again. He kissed her neck while he brushed her clit with his finger. Then he picked her up and brought her over to the bed.

"Hawk," she said he laid down on top of her, "take off your jeans."

"Not yet," he said as he worked his way down her body, dropping butterfly kisses here and nipping her there. He finally hovered above the apex of her legs. He blew on her hot center, and she sunk her fingers into his hair and squeezed her thighs against his ears. He leaned forward and licked her. She tasted so sweet. He swirled his tongue around her clit, and she cursed breathlessly.

He lifted her ass and held her in place as he sucked and licked her, driving her higher and higher with his lips, teeth, and tongue. Then he slowly eased one finger inside her tight sheath. He was hard as granite, his erection pressing painfully against his zipper with an intense need to be in her, instead of just his fingers. She arched to meet him. He added another finger while he sucked her clit. She flexed her hands on his scalp and lifted her hips to meet his fingers and mouth. As he increased his rhythm, she rocked with him. The way she was losing control was so fucking hot. He swirled his tongue and kept her right on the edge until he nipped her clit with his teeth.

She called out, "Hawk!" as she came hard, his head clamped between her legs. Then after her breathing settled, she said, "Jesus, you're trying to kill me."

He grinned. He loved that she enjoyed sex as much as he did, and it drove him wild that she called his name when she came. It was as if something primal inside him came alive.

She was his now and only his. For as long as she wanted to be. And then some.

"It's my turn," Remy said. She needed to touch him. To taste *him*. She undid his belt buckle and slid his jeans down over his hips. He helped her, and she dropped his clothing on the floor.

She lay down on top of him and kissed him, letting her flesh sink into his. This was what she needed. The feel of Hawk against her. The knowledge that he wanted her. That she was safe in his arms and nothing bad was going to happen. At least, not at this moment.

She kissed his neck and ran her hands down over his chest. She used her teeth on his nipple, and he swore. He grabbed her ass, but she wiggled him off.

"Remy." His growl sent shivers across her skin. His body was something to behold. Chiseled and steely, as if carved in stone. Not an ounce of fat anywhere, which might have been damned annoying if he wasn't so fucking hot. She went back to his nipples and then headed lower.

He swore in response, and she moved farther down his body until her mouth hovered over his cock. She touched the tip with her tongue, reveling in the salty taste, and then made small circles on the crown, first one way, then the other. Slowly, she drew more and more of him into her mouth, sucking and twisting her tongue.

"Honey," he said, his tone spreading heat in her girlie bits. She wanted him inside of her, but first she wanted him to yell *her* name. His hips started to move, and she matched the rhythm with her tongue.

"You're killing me. I want to come inside you. I won't make it if you keep that up."

She stopped and smiled, catching his gaze and holding it. "No, you won't. That would be disappointing, and you won't disappoint me. I know you won't." And she did. She knew it as fundamentally as she knew the sun would rise in the east. Hawk would never purposely disappoint her. Or hurt her. Or do anything that he didn't think was in her best interest. Another bit of knowledge settled in the pit of her stomach. What he *thought* was in her best interest was not the same as actually *being* in her best interest. Hadn't she learned that from her family? She pushed that thought aside as she returned her focus to Hawk.

"Fuck, Remy," he said through gritted teeth. "It feels so good."

It made her soul sing that he wanted her that badly. Just her. Almost as much as she wanted him. She was wet and ready. She moved back up to cover his body with hers and kissed him fiercely with all the passion and intention she felt. Then she started to lower herself on top of him, but he flipped her over and suddenly she was beneath him.

"I need to be deep inside you," he said, his voice just above a whisper in her ear.

God help her, she wanted that, too. He was so fucking hot. She was drenched and so ready.

He grabbed her ass cheeks as he slowly slid inside her. She wrapped her legs around his hips, and he brought her up, so they were both sitting, and she was in his lap. He moved her hips back and forth. Pleasure radiated through her, and she tried to move her hips faster, but he held her in a measured rhythm.

"More, Hawk." she moaned as she tried to speed up the pace.

Hawk stood from the bed while holding her in place. He pushed her back against the wall and then drove himself inside of her.

She let out a yelp of surprise. "Hawk," she grunted. "Oh my god, yes. You're so damn deep."

He drove into her again and again, the rhythm ever increasing. She struggled to lift her knees higher around him, wanting him even deeper.

He thrust all the way inside her and then drew out and did it again. She arched her body as he slammed into her, and she yelled out his name again as she orgasmed. A few strokes later, he was right there with her.

"Jesus, Remy," he mumbled as he gasped for breath.

She rested her forehead on his shoulder, her breathing still heavy. "Yeah, I know. I feel the same way." And she did. This was by far the best sex of her life with the best man she'd ever known. But it wasn't just sex. She'd fallen for him. Hard. He was the perfect match for her. He even knew what she was thinking but if life had taught her anything, it was that good things came and went. Her time with Hawk would be over soon and her heart would hurt. He'd brought her peace. Too bad it wasn't going to last.

CHAPTER TWENTY

R emy held her breath as she left her room, doing her best to avoid waking Hawk. As soon as she heard the quick *snick* of the closing door, she moved swiftly down the hall. She wasn't sure where to find Lacy and Alex, or if they were even in the building. Lacy had an apartment with Logan not too far from here, but she wasn't sure if they'd gone home last night or not.

When she rounded the corner into the bar area, she heard voices coming from the kitchen. She ducked through the door and found the two women she was seeking.

"Morning," she said as she approached.

The space was a professional grade chef's kitchen, with two huge stainless-steel fridges and two wall ovens along with a separate cooktop and a full range along the outside wall. In the middle of the kitchen was an island where she guessed most of the prep work was done. The two women were leaning on it.

"Good morning to you." Lacy narrowed her eyes. "You didn't get much sleep by the look of things."

"Are you telling me I look awful? Thanks."

"Nope. I'm pointing out that you didn't get any sleep. You have that after-sex glow. My guess is you spent the night having fun with Hawk."

"Don't blame you one bit," Alex said as she grabbed a mug from the cupboard and poured a cup of coffee.

Heat climbed up Remy's neck into her cheeks. "Is it that obvious?"

Both women nodded. Alex handed her the mug. "Milk is in the fridge. Don't be embarrassed. Hawk is one good looking man and sexy as hell."

She accepted the coffee and took a sip. Black would be good this morning. She *didn't* get much sleep, and it wasn't just the sex. She was worried about tonight. Long after Hawk had fallen asleep, one arm slung over her hips, she stared at the ceiling and wondered what the best course of action was for her.

She'd come to a decision just before dawn, which led to an hour of fitful sleep before she got up and had a quick shower and then sneaked out of the room. Remy leaned against the opposite side of the counter and took a second sip of coffee.

Lacy eyed her friend over the rim of her mug. "I think we're good to go for tonight, barring any unforeseen events."

"About that," Remy started, "I want to help. I— It's bothering me that you guys are taking all the risks. I—I just can't let you do that for me. It just feels wrong."

Lacy and Alex exchanged glances, and then Lacy smiled. "See, I told you she would try to talk us out of it and then volunteer to be a part of it. She's one of us for sure."

"That you did." Alex grinned.

"One of you?" Remy asked puzzled.

"Women of action," Alex replied. She added a deep southern drawl to her voice. "We're not so good at sitting around letting the men folk make the decisions and do the work while we wait and worry."

"Yeah, fuck that," Lacy said rolling her eyes. "So, what do you want to do?"

Remy blinked. "Well, I hadn't really thought about an exact role. I don't even know what the plan is yet really."

"Right." Alex looked her over for a second and then drained her mug and went back for a second cup. "As chief thief around here, I have some ideas. The guys think Najeddine will use this biometric wallet, and we're prepared for that, but in my experience, no one at his level in terms of work and accomplishment would walk into that party without some kind of backup. He's not a stupid man. He advises part of the Moroccan royal family. He's on his game."

Remy frowned. "Two things. One, do you have a clue what his plan might be? Two, what is your experience exactly? What is a 'chief thief'?"

Alex burst out laughing. "That's a fair question. I'm what I like to refer to as an Asset Repossession Specialist Extraordinaire."

Remy cocked an eyebrow. "You're an ARSE?"

Lacy spit out her coffee all over the counter and broke out into gales of laughter. She laughed so hard she had tears running down her face.

"It's not that funny," Alex snarled, hands on hips. Then she relented. "Okay, maybe it's a bit funny."

Lacy finally got herself under control. "I'm sorry. I've just been telling her that she can't use that title because everyone thinks ARSE, but she always argues with me, but you just proved my point."

"Fine," Alex said, "I will call myself something else."

"What exactly does an Asset Repossession Specialist do?" Remy asked as she pulled herself up onto the opposite counter next to the stove.

"I'm a master thief," Alex said proudly. "I steal things back for people who lost them somehow. Mostly for women." She paused. "It's a long story, but that's really what it boils down to."

Remy took a sip of her coffee and swallowed. "So, with your experience as a thief, you think Najeddine will have a backup plan of some kind?"

Alex nodded. "I would."

"But what does that mean?"

Lacy also pulled herself up onto the counter. "That's the million-dollar question. He could do anything."

"So, what should we do to prepare?" Remy asked.

Alex sighed. "That's the hard part. It's going to be one of those situations where we just have to go with it and improvise on the fly."

"I'm not a huge fan of improvising," Remy admitted.

"Unfortunately, that's part of the game when you're in the thievery business." Alex tossed her long blond hair over her shoulder and stretched her arms above her head. "The plan we have so far is for you to help distract Najeddine since he's going to be focused on you anyway, while I cause a diversion and make a play for the wallet."

"Don't you think that might be a bit obvious? Not to criticize or anything," Remy said quickly, "but won't he be expecting it?"

"That is the difficulty, yes." Lacy let out a big sigh. "Alex is going to have to be very fast. She needs to be gone before Najeddine puts two and two together."

"Still, it seems risky." Remy put her mug down on the counter. "What happens if he catches you?"

"That's another big unknown," Alex agreed.

Remy shook her head. "I don't like this. Is there anything else we can do?"

Alex shrugged. "We can be prepared. With all of us at the

party, maybe we can find the right opportunity to get the wallet with Najeddine none the wiser. Or, at the very least, get the wallet. From there, we can deal with the next hurdle, which is keeping you safe until the meeting begins."

"So, then what can I do to be prepared? I want to help," Remy stated firmly.

Alex narrowed her eyes. "Hmmm. Let me see your hands."

Remy checked her look once more in the mirror. Any other time, she'd be thrilled to be wearing this dress. The floor length-affair with a slit almost to her hip bone in a soft purplish-gray fabric hung perfectly off her curves. The halter neckline emphasized her chest and showed an almost embarrassing amount of cleavage. She couldn't remember any other time when she showed this much skin. Her hair curled in loose waves around her shoulders.

She checked her makeup. More intense than she usually did it, but it suited the gown. She had chosen a smoky gray-purple eye shadow and used it to line the underside of her eye as well. It was the perfect smoky look that made her eyes seem huge and brought out their distinctive color.

All in all, she looked good, which was going to be helpful. She just hoped Najeddine bought it.

"You look stunning," Lacy said as she came into the room behind her.

"Thanks. You, too. That purple really sets off your eyes."

Lacy smiled. "He won't know what hit him."

"Let's hope so. Najeddine better be distracted, or this whole thing falls apart."

"I was talking about Hawk."

She met Lacy's gaze in the mirror. "I…"

"Did you think we didn't notice? We teased you this morning about the sex, but it's easy to see there's something real between you two. Hawk has been super protective of you. And you only seem to really relax when he's in the room."

Heat rushed up her cheeks. "It was his job to keep me safe. That's why he's protective. He's worried I will do something stupid. Again."

She snorted. "Is that what he's selling you? Don't believe a word of it. That man cares about you, very much if I'm not mistaken. That's a good thing. Hawk is truly one of the good guys."

Remy's stomach rolled, and her heart rate ticked up. She didn't need this now. She needed him *not* to care about her. She didn't want to care about him either. *Too fucking late*. She had no idea what the future would bring. Hell, she didn't even know if she'd be alive after tonight. Anything could happen. She didn't want Hawk worrying about her, or worse, doing something stupid to protect *her*. Just the thought of Hawk getting hurt made her feel physically ill.

She took a deep breath. Lacy was wrong. She and Hawk were done now. They'd had their fun, but tonight would determine the rest of her life in so many ways. She would not be distracted by anything, not even Hawk.

She smiled at Lacy through the mirror. "Let's do this."

Thirty minutes later, they were pulling up in front of the Museum of Art with Gunnar behind the wheel of the Escalade. Logan had introduced him earlier and told her that Gunnar was one of the best. She hoped that was true since he would be the getaway driver if everything went to shit.

"You ready?" Alex asked.

"As I'll ever be."

Alex smiled. "You're gonna be fine. You'll knock him dead in that dress. Trust me." She adjusted her vest and pants. She'd added glasses and a red wig. Remy wouldn't have recognized her at all if she didn't know who she was.

Lacy leaned over and brushed a piece of lint off Alex's shoulder. "You look awesome. Now, remember, we are just here for the key," she said, staring directly at Alex.

Remy frowned. "Er, what's going on?"

"As we told you, Alex is a master thief, and she can get distracted when she's around pretty things, like the paintings in the museum. I'm trying to make sure she's not going to steal anything else while we're here."

"Would I do that?" Alex asked, trying to look innocent.

Lacy snorted. "If you thought you could get away with it, yep. In a heartbeat."

Alex laughed. "Okay, you got me. I would be tempted to steal one of the pictures that I happen to know was stolen from its rightful owner but," she said and turned to Remy, "tonight is all about Remy, and I won't do anything to jeopardize that." She reached out and squeezed Remy's hand. "None of us will."

Lacy looked out the car window. "Do you see the guys?"

" Hawk is standing by the door with Logan," Gunnar said.

"I see him," Remy said. "I guess it's time to go."

Gunnar got out of the car and hurried around to open their door. Lacy got out first and then Remy. "Thanks, Gunnar," she said. "Wish me luck.".

"Good luck. You won't need it. You've got one of the best teams on the planet with you and may I say you are looking damn fine to boot," he said with a wink, and she giggled.

"Good luck," Alex said from the back of the car before Gunnar shut the door.

Remy secured her black cloak more tightly around herself. The store had sent it over with the dresses to try on, and she'd fallen in love with it. It was mystical and romantic somehow to turn up in a cloak, like one of those old-fashioned mystery movies set in Victorian times. She glanced around and laughed a little to herself. The temperature had warmed up, and the snow on the ground was creating a low-level fog. It was just like the movies.

She sobered instantly. This wasn't the movies. This was life and death. Hers. And others, her friends. If she didn't get the key back tonight, she would not only lose her family legacy, she might even lose her life. She swallowed and followed Lacy up the walkway.

"You made it," Logan said with a smile. "I was starting to worry. You look beautiful, my love." He bent and dropped a kiss on Lacy's cheek.

"You look rather handsome yourself," she replied.

Remy looked at Hawk. He was magnificent in a tux. A lock of his dark hair curled over his forehead in a way that made her want to touch it. He filled out the lines of his tux so well she knew it had to be expensive. His cuff links looked like they might be real diamonds. He reminded her of James Bond, only more dashing and debonair. His eyes raked over her, too. There was a fire in their depths, but all he said was, "Ready?"

She nodded. So, it was going to be like that. She really shouldn't have expected anything else. He had been irate when he discovered that she was part of the plan to distract Najeddine. He'd probably spoken to the Callahan brothers to make sure they wouldn't involve her, but she'd gone to Lacy and Alex. They were more than happy to include her. As Alex said, it was *her* life. She had a right to play a role. It made her feel better to be involved. How could she ask others to risk everything for her if she wasn't willing to risk it all herself?

Still, she was annoyed that Hawk was so upset. She would have felt much better about the whole event if he wasn't so angry with her. But he was, and it was time for her to pull up her big girl panties and get on with things.

They walked up the museum steps and showed their tickets to the guard. Then they each went through the metal detector. Lacy had explained that Alex would smuggle their weapons into the museum through the back entrance inside some catering equipment. Remy handed her cloak off to the coat check attendant, a young, well-groomed man wearing a traditional black tuxedo with bowtie. She turned to find Hawk assessing her one more time. His gaze lingered on her cleavage before he raised his eyes to meet her own. The fire burned brighter now. Anger came off him in waves.

She shot him a bright smile and then took Lacy's arm. "Shall we go get some champagne?"

Lacy nodded, and off they went through the crowd.

The room was huge and stunning. The cream-colored marble floors set off the various pieces of sculpture scattered about the room. People in austere tuxedos and glittery dresses that sparkled as they moved around, examining carved statues as well as the art that was hung on the walls. An upper balcony ran all the way around the room with a balustrade also made out of marble. She glanced up and noted Gage in the far-right corner. Mitch was all the way opposite in the left corner. The tension in her belly eased slightly. She had a lot of eyes on her. They were here to help.

"Hawk is not pleased with you at all," Lacy murmured in a low voice. She nodded to Remy's right. Hawk was glowering at her from the corner of the room, standing by a statue of a man who looked like he was in pain.

"Well, at least he picked the right sculpture to stand by," she murmured back. She was trying to keep her voice low because they were all wearing ear buds, and she didn't want Hawk to hear what she said although it was probably pointless. Maybe he needed to hear he was being an ass anyway.

Lacy giggled. Then she grabbed two glasses of champagne off a waiter's serving tray and passed one to her friend.

Remy did her best not to touch her earbud but it felt weird. It was similar to her airpods but smaller, flesh colored and she only wore it in her right ear. Lacy had told her to wear her hair down specifically so no one would notice it. She had to admit, it kind of made her feel like she was a spy.

After taking a sip of champagne, Remy swallowed and asked, "Do you see him?"

"No," Lacy responded, and they clinked glasses, then each took a sip.

"Does anyone see him?" Lacy asked.

"Negative," Logan said. Gage and Mitch both responded in kind.

"Hawk?" Gage asked.

"Nothing," was his curt response.

Remy's palm was sweaty against the champagne glass. Her heart was doing a quick beat against her ribcage. She turned slowly as if studying the art in the room, but she was scanning the crowd. Her heart stuttered in her chest when she spotted the Triad group. "The Asian guys from your apartment building, Hawk. They're by the statue of—" She broke off. What the hell was that statue supposed to be anyway? "The slab of rock in the corner that looks like a badly mutilated rooster."

There was laughter in her ear. "I thought it was a duck," Mitch responded. "Glad it's not just me who thinks that's awful." Then he sobered up. "I have eyes on the gang members. There are four of them. They look mighty uncomfortable in those suits. They're with an elderly Asian gentleman."

"Ying Chan. He lives in my building," Hawk's voice sounded in her ear. Even though he was being an ass, it was comforting to know he was there.

"Did he see you?" Gage asked.

"Not yet, but once he sees Remy, he's bound to know I won't be far away. He had his goons search my apartment."

"Keep out of sight as long as you can, then."

"Roger that."

Remy took another sip of champagne and then winced. The sound of that brash Texas voice was unmistakable. Austin Davis was in the middle of the room, holding court.

"Great, another asshole to add to the crowd," she said, hiding her lips behind the rim of the champagne flute.

"I hope you weren't talking about me," a voice said behind her left ear.

She whirled around to find Asad Najeddine standing in front of her.

With a slight smile, he said, "I've been wanting to meet you for a long time. I knew your grandfather." He brought her hand to his lips and dropped a kiss on the back. "It's such a pleasure to finally meet you in person." But the smile didn't reach his eyes.

CHAPTER TWENTY-ONE

awk's entire body tensed as he fought the instinct to march over and snap Najeddine's neck. He whistled out a long, low breath and tried to get his focus back. To be available to help Remy, he needed to maintain his distance and not blow his cover. It just rankled him that Najeddine even thought about touching Remy, let alone was actually doing it. He'd make sure the man paid for taking that liberty and enjoy every second of it.

"Hawk, do you have eyes on Najeddine?" Mitch asked.

"Yes. Nothing stands out so far. He seems to be by himself." Hawk scanned the crowd. "Scratch that. At my ten o'clock. The dark-haired guy in the tux that's next to the post. He's one of Najeddine's. He's the fucker that held Remy on the roof.

He was another one Hawk would enjoy making pay for his crimes. If only the opportunity was afforded to him. He scanned the room again. A sudden movement on his right caught his eye. He zeroed in, but what was it that had caught his attention? There. The blond man. What was he doing? Hawk couldn't tell from the angle he was at because the blond man had disappeared behind one of the statues. The vibe he'd gotten though was of a fellow soldier. A tier one operator on the prowl. He was involved in this mess somehow. Hawk knew it in his bones.

"Changing location." He moved through the throng of people. The crowd was growing, which was good for cover, but bad for anything else. He hated being this far from Remy. The thought was that Najeddine wouldn't kill her as long as he had the key and she was on her own, therefore not a threat to him. Mitch had pointed out that if Hawk was beside her, Najeddine might think twice about keeping her alive. Better to let her appear to be vulnerable, and therefore less of a threat. That whole line of thinking was killing Hawk.

"Mr. Hawkins, how nice to see you this evening. I didn't know you were a lover of the arts."

Hawk looked over his shoulder and found Ying Chan standing there. How the hell had he missed Chan on the move? He fuckin' dropped the ball because he was too focused on Remy, emotionally focused, not militarily focused. He needed to up his game in a big fucking hurry.

He offered his hand. "Mr. Chan. Nice to see you as well. Are you a big supporter of the museum?" he asked as he assessed the muscle Chan had brought with him. One had wandered off to stand by a pillar to Hawk's left. Another drifted away about ten feet, but still alert and ready. Guards flanked Chan on each side, maintaining a respectful distance, but close enough to stop anything bad from happening to their boss.

Chan inclined his head. "I do like art, but my taste runs more toward my country's offerings than this"—he waved his hand at the room in general, and ended with the word—"stuff."

Hawk grinned. "Yes, some of the sculpture is not to my

taste either." Then he sobered. "I was surprised to find your men in my place the other day. Perhaps you would like to explain?" He'd decided a full-frontal assault would be better than beating around the bush, mostly because his patience had left the building.

Chan eyed him and then gave him a little nod. "So, we are dropping the pleasantries already?"

"It would seem so," Hawk agreed.

"I am in need of that key."

Hawk cocked his head. "In need. That is an interesting way to say it. I assumed you wanted the key, but 'in need' sounds more desperate."

Chan looked around the room. "Mr. Hawkins, I enjoyed our encounters immensely at our mutual residence. You have struck me as a very intelligent and thoughtful individual with a strong sense of respect for your elders. You were very respectful to me and my wife as well as several of our contemporaries in the building. That is to say, you are well thought of and well liked.

"Unfortunately, that cannot factor into my current situation. Yes, I am in *need* of the key. I need the protection it affords its owner. I am sorry that your lady friend is involved but, again, I cannot let that affect my desired outcome."

He was giving Hawk fair warning that the gloves were off. It was a sign of respect. Hawk gave him a little bow. "I am sorry to hear you are in a difficult situation. I assume past indiscretions have come to light back in Hong Kong, and now your days may be somewhat numbered?"

Mr. Chan merely smiled in response.

"Well, I appreciate the warning. I, too, enjoyed our encounters. Let's hope we both live long enough to have more." Hawk gave him another small bow and moved across the room in search of the blond man.

"Well, shit. That was the most civilized declaration of war I have ever heard," Mitch said. His voice came through loud and clear through Hawk's earpiece.

"Yeah," Gage agreed. "It's quite worrying actually. I don't like it. Not one bit."

"Join the club," Hawk grumbled. "I'm pretty sure he's a former Triad member. Like I said to him, something must have come up from the past, and now he's in big-ass trouble."

"I'm still unsure how having the key would keep him safe, though," Logan added.

"No society member is allowed to kill someone on the board, but that only protects him from the society members and those who are in the know." Hawk moved to the left to avoid a woman who'd already had too much champagne. "I don't know how that would affect the whole Triad situation."

"Safe to say there are probably details of the society that we don't know," Gage said. "But I think Dragan mentioned that Archer Gray would also have to provide some security for members, especially board members, so maybe that's what he's after. Maybe he moved into a Lock and Key location and never leaves again."

That was a hell of a thought. He couldn't imagine spending the rest of his life in the equivalent of a luxury hotel, it didn't matter how many stars it was.

"Where are you going, Hawk?"

"I'm looking for the blond man. He caught my eye. I think he's at the very least someone's security, if not a society member himself. I need to find him again."

Mitch cut in. "What does he look like?"

"Blond. Over six feet. Slim build. Mid to late thirties. There. By the bar." Hawk started moving toward a statue on the left to give him cover. He glanced over at Remy. She seemed to be holding her own, which wasn't surprising.

Najeddine was looking at her chest. Hawk fisted his hands. When someone bumped into him, he swung around, ready to address any threat, but realized the woman was just an art lover. When he turned back around, he couldn't see Remy anymore, but the blond man was moving away from the bar. Where the hell was he going?

CHAPTER TWENTY-TWO

"I'm sorry. I don't believe I know you," Remy said once she found her voice again and pulled her hand from his grasp.

"Come now, you must know who I am."

"Er, no, sorry. I'm finding that my grandfather had many friends I didn't know about."

Najeddine chuckled. "I'm sure that's true. Well, allow me to introduce myself. I'm Asad Najeddine."

She nodded. "Mr. Najeddine, how did you know my grandfather?"

"Please call me Asad. Your grandfather and I were in the same social club, I guess we'll call it."

Remy tried to look mystified, but it was hard. She wanted to smash the guy's face in. She also wanted to wash her hands.

"I see, and what club would that be?" she asked with a smile.

He shook his head. "Come now. You know exactly what I'm talking about. You had the key after all. And now I have it."

The look of triumph in his eyes made her seethe. "Oh, I see. So, it was you who held me hostage? I'm afraid I didn't see my captor's face."

He frowned. "I do apologize for that, my dear." He offered her a small bow, which was supposed to be respectful, but since his eyes wandered down to her boobs and stayed there, it was hard to find it anything but gross. "It was not I who did that necessary but unfortunate task. I'm sure it was unpleasant."

"On a scale of one to ten, being dangled by your ankles over the side of a six-storey building is a negative five-hundred. How are your other men from the roof? The ones that didn't try to drop me off the edge." *Two could play this game, asshole.*

"My men are all fine." His face had gone hard. "Their actions were necessary to retrieve the key. Surely you can see that."

She shrugged. "You could have just asked. You never know what could have happened."

Najeddine's smile was cruel as Alex, masquerading as a server, approached with more champagne. Alex offered the tray to Remy. She put down her empty one—how had that happened?—and picked up a full one. Najeddine did the same. Alex gave her a wink and disappeared back through the crowd with Najeddine's fingerprints on the champagne glass.

She reached out and touched his arm. "Tell me, Asad, why did you need the key so badly?"

He narrowed his eyes at her as if trying to discover a motive for her question. "I would like a seat on the board."

"I see. And what does that give you?" She was genuinely curious. "You're already a member so what is the extra benefit of being on the board?"

He seemed to sense this. "You really have no idea, do you?"

She shook her head. "Why don't you enlighten me?"

"Power. It is the key to riches and power."

So Gage had been right. The people after the key were all already members of the society. They just wanted...more. "I see. My understanding was that you are quite powerful already."

Najeddine smiled. "So, you do know who I am."

She gave a small shrug. "A woman likes to know about the man who intended great bodily harm to her. But seriously, Asad, I know you're already a powerful man." She reached out and touched his arm again. "So, why do you need more power? What exactly does the key give you?"

He leaned in slightly. "It is the power to make decisions and the protection of the society that makes the key so very valuable." He grabbed her hand and put it over his arm and placed his hand on top of hers. "You see, your grandfather did you a great disservice by not allowing you to join the society sooner."

"How so?" She moved along with him, taking small steps and watching out for anything that looked out of the ordinary. Lacy was off to her right. She lost Hawk behind some statue. Gage, Mitch, and Logan probably had eyes on her, but she couldn't confirm without drawing attention to them.

"...needs change," he said. "If it doesn't change, then it doesn't serve the needs of its community. I want to direct that change. Being on the board makes that a reality."

She cocked an eyebrow at him. "So, it's all for the good of the society, is that what you're saying? Somehow, I don't believe that."

"I'm not convincing you of my altruistic nature?"

She snorted. "No. Sorry. I'm not buying it. You strike me as a lot of things, but altruistic is not one of them." She flashed him a charming smile. "I think you are more intelligent than that. I think you have your eye on something specific."

He chuckled and pulled her in closer as if he was going to share a secret. "I think you're trying to manipulate me."

She gave him a coy smile. "Can't blame a girl for trying." There was no point in lying. She was already losing Najeddine. She glanced over at Lacy, who shook her head. It wasn't time yet. Shit. Alex wasn't in place.

"Seriously, Asad," she said and shifted slightly so her breasts rubbed against Najeddine's arm, "what is the power of the society? As you pointed out, my grandfather didn't tell me anything. I'm completely in the dark."

Najeddine hadn't missed the use of his first name or the fact that her breasts had touched him. He glanced down at them and then back at her face. "It's too bad we are enemies. I think we could have a lot of fun together otherwise."

"Do we have to be enemies?" she asked in a soft voice. "Maybe we could be friends." It took everything she had to utter that statement without gagging.

The sound of someone tapping a microphone caught her attention, and she looked up at the stage. It was time for the speeches. She glanced around looking for Alex. She spied her making her way across the room with a tray of champagne. Soon this part will be over. *Thank God!*

"We've got a problem," Hawk's voice sounded in her ear. "The blond man just exchanged looks with Najeddine. A small nod. They are working together."

"Shit. Do you think the blond man has the key?" Logan asked.

"I can't tell," was Hawk's response.

Remy knew instinctively that Najeddine would never let someone else hold the key. His ego wouldn't let him. She cleared her throat. "I'm always amazed at the amount of money these types of things raise. It's almost as if *no* one says '*no*'." She tried to emphasize the no's enough that Hawk and everyone else could pick up on what she was saying without alerting Najeddine.

Alex was still working the room, but she was moving more slowly now.

"I think Remy is saying she thinks Najeddine has it."

"Then what's the blond guy doing?" Mitch asked.

Hawk briefly popped into Remy's line of sight and then disappeared again. "If Remy is right and Najeddine has the key, then the blond is the decoy. The guy Najeddine set up to look like he has the key, making *him* the target."

Gage commented, "Agreed. The nod was pretty obvious if you were looking for it. I think that's Najeddine's play."

"I agree with Remy." Dani's voice came through the earbud. Remy had almost forgotten she was there. Dani continued. "Najeddine won't trust anyone else with it."

"So, what do we do now?" Lacy asked.

The applause sounded, and people went back to chatting and drinking champagne. The speeches were much shorter than they'd anticipated. They'd missed the window. *Shit. Shit. Shit.* Now the place would start to empty out.

"Get Najeddine over by the blond guy," Alex directed. "I have an idea. Remy, you're going to have to put your newfound talent to work."

Hawk's voice cut through the din. "What newfound talent?"

CHAPTER TWENTY-THREE

Hawk was trying to keep one eye on Remy and the other on Chan. It wasn't working. Now they were talking about changing the plan. He didn't like it. Not one bit. All his senses were on high alert. Chan's men were circling Remy and Najeddine. Najeddine's men were now closing ranks. It all looked like it might go south.

Hawk started across the room, but then a loud voice said, "Well, now, I've got to go to meetin'. Y'all enjoy the rest of your evenin'." Austin Davis stepped away from the crowd he'd been talking to. Hawk's gaze locked with Remy. Was Austin Davis in the Lock and Key Society? Was he on the board?

Remy turned to Najeddine. "Asad," she purred, and Hawk's stomach knotted. He wanted to kill Najeddine just because Remy said his name in that voice. She continued. "Is Austin Davis a member of the society?"

Najeddine smiled down at her. "You know, I can't answer any questions about the society. It's against the rules."

"Hypothetically speaking then... There could be other

members just like you who want the key so they can be on the board. Could Austin Davis be one of those people?"

"I don't care how many others are looking for the key because I have it, but hypothetically speaking, Austin would not be among them."

She frowned. "Why not?"

It was a good question. Hawk was wondering the same thing. Why wouldn't Davis want the key? He was a definite power monger. Two minutes of listening to any interview with him and it was obvious.

Najeddine stayed silent and just smiled at Remy.

What? Then it clicked. Hawk said, "Davis already has a seat on the board," He'd been thinking he was behind the third group that were after the key. The one Connor had mentioned but if he was already on the board, then that couldn't be the case. Remy repeated aloud what Hawk had said into the earbud.

Najeddine ignored her statement. "Well, my dear, it has been so interesting speaking with you," He looked down at Remy's chest one more time. "But I must run off to the meeting."

Hawk still wanted to kill the guy. Every time he looked at Remy's chest, Hawk felt a strong urge to punch something.

"Wait," she said. "I have a couple more questions." She leaned in a bit and brushed him with her breasts again. "Just a few. Promise." She gave him a huge smile.

Hawk was grinding his teeth. This was so painful to watch and listen to.

Remy was slowly moving Najeddine over toward the stairs to the upper level, where the blond man was standing at the bottom.

"I guess I can be a few minutes late." He smiled back and glanced down at her boobs.

"What kind of danger am I in?"

CHAPTER TWENTY-FOUR

Najeddine stared at her. "That's a rather bold and loaded question."

Where the hell was Alex? They were almost at the stairs. The blond man was there waiting. She glanced around the room. It seemed to be emptying out. She didn't see the Asian men, but Najeddine's guys were moving in.

"It's my life. It seems now might be the time to be bold."

He nodded. "I regret to tell you that you are in a fair bit of danger. You see, as a legacy member, you can still ask for, and possibly receive a token, even if you don't have the key. The board would vote on such things. I'm unsure how that vote would go but..." He smiled at her again, which was more like a wolf baring its teeth. "My guess is they would let you in, so to the key holder, you will always be a threat. You have a legitimate claim to that seat at the table. Should the key holder do anything outside the rules, you can challenge *him* and claim the seat. It is most unfortunate that your time on earth seems to be rather limited." He looked up and nodded to one of his men.

Suddenly, there was a loud crash. Alex dropped a tray of

champagne on the blond man who was now only a few feet away. "I am so sorry, sir," she said as she tried to dry him off.

Remy's heart double-timed in her chest and sweat broke out across her back. It was now or never. Najeddine turned to look. Remy said a small prayer and braced herself before she was shoved from behind and pushed into Najeddine's chest.

"Seriously," a voice said. "You stop fussing with this man." The man who appeared to be the head waiter hurried over. Logan was unrecognizable. He wore the vest of his tux, but he had huge glasses, and he was using some weird accent.

"I'm so sorry, sir," Alex said again.

Remy reached into Najeddine's breast pocket and quickly pulled out the wallet. She brought it down to her side as she straightened up again. She was holding her breath. *Please don't let him notice.*

Logan hissed, "Back to the kitchen," at Alex, who then brushed by Remy and took the wallet with her. "I am so sorry, sir." Logan said again as he brushed at the blond man's suit. The blond man pushed him off and glared.

Logan bowed and disappeared back into the crowd as another man appeared with a broom and a dustpan to pick up the glass.

"Well, thank you for being honest with me," Remy said, her heart still pounding against her sternum. She started to step away from him, but he grabbed her arm. Her stomach clenched. She needed to get away before he found out the wallet was gone.

"Suddenly, you're in such a rush to go. Why is that?" He narrowed his eyes at her.

"Forgive me, but you've just told me that I could be a threat to you, so I don't think there's a need to stay here and see if you decide to act on it."

He smiled his wolfish grin and then tugged her close.

"Until we meet again." He raised her hand and kissed it once more.

She pulled away from him and went back through the thinning crowd. Where the hell were the bathrooms?

"Go straight, and the ladies' room door is on the left." Lacy's voice sounded in her ear. "I'm right behind you."

Remy opened the ladies room door and almost bumped into an elderly woman coming out. "So sorry," she said and moved out of the way. The woman finally made it out the door and Remy entered. There was a rest area outside of the bathroom stalls that had a round seat for women to relax. Dani and Alex were seated there.

"Great job!" Alex said. "You did it! I told you you'd be a natural. You've got the hands for it."

Remy collapsed onto the seat. "Oh, my god! That was nerve-wracking. Wait! Are we alone?"

The two women nodded. Dani pulled out her cell phone.

"How's it going?" she asked as the door opened again and Lacy entered.

"Hey," Lacy said. "We have to hurry this up. The crowd is really thinning out there, and we need to get this done before we don't have any cover."

"I've almost got it, but the iris scan isn't working." Dani swore.

"What do you mean it's not working?" Lacy asked.

Dani huffed. "It's not reading the screen." She held up the phone that had a closeup of Najeddine's iris on it."

"Maybe you're too close?" Alex suggested.

Dani moved the phone further away from the wallet reader and tried again. Nothing happened. "Shit," Dani mumbled again. "It worked when I tested it back at the office with the identical new wallet we got for Remy."

Remy tried to breathe. She was starting to freak out. If this didn't work, she'd be dead. "Najeddine won't let me live after this, regardless of if he has the key or not. He doesn't want me around to challenge him anyway. He'd only hesitate if he thought I'd sleep with him for it. If he can get me into bed, then he'll let me live until after we have sex. Otherwise, I'm dead at his earliest convenience."

Lacy squeezed her arm. "We'll figure this out."

Remy wasn't so sure. She watched as Dani struggled with the phone and the reader. "Did you wipe the screen?"

"What?" Dani asked.

"Well, you got prints off the glass, right? The screen probably has goo on it from the fingerprint stuff you used to transfer the print."

"Shit," Dani said. She wiped both the scanner on the wallet and the phone screen with the fabric of her dress. She held both. There was a click and the wallet opened.

"Thank God," Alex mumbled.

Dani took out the key and handed it to Lacy. Then she took another identical key and put it back inside the wallet. She clicked it closed.

Lacy let out a breath. "Alex, make sure you get that to the guys so they can put it where Najeddine can find it. If he figures out he's lost it…" her voice faded out.

Remy shuddered. "He'll kill me. Probably stand right outside the space where the board meeting is supposed to take place and kill me the moment I try to enter."

Lacy touched her friend's shoulder. "Let's just say it's better he gets the fake and thinks he can claim the seat on the board until you can claim it with the real key, Remy."

Alex nodded. "Got it." She smiled at Remy. "Good luck." Then she was gone.

Lacy put the key into another wallet. "I'll keep it until we get you to wherever the meeting is." She raised her voice. "Which is where?" She was asking the guys.

"Upstairs. Take the stairwell to the right of the bathroom. At the top of the stairs, turn left and then right. Then go to the far end. It's the last door on the left," Gage said. "Best hurry."

Remy stood but then promptly fell back down on the seat. Her knees didn't want to hold her.

Dani squeezed Remy's bicep. "You can do this. You just successfully pickpocketed a guy who was expecting it, all the while keeping him amused and scanning the room for trouble. You've got this."

"She's right." Lacy helped her up. "You do have this." She gave Remy a hug. "I'll be ahead of you. The guys will be in the hallway to help if you need it. I'll meet you at the door."

She nodded.

Dani stood. "How do I look?" she smiled. She was wearing the same dress as Remy, and she had a matching wig. If someone didn't look closely, they would never know it wasn't Remy, which was the whole point.

Gage's voice was back. "Dani, go up the same stairs and turn right and then left. You'll be walking down a parallel hallway. Drop the case in the third plant down. Make it obvious but not too obvious."

Dani rolled her eyes. "Yes, dear." She shook her head. "See you guys soon." Then she and Lacy left the bathroom. Remy wanted to walk out the door and go back to the car and get Gunnar to just drive. Take her anywhere but here.

Instead, she took a deep breath and squared her shoulders. *This one is for you, Gramps.* She headed out the door.

CHAPTER TWENTY-FIVE

"Where is she?" Asad Najeddine demanded. "You were supposed to keep an eye on her," he seethed. "She has the key!" He broke off abruptly and smiled at a couple passing before he demanded from his men, "I want it back now."

"There," said the man who had held Remy hostage. "She's walking in the upper gallery."

Hawk leaned back behind the sculpture that looked like a mashed-up cookie. "You're up, Dani. He's sending his goon after you."

"Got it," she responded. She slowed her pace.

The man hit the stairs and took them two at a time. "

"He's coming up ahead of you," Hawk confirmed.

"I'm here at the end of the hallway, Dani," Gage said. "If there's trouble, I've got you."

"Got it." Dani waited until the man appeared and then she turned and ran down the upper gallery. She dropped the wallet and then turned back like she was going to go back for it but glanced at the man chasing her and then started running again. She disappeared from Hawk's view.

The man disappeared from sight as he bent over, then reappeared. "Did he get the wallet, Gage?" Hawk asked.

"Yes. Dani played it perfectly. I'm pretty sure he thought she dropped it by accident."

Hawk waited as Najeddine fumed in the corner. He looked around, but Mr. Chan was nowhere in sight. Neither was Austin Davis. The meeting had probably started. No wonder Najeddine was livid. No key and missing the meeting. He was not a happy camper.

Najeddine's cell rang, and he answered it as he looked up. Then he smiled and nodded. He put his cell back in his pocket and headed up the stairs.

"Looks like he took the bait." Hawk asked, "Dani, are you clear?"

"Yes, I'm good."

"Alex?"

"All clear. Here with Dani."

His gut loosened ever so slightly. He started up the stairs that the girls had just ascended. He turned left and then right. Remy was at the very end of the corridor, about to turn into the meeting room. Lacy was a few steps behind.

"Um, guys?" Remy's voice came through his earbud. "This isn't a room. It's another hallway."

Shit. He picked up speed. Across the way, Najeddine met his guy and put the wallet back in his pocket. He hadn't seen the girls yet, but he would.

"Get out of there, Remy. You too, Lacy. Hide. Najeddine is headed your way."

Both women ducked into a different doorway and closed the door after them. He secreted himself behind yet another large sculpture. This one looked like two people having sex or doing some kind of dance. Sculpture just wasn't his thing.

He waited a beat and then peeked out. Najeddine came down the hallway and opened the door they had thought led to the meeting room. He disappeared and closed the door after him.

"It's clear." Hawk came out from behind the statue, and the girls came out of the room. They met in the hallway.

"What do you want to do?" Lacy asked.

Gage, Logan, and Mitch arrived.

"It looks like we have no choice. I have to go down that hallway. You heard Najeddine. He wants me dead even when he believes he has the key, and I can guarantee that situation won't improve when he finds out he doesn't."

Hawk's breath hitched in his chest. She sure as hell wasn't going alone. "Fine, but I'm going with you."

"They aren't going to let you in," Mitch said.

"I can't let her go on her own." It didn't matter if he wasn't welcome. He wasn't leaving her to the wolves.

Mitch eyed him and then nodded. "Okay then. We'll all go—"

"You can't." Hawk cut him off. "If we show up en masse, it will be seen as hostile. If I show up, I look like her date, or at least less hostile."

Gage nodded. "He's got a point." He glanced around. "Keep your earbuds in, and we'll stay close. Yell if there's trouble, and we'll get there as fast as we can."

Hawk nodded. He looked at Remy. "Ready?"

She gave a single nod, but Lacy grabbed her hand and gave it a squeeze. "You've got this," she said.

Remy gave her a brief smile, then turned and headed for the door.

Hawk came up beside her. "Do whatever I tell you, when I tell you. Do not hesitate."

"Got it."

"We'll discuss your pickpocketing escapade later." He said it so she'd get mad. Mad was better than scared. Anger provided energy. Fear drained energy. At least, that was what worked for him.

She shot him a glare as she pulled open the door.

"Hawk," Lacy called and tossed him the wallet. He put it in his pocket and then followed Remy through the door. She was already a good twenty feet ahead. He was about to call to her when he saw movement out of the corner of his eye. His spine tingled, and his hair stood up. "Get down," he ordered.

To her credit, she dropped like a stone, and the knife that came out of the darkness on the left hit the wall. Then the four Asian men emerged. Hawk pulled the gun that Alex had dropped off to him earlier.

He pointed in the general direction of the men. When they started separating, he said, "Don't fucking move." He didn't have a silencer this time, so it would make an awful boom, but he was prepared to pull the trigger.

The door opened behind him. "We got your back," Mitch said, and he came to a stop beside Hawk. Gage was on his other side along with Logan.

"Remy, stand up and go to the wall," Hawk instructed.

Mitch and his brothers moved forward and frisked the men, taking various guns and knives off them. Then they turned them around and walked them back down the hall and out the door. "Good luck," Mitch said as he went by.

Hawk nodded and then went to Remy. "Are you okay?"

"Yes." She sucked in oxygen like she'd been holding her breath. She leaned against him for a second. "Sorry. It's just a bit overwhelming."

He wanted to take her in his arms and get the fuck out of there, but Najeddine's words haunted him. If she didn't claim her seat on the board, she would always be in danger. Looking over her shoulder for the rest of her life was no way to live. His heart hurt for her. A fierce fire of protectiveness ran through his veins.

She straightened up. "Let's go."

He nodded. They took another few steps down the hallway before a gun was stuck in Hawk's ribs. He froze. He'd had no warning sign. How could this have happened? He looked over at Remy who stopped and looked at him.

"What?" she asked.

Of all the times for him to lose his sixth sense. He closed his eyes and tried to see what he'd missed. Nope. He wasn't getting anything.

"I am sorry, Mr. Hawkins, but as I said, I am in *need* of the key." Mr. Chan's voice echoed around them.

As Remy looked over his shoulder, her eyes got big. She looked back at Hawk, and their gazes locked. He tried to tell her how sorry he was with his eyes, but she just seemed confused.

Hawk turned around, and Chan pulled Hawk's gun out of his waistband. He moved to put Remy behind him. "You're already a member then."

He hesitated. "I used to be. Due to circumstances beyond my control, I lost my membership."

"I see. So, you need the key so you can not only be a member again but be on the board." Was that a flash of movement he saw? A shadow of some kind? He moved to his left, keeping Remy behind him. Chan moved across from Hawk in the hallway, far enough away that Hawk couldn't strike, but close enough so Chan couldn't miss.

"Yes, it would provide me membership again, but more. Only board members are protected to the degree I need protection. There is much they offer. I cannot divulge anymore. You understand."

He waved the gun slightly. "The key please."

Hawk didn't move. He wasn't going down without a fight. He glanced over Chan's shoulder. Definitely movement that time. Friend or foe?

"I appreciate that you want to protect your lady friend, but there is no need for you to die this evening. Give me the key, and I promise I will not harm Ms. Tanger."

"Unfortunately, there are others who will still see her as a threat, as someone who can still claim the seat."

Chan gave a small shrug. "If that situation arises, then I am already dead and cannot help you." His face hardened. "The key."

Hawk still didn't move. Out of the corner of his eye, a shadow detached itself from the wall.

Chan raised the gun.

"Hawk," Remy said. Her voice trembled.

He reached back, and she gave him her hand. He squeezed it. He wanted to make sure she knew he was okay, but more. He needed to know exactly where she was in case this all went south.

"Now, Mr. Hawkins." Chan put his finger on the trigger.

A quick flash as the light reflected off another gun, Dragan brought it down on Chan's head. Chan slumped to the floor.

"Sorry it took so long," Dragan said as he checked Chan's pockets. "I wanted to make sure there was no one else lurking in the shadows." He handed Hawk back his gun.

"Dragan," Remy gasped, relief pouring off her. "Thank you."

Dragan nodded. "Thank Hawk. He kept the man talking. He also positioned him to make it easier for me."

Remy immediately curled under Hawk's arm. He gave her a quick squeeze and let her go. No more distractions. If it hadn't been for Dragan, they both might be dead.

"You ready to go to the meeting?" Dragan asked.

Remy shot a glance at Hawk. He thought he saw hurt on her face, but he wasn't sure.

She smiled at Dragan. "As I'll ever be."

"Then follow me." Dragan moved quickly down the hallway. Remy followed, and Hawk brought up the rear. He kept his eyes open for any dangers. They came to what looked like a dead end. Hawk studied the wall ahead of them. There, in the corner near the ceiling, the logo just like at Remy's shop.

Remy looked around. "Is this another secret room?"

Dragan nodded.

"How do you know about this?" she asked.

He just gave her an enigmatic smile and then reached over and pulled the statue on the left. The door, which was more like a panel, slid into the wall. Beyond was a room full of people. He gestured for her to enter. Remy stepped inside, and Hawk followed. Dragan slid in as well, and then the door closed behind them.

The room was like any other room in the museum. It was filled with artwork on the walls, paintings by famous artists, and a few sculptures in the corners, but there was also a long table in the middle with twelve chairs around it.

On the right side of the room was another table laden with food. On the left side, a bar. People mingled and chatted. It was a cocktail party like any other.

Archer Gray froze when he noticed them by the doorway. Then he made his way over to them. Gray addressed Hawk's friend first. "Dragan Maric, it's been a while.

"Archer," Dragan said and inclined his head slightly.

"Ms. Tanger, Mr. Hawkins. May I ask how all of you got in here? It is most unusual." He nodded to two rather large men who came over and searched the three, taking Hawk's and Dragan's guns and all three sets of earbuds.

Remy frowned. She felt naked without the Callahans in her ear. "Well, you didn't have any code locks or retinal scanners on the door. It wasn't exactly hard to figure it out."

Archer narrowed his eyes at her but nodded. "I see. This is just a meeting space, not an actual..." He paused. "Usually, we kill people who wander into one of our spaces uninvited."

Remy snorted. "You know, I'm kind of tired of people telling me they're going to kill me. There's been a lot of that tonight. Let's just skip the bullshit and move on to business. Besides, I think I *was* invited." She put her hand up. Hawk took out the wallet and placed it in her upturned palm.

Archer seemed to smile. "Yes, I guess you were, but your friends weren't."

Hawk tensed.

"Well, if you want to give it a try, be my guest," Remy said, "but so far, no one has succeeded in killing them, so I'm not liking your odds."

Hawk had the serious urge to laugh. That was his girl defending him. It made his heart swell just a bit. She was so fierce and strong. He loved it. He loved her. That thought froze his lungs. No. He couldn't think about it now. That was just crazy. *Focus.*

Archer's eyes opened slightly wider, but he said nothing.

"Maybe we could get this meeting underway?" Remy asked. "I'm tired and want this sorted."

CHAPTER TWENTY-SIX

Remy let out the breath she'd been holding when Archer walked away from them. She wanted to collapse onto the floor, but she managed to stay on her feet. What she really wanted was to be in Hawk's arms, but that wasn't fair to him. She was involved in this up to her eyeballs for the rest of her life. He didn't need that. He had his own life to live. He had freedom that she just didn't have.

"Gentlemen, ladies," Archer said, "if you could take your seats."

Remy studied the people as they all moved about, taking their seats. She recognized two Fortune 500 company CEOs, and even one congresswoman, but for the most part, the people in the room were a mystery to her. Except Austin Davis. So he *was* a board member. He took a seat. There was one empty seat at the end of the table.

Najeddine was standing at the far end of the table speaking with one of the CEOs. He hadn't noticed them yet. It was just a matter of time, Remy knew, and then things would get ugly. She braced herself for the onslaught.

"Austin has a seat," Remy said quietly. "Then why the hell

did he want my key? Maybe we were wrong. Maybe it wasn't him but someone else."

Hawk shrugged. "I have no idea. With this crowd, nothing is as it seems."

It was then that Najeddine noticed them and said out loud to the room, "What are they doing here? They aren't members. They aren't allowed in."

All faces turned in their direction. Remy swallowed but walked closer to the table. "I believe I have a right to be here." She held the wallet in her hand.

Najeddine began to protest, but Archer sent him a look, and he promptly shut up. *Interesting.* Archer Gray was the man with all the power by the looks of things. Even Austin Davis seemed to be toeing the line.

"You all remember the passing of Remington Tanger, Jr. Well, this is his heir. Remington Tanger the Fourth."

All the heads in the room nodded at her. Then a bald man, who looked to be in his fifties, sitting about midway down the table, spoke up. "Najeddine is still correct. Those men have no place in here."

Archer studied the man for a beat. "This is a meeting space and not one of our facilities. There are no rules specifically about meeting spaces. In the past, many non-members have been allowed in this space. At this time, those gentlemen may remain. They will follow all rules, or Ms. Tanger suffers the consequences." Archer turned toward her, and she nodded as if she understood but she had no clue. What could the consequences be? Removal? Torture? Death? These people scared the hell out of her.

Archer continued. "Ms. Tanger has a birthright membership to the Society. She, being a direct descendant of one of our founders, has a claim to one of the seats at this table if she can produce her family key."

"She cannot," Najeddine said in triumph. He held up his

biometric wallet. "I have the key. I'm claiming the seat at the table."

Was she mistaken, or did Davis just swear?

Archer cocked his head and then put out his hand. Najeddine walked over, opened his wallet, and handed it over. He looked at Remy, his face smug. She stifled the urge to smile but it was hard. He had a comeuppance coming, and it was going to be ugly. It thrilled her to know she'd be delivering it.

Archer took the key out of the wallet and looked at it in the light. He closed his hand around it and then looked over at her. He put his hand up and beckoned her. Remy walked over, opened up her wallet and placed it on the table in front of Archer.

"What's this?" Najeddine sputtered. "She made a fake. My key is the real one."

Archer spoke in a clear voice. "If that is the case, then she will suffer the consequences, as will you."

"Consequences?" she tipped her head, forcing a calm she wasn't really feeling into her voice. "What are those?" Sweat broke out across her body. It was one thing to trick the guy. It was another to have him killed because of it. These people were all so keen on death as a penalty, but she couldn't do that. She couldn't be responsible for someone's death. She needed details.

"Is your key a fake?" Archer asked.

She shook her head.

"Then you don't have to worry about the consequences."

"Yes, but—"

Archer gave her the stare, and she suddenly understood why the world shut up when he looked at them. It was a cold stare that promised nothing good if he was not obeyed. So she stayed silent, her heart beating rapidly against her ribs.

Archer looked down at the key Remy had given him. He didn't touch it. He didn't take it out of the case.

Shit! Did they mix them up in the bathroom? Did they give Najeddine back the right key? What the hell were the consequences?

"Mr. Najeddine, your key, sir, is the fake." He threw the key across the room, and it landed in a garbage can. "You have no claim to the chair."

"What?" Najeddine's face lost all its color. "But—" Then he looked up. "You!" he yelled and lunged at her. Remy moved backward too quickly and stumbled over her dress. She was falling. Hawk caught her and immediately righted her, putting himself in between her and Najeddine.

"You bitch!" Najeddine bellowed. "She tricked me!" He lunged again, and Hawk dropped the man with one massive right cross to the jaw.

Remy blinked. How the hell had Hawk gotten across the room so quickly? How had he stopped her from falling? She stared up at him. He merely nodded at her and then stepped back against the wall.

Archer looked at Hawk and gave a curt nod of approval. "It appears Ms. Tanger has claimed her family legacy and her seat at the table." He gestured toward the empty seat at the head of the table.

Remy pulled the chair out and sank onto it.

Archer then gestured to the two security guards. They walked over, picked up Najeddine, and carried him out of the room.

"We need to vote on the acceptance of Remington Tanger the Fourth as board member and founding family member. All in favor?" Archer's voice carried across the room and resonated in Remy's chest. If this was what she wanted, then why did she feel terror clawing its way up her throat?

Slowly, every person at the table raised their right hand

except Archer and Austin Davis. Finally, Davis raised his hand, but he glared at Remy, hatred in his eyes. What the hell had she done to him?

"It is settled. Ms. Tanger, Remington, you are now a member of the Lock and Key Society until death do us part."

A chill went down her spine at Archer's words. His gaze suggested he was serious. What the hell had she just done?

"Now," Archer said, "on to other business."

"But, Archer…" the congresswoman spoke. She indicated Hawk and Dragan with her chin.

Archer let out a sigh. "I can ask the gentlemen to leave, but given what's transpired, chances are good they won't, and then it will all turn ugly." He looked down at the table. "I'm not in the mood for ugly tonight. We will reconvene in two weeks at our usual location. All rules apply."

People stood and made their way out of the room, exchanging a few words on the way out. Every single person came up and congratulated Remy before leaving the room. Everyone except Davis. He just walked out. Najeddine was hauled out by the same two burly looking men who took their earbuds and weapons earlier.

Remy stood up. "What happens now?" she asked Archer. He was the only other member left in the room.

He studied her for a moment. "Your grandfather did you a massive disservice." He stood and moved down to her end of the table. "He should have told you everything. Instead, you just signed your life away to something you know nothing about."

Despite the cold sweat breaking out on her body, she squared her shoulders. "It wasn't like I had a choice really. It became pretty clear I either joined or I died, so here I am."

He nodded. "It's true. Your grandfather was of the old ways. The last of the dinosaurs. He was also the collective conscience of the society. With him gone…." Archer let out a sigh. "Well, let's just say the days ahead will be challenging."

"You still haven't really told me anything." Remy was tired and scared. She just wanted answers.

"I can't." He looked over at Hawk, who stood a few feet away and then over to Dragan, who was posted by the door. "There are rules that must be obeyed."

"I get that. You all seem to favor death as the punishment for breaking them."

Archer nodded. "In many circumstances, yes."

Remy put a hand over her stomach. She was nauseated. "Is that what will happen to Najeddine? I don't want him to die. He tried to—"

Archer put up his hand. "Please don't tell me what he or you did. The more I know, the worse it will be for you both. There are always consequences. Currently, he will be banished from the society. If he breaks his vow, then, well… You get it?"

She did. She closed her eyes for a second and tried to regain her equilibrium. "What vow?" she asked.

Archer smiled slightly. "I can't tell you now. You and I will meet later this week or at the beginning of the next. You can come down the stairs to the door, and you will be let in. Just make sure you have your key with you. We will go over everything you need to know then."

She nodded.

"And Remington," he sent a pointed gaze toward Hawk and Dragan. "Come alone."

She let out a sigh and headed for the door. Hawk and Dragan fell in behind her.

"She has the protection of the society now, gentlemen. No one will hurt her."

Remy stopped and looked over her shoulder.

"Forgive me if I don't take your word for it," Hawk said.

Archer's lips curved slightly upward. "Suit yourself." He looked at Dragan. "I would like to meet with you."

Dragan's face remained impassive. "When?"

"I'll get back to you."

"Fine." Dragan leaned over and pushed the button for the door, and they all exited the room.

"Are you okay?" Hawk asked in a low voice as they walked down the hallway and entered the upper gallery once again.

Was she okay? She had no fucking clue. "I think so," Remy said.

"I'm going to leave you two here. I have things to do," Dragan said.

"Thanks for coming to our rescue," Remy said and then leaned up and beckoned Dragan down so she could kiss his cheek.

"It was all Hawk. I was just window dressing." The two men bumped shoulders and nodded at one another and then Dragan disappeared down the dark hallway.

"He's right. You saved my life."

Hawk grimaced. "I almost got you killed. I didn't sense Chan."

"You can hardly be blamed for that. There was a lot going on and, to be fair, since Dragan was also there, maybe we weren't in quite as much danger so you didn't pick up on it."

He glanced at her. "Nice try." Then he froze and cocked his head. In a split second, he whisked her behind a sculpture of a young woman with an umbrella and into the shadows.

"What?" she murmured, but he shook his head. Then voices reached her.

"I thought Najeddine was taking care of it. That's why I had you back off getting the key. It was a mistake. I should have taken the key. Then the place on the board could have been eliminated all together. It will be a nightmare with her in control. Mark my words, she'll be just like her grandfather."

A second man spoke. "I took care of him. Let me take care of her."

Remy's heart went into her throat, and her stomach nose-dived to her feet. She looked at Hawk. He squeezed her shoulders. She leaned over just a bit to see who it was that had killed her grandfather.

"No. At least not yet. She's new. If anything happens to her now, it will be suspicious. We'll wait. See what transpires. We have time."

She squinted, and the two men came into focus when they stopped a few feet away. Austin Davis and the bald man with the scar. Archer's man! Did Archer have her grandfather killed?

Hawk squeezed her shoulders again and gave her a very small shake. When she looked back at him, he raised his chin toward the statue that was just down from them. She peered into the darkness. Archer moved forward just enough so she could see him, and then he slunk back into the darkness.

Davis pulled out a cell phone and started to make a call as they went down the stairs. Hawk made her wait a few minutes, and then they came out from behind the sculpture. They looked for Archer, but he was nowhere to be seen.

They started down the stairs. "Hawk," she said, her voice somewhat shaky, "what the hell have I gotten myself involved in?"

He reached over and squeezed her hand. "I have no idea."

"Did you notice that Davis didn't have an accent? His whole demeanor was different. It was like he was a totally different person."

"I noticed," Hawk agreed.

"I'm scared," she said, her voice barely above a whisper. She wanted him to take her into his arms and tell her everything was going to be okay, but he remained silent. Great. Who could blame him, though? He had no clue what was going on any more than she did.

Then it hit her. This, right now, had to be the end of anything between her and Hawk. She couldn't ask him to be a part of this world. It was dark and dangerous and deadly. He deserved a life full of light and love. She couldn't offer that now. Not ever. Her heart broke, and pain radiated through her chest.

They had just reached the bottom step when Hawk suddenly stepped in front of her. A shot rang out, and she screamed. Hawk fell against her, knocking her down to the steps, Hawk's body covering hers. He didn't move.

"You're a conniving little bitch!" Najeddine came out of the darkness, a gun out in front of him. "You cost me everything. Everything! You won't live." He raised the gun again.

Remy couldn't breathe. Couldn't speak. Why wasn't Hawk moving? She tried to move him. "Hawk," she managed to whisper. She tried again, louder this time. "Hawk!"

"He's dead." Najeddine smiled and then aimed the gun at her head.

The sound of the shot echoed around the foyer. Remy's heart stopped. Najeddine fell where he stood, and Austin Davis came up behind him. "I should have let him kill you," he hissed. "Be warned, your days are numbered." He glowered at her.

Archer appeared at his side a second later, and Davis's whole demeanor morphed back into his good ol' boy southern thing. "It's Najeddine. He tried to kill Mizz Tanger."

Hawk groaned.

"Help me," she said as she tried to lift Hawk.

Archer and Davis moved Hawk and flipped him over. There was a large red stain on his chest.

Remy let out a small scream. "Oh, my god! He's hit." She put her hands over the wound and applied pressure to stop the bleeding." Where's a phone? I need a phone. Call nine-one-one!"

Archer put his fingers on Hawk's neck and checked for a pulse. Then he pushed Remy's hands out of the way, yanked opened Hawk's shirt, and assessed the chest wound.

She put her hands back on Hawk's chest and applied pressure. "Why aren't you calling the ambulance?" she demanded.

"Remington, you have a choice to make. Hawk is not going to make it to the hospital. The ambulance will take at least ten minutes to get here. He needs treatment now."

"What are you saying?" What the fuck was he going on about?

"I have a fully equipped ambulance outside. We can take him to one of our facilities."

"Yes! Let's do that!"

"Wait." Archer's voice was harsh. She stared at him. "Hawk can only come if he's your permanent partner. As a board member, you get this…perk. Regular members aren't allowed to do this. But Hawk can never leave the Society, and you can never break up. You must marry Hawk, and you must stay together until death. If he tries to leave or you break up, Hawk will have to die. He'll know too much, and he won't be allowed to live."

She stared at him. What the fuck was he talking about? She wanted Hawk to live.

"Do you understand what I'm saying to you? You must marry Hawk and never ever divorce or even be separated, otherwise he dies, and you will be forced off the board."

She stared into Archer's green eyes. He was telling her the

only way to save Hawk was to force him to marry her and be part of the society. She glanced down at Hawk. She loved him. She had since he first came to her rescue. He was who she wanted to spend the rest of her life with, but what did he think? Did he love her? If she did nothing, he died. She must be a better choice than death. "Save him," she said in a clear, calm voice. "I won't let him die because of me. Surely, being with me is better than being dead."

Archer nodded and then whipped out his phone. Within seconds it seemed, she and Hawk were in the back of an ambulance. The two EMTs worked on him as the ambulance went somewhere in the city and disappeared into a parking garage. Then they went down in a car elevator. The back doors of the ambulance opened to what appeared to be a fully functional hospital. They wheeled Hawk away, but Archer remained standing with her.

"They'll take care of him. If he can be saved, they'll do it."

She looked up at him. "Thank you."

He shook his head. "Don't thank me. You are the one who made the choice. You saved him." He glanced down at her dress. "Would you like to get changed? The doctors will find you when they know something."

She nodded. She had blood, Hawk's blood, all over her dress. She wanted a shower and clean clothes. But more than anything, she wanted Hawk to live.

CHAPTER TWENTY-SEVEN

Hawk opened his eyes slowly. His chest hurt like a bitch, as if someone had hit him with a sledgehammer.

Remy. Was she okay? He tried to look around and see if she was there, but pain lanced through his head as he moved. He flopped back with a moan.

"You'll want to keep still. It will hurt otherwise."

Hawk turned his head to find Archer Gray sitting in a chair next to his bed. Was he in a hospital? The room looked more like a swank bedroom with its warm gray walls and overstuffed off-white furniture. The beeps and whirring of the machines were the only thing that said this wasn't a hotel room.

"Remy?" he croaked. "Is she—"

"She's fine. You saved her life."

Hawk closed his eyes again for a moment. He remembered the tingling at the base of his spine and his hair standing up. He had stepped in front of Remy. But after that, the rest was blank.

Thank God, she was okay. If he'd done nothing else right, at least he'd kept her safe.

"You took a bullet for her. Najeddine shot you. He's dead."

"Did you kill him?" Hawk croaked. He opened his eyes and stared at Archer.

"No, you can thank Austin Davis for that."

"Really?" Drawing a full breath in order to get words out was a massive struggle. He rested his head on the pillow and focused on breathing shallowly.

Archer nodded. "I know, surprising. I was surprised, too. I think— It's not important what I think. You need to save your energy and get well."

"How did I get here? This is part of a Lock and Key Society facility, isn't it?"

Archer nodded. "I will let Remy explain that to you."

Hawk had the distinct feeling he wasn't going to like whatever Remy had to tell him. "Why are you here?"

Archer stood. "I came to make sure you're okay. It's part of my job," he said in a clear voice as a nurse entered the room. She checked the machines, offered Hawk some water and then adjusted his blankets. "Not too long, Mr. Gray. Mr. Hawkins needs his rest," she instructed, then she bustled out.

Hawk looked back at Archer and raised an eyebrow. "I thought the society was supposed to be secret. How can all these people work here? Are they members?" he asked. Talking was taking more out of him than he liked but he needed answers.

"We have many employees who work for us. They only see the area they work in and are sworn to secrecy. They are well paid for their silence."

"I see," Hawk said.

Archer leaned forward. "Remington," he said in a voice barely above a whisper, "is in danger. She is not supposed to be, but certain factions want to change specific things in the society. Her seat holds special…privileges. People want those. They won't kill her today or tomorrow, but know there's a big shit storm coming, and she might end up in the middle of it. I will do my best to protect her, but I think she will need all the help she can get."

Hawk nodded once but even that small movement jarred him with pain.

"I'm sure Remington will be by to see you shortly. Rest up." He dropped his voice again. "You're going to need it."

CHAPTER TWENTY-EIGHT

"I'm sorry I took so long to get here," Remy said as she brushed a stray hair behind her ear. "You all saved my ass, and I feel like I've treated you horribly. It was just I didn't want to leave until I knew Hawk would be okay."

"Totally understandable," Logan said as he handed her a cup of tea and then sat down on the sofa beside Lacy. "He's doing okay?"

"Yes, the doctors say he'll make a full recovery. The bullet missed his heart but nicked his lung. He should be up and around shortly. He'll have some rehab to do after he gets on his feet, but he should be good as new."

Lacy narrowed her eyes at Remy. "Why don't you seem happier?"

Happy that she was going to have to tell Hawk that he was forced to marry her? That he could never leave the society or they'd kill him? Yeah, that was going to go over well. She took a sip of tea and immediately tasted the rum. She glanced at Logan, who winked at her. She must look worse than she thought if he was giving her shots of rum at one o'clock in the afternoon.

"The answer to your question is I can't tell you. I can't tell you anything. If I speak, then"—she dropped her voice to mimic Archer Gray's—"there will be consequences." She shook her head. "All of their consequences seem to involve death and disowning."

"What *can* you tell us?" Mitch asked.

She thought for a moment. So much had happened. She was learning about the society and all of its rules but, more than that, she was realizing it was a whole way of life, and that was truly overwhelming. She didn't know how the other board members did it. Of course, they weren't direct descendants of the founders. Only she had that distinction. Only she owned that responsibility.

"I can tell you what happened." She proceeded to tell them how Hawk got shot, and she had made the choice to bring him into the society in order to save his life.

Alex, who was sitting across from her said, "You're worried Hawk isn't going to like the fact that he's now part of the society. You made the choice for him, and he didn't get a say."

She tapped the end of her nose. That and the fact he had to marry her or die. Just a small detail.

"Stop worrying. Hawk would rather be alive." Mitch grabbed a cookie off the plate on the coffee table. "He'll figure out a way to make being a part of the society work for him. He's a smart man. He's already reinvented himself once. He can do it again."

Twice. He'd done it twice. Remy didn't say anything because Hawk was such a private person, but he'd come out of an extreme situation and reinvented himself twice, once in the SEALs after his true parentage was revealed, and then again when he was burnt out and decided to take up law after getting out of the Navy. He made it work before. He could do it again, couldn't he?

"What are you going to do with the shop? Will you run it?" Gage asked. He was resting a butt cheek on the back of the sofa behind Dani.

"I haven't gotten that far yet." She let out a sigh and ran a hand over her face. It had been thirty-six hours since Hawk had been shot. She hadn't figured anything out yet.

"I saw that it was open this morning when I went by," Lacy said.

"It was open?" Remy frowned. *Archer.* He must have opened it.

"Emily was working."

"Right." Remy nodded. "I had forgotten she was back." *Liar, pants on fire.* This was going to be the way of things. She needed to get used to it. She wasn't allowed to tell the truth to anyone except Hawk, and who knew how well that truth would go over with him?

"I read in the paper that Asad Najeddine died of a heart attack in his hotel room. The Moroccan royal family is in mourning." Gage pinned her with his gaze.

She shook her head. "I...have no idea how they pulled that one off. Austin Davis shot him. I think I can tell you that because it happened outside of the society facility. Honestly, I don't know what I can and can't say. Just don't tell anyone, and I think we'll be fine."

She took a sip of tea. "Oh, and don't trust Austin Davis. That whole good ol' boy thing? Just an act. He doesn't even have a southern accent in real life."

"Seriously?" Alex asked.

She nodded. "Yup. It's just weird, and he's scary as hell. Avoid at all costs." She shuddered and then took another sip of tea before setting her mug on the coffee table. "I want to tell you again how grateful I am to all of you for your help. You really stuck your necks out for me, and I am just so thankful."

"You hired us. It's our job." Logan smiled as Lacy elbowed him. "And beyond that, it was our pleasure."

When she stood, so did everyone else. Lacy moved past Logan. "Seriously, we did it because you and Hawk, you're family. If you ever need us, just let us know. We'll do whatever we can to help you."

Remy hugged her friend. She was so filled with gratitude that, for the first time since Hawk was shot, she almost relaxed. Going forward, moments like this would probably be few and far between. She was determined to enjoy them as best she could.

An hour later, she walked into Hawk's hospital room. What she'd thought was a full-fledged hospital was actually only a six-bed affair with two surgical suites. It was amazing, nevertheless, and she was beyond impressed.

"You're awake," she said as she approached the bed. Her stomach rolled. He still looked pale to her and had way too many machines attached to him for her liking, but he was no longer at death's door.

He smiled at her. "You okay?"

She smiled back "Now that you're awake. You had me worried." The tightness in her chest had eased ever so slightly at seeing his beautiful blue eyes. "I'm good. How are you feeling?"

"Like someone hit me in the chest with a sledgehammer, but I guess it's better than the alternative."

The restriction in her chest eased a bit more. "Um, about that." She sat down on the edge of his bed. "I know you must be wondering how you got here and why." She started fidgeting with the blankets. "Hawk, it didn't look like you were going to make it when we saw the wound. I swear, I almost died when I saw you were shot." She swallowed. She'd promised herself she wasn't going to cry. The danger was past. Now wasn't the time for tears.

She cleared her throat, but her racing pulse clogged it back up again. She had to tell him the truth. She had no choice. More importantly, he had no choice, which was the entire problem.

She coughed, then plunged in. "It didn't look like you would make it if we waited for an ambulance." She met his gaze. "Archer gave me a choice; let you die or make you my permanent plus-one. As a board member, I'm allowed a permanent partner. You are now a full member of the society but not a board member. I'm allowed to discuss everything with you, though."

Hawk narrowed his eyes at her. "What is it? What aren't you telling me?"

Her palms became sweaty. She couldn't look at him, so she fiddled with smoothing the blanket, over and over. "To be my permanent plus-one means we have to get married." There, she'd said it.

He opened his mouth, but she put up her hand. "There's more. Hawk, we can never separate or divorce. You can never leave the society. They'll kill you if you do. Unless I do something stupid and they kick us both out at which time they'll kill us anyway because that seems to be the consequence they like the most."

She hazarded a glance up at Hawk but quickly went back to staring at the blankets. "As a plus-one you have access to more information than a regular member. You will know where all the bodies are buried, and if you choose to leave the society, or leave me, you will die."

When she finally did look up, their gazes locked. She tried to read what he was thinking, but his face was blank.

"I know this is not what you wanted. The last thing you need is to be hooked to me and this…mess for the rest of your life, but it was either that or watch you die. I—I know it was selfish, but I just couldn't take the chance that you would die on the way to a regular hospital. I couldn't live with it if that happened."

Hawk stared at her for a moment and then opened his mouth to speak just as the doctor breezed in. "Mr. Hawkins. Glad to see you awake." He smiled at Remy. "If you wouldn't mind giving us a minute, Ms. Tanger. I need to check my patient."

Remy nodded and got off the bed. "I'll be back later."

She hurried from the room and fled down the hallway. She was a coward for not waiting, but she just needed a break. She headed up the stairs and used the retinal scanner to call the elevator. The doors opened and Jerry, the elevator operator and security guard motioned her in.

She entered and rode the elevator silently up to the underground parking garage. Jerry hit a series of buttons and the doors opened again. She exited into a small non-descript room where she used another retinal scanner to unlock the last door. She walked out into the parking garage and headed for the stairs. A minute later she went out into midtown.

It was cold, but she decided to walk all the way to her shop. Good exercise. Good time waster. She didn't have it in her to face Hawk right now. What if he didn't want to be married to her? What if he yelled at her that her decision had been a huge mistake? Her heart couldn't take that. She was in love with Hawk. If he rejected her, the next fifty years were going to be long and painful.

Later that evening, Remy walked down the hallway to Hawk's room. She'd stayed at the shop much longer than she should have, but it was nice to do something normal, something ordinary. As she approached the door, a young nurse with a high blond ponytail and big brown eyes stepped in front of her. "I'm sorry, Ms. Tanger. Mr. Hawkins has asked not to be disturbed."

She stopped. "Oh, okay. I'll stop by in the morning then."

"Actually, Mr. Hawkins has put a do not disturb notice on his room for the foreseeable future." The nurse smiled brightly. "I'll be happy to let you know when he lifts it, if you'd like."

Her stomach churned, and a corner of her heart splintered. Hawk was rejecting her. What the hell did she expect? She'd just tied the man to her for life, his life, and they'd only known each other for less than a week. Could it really be so little time? Nausea hit her, and she put her hand on her stomach. "That's... I'll... Thanks, I'll reach out in a few days."

She turned and headed back down the hallway. She didn't blame Hawk. Not one bit. It wasn't fair. It wasn't right, but there was nothing she could do to change it now.

CHAPTER TWENTY-NINE

Eight Weeks Later.

"You're still dropping your left," Archer said as he watched Hawk hit the heavy bag.

"Thanks," Hawk grunted. "Don't you have anything else better to do? Or is harassing me on the top of your to-do list today?"

"I have to have some fun." Archer gave him a ghost of a smile. Archer caught the bag and stopped it. "Actually, we need to talk."

Hawk stepped back and grabbed his water bottle. He took a long swig. Then he wiped his face with his towel. "What?"

Archer leaned on the bag. "You're better. Your doctors all agree you've made a miraculous recovery. You got the all-clear this morning, or so I'm told."

"So much for privacy."

"There is no privacy in the society. Know that. It's true." Archer continued. "I'm getting pushback from some of the board members. You and Remington need to get married as soon as possible. They are quoting the rules to me. Me! I fucking hate that," he growled. "I've bought you as much time as I can. It needs to happen now."

Hawk glared at him. "And then what?"

Archer shrugged. "What do you mean?"

"Am I supposed to sit around here all day? Go back to normal life? What?"

"Do whatever the fuck you want to do. Just obey the rules."

Hawk stepped closer to Archer. "You've been watching me like a hawk, no pun intended, for the last six weeks," he snarled. "What gives? This isn't about the wedding. What do you really want?"

Archer glanced around the gym. It was empty except for the two of them. "Not here. Not now. But you're right. I need your help. I have a job for you. One that will use *all* your skills. One that will allow you to keep Remington safe and still enjoy life. One that will make you lots of money. Are you in?"

"Do I have a choice?"

Archer smiled. "Not really."

"Then I guess I'm in."

Archer nodded. "Get married," he demanded. "Sooner than later." He pivoted and marched out of the gym.

Hands hanging limp at his sides, Hawk stared at the heavy bag. He knew Archer had run interference for him about getting married. It wasn't hard to notice the grumblings. Several members had dropped by his room to inquire about his health and his impending nuptials. He used the society's gym because it was state of the art and because no one else was ever there. Also, because he didn't want to have to explain to the rest of the world that he'd gotten shot. It felt like a failure somehow. If he'd only been faster, he could've...what? He didn't have a gun. No other weapon. It was stupid, but there it was. He was having problems dealing with getting shot. In all his time with his SEAL team, he'd never been injured. Who would have guessed that civilian life was more dangerous than special ops? He felt like he'd failed Remy and that was the last thing he ever wanted to do.

Which led to his other major problem. He did not want to marry Remy because she was being forced to. It wasn't fair to her to be saddled with him. He'd picked Archer's brain many times over the last six weeks, and there was just no way out for her. Hawk knew he could go on the run, and he had a fifty-fifty chance of surviving, but the repercussions on Remy would be extreme. He did not want to bring her any grief. He was in love with her. Pain was the last thing he wanted for her.

He hit the shower and got dressed. It was past time to talk to her. He'd managed to keep their conversations to short chats over the last six weeks. He made sure other people were around, offering no opportunity for her to talk to him about them getting married. It galled him that she'd been forced into it. He wanted her to marry him because she loved him, not because she was forced into it.

He picked up his cell and dialed her number. "Remy," he said when she answered. "We need to talk. Can you meet me at my place in about an hour?"

"Sure." Her voice was guarded.

He didn't blame her one bit. "Great. See you then."

He arrived home thirty minutes later and took another shower. He pulled on fresh jeans and a blue button-down shirt. He was just pouring himself a drink when the doorman buzzed him. "Send her up."

Remy knocked on the door a few minutes later. Hawk took a deep breath and opened it. His heart gave a lurch as it always did when he saw her.

"Come in," he said. She entered, and he took her coat. "I was just about to pour myself a drink. Would you like one?"

She nodded. "Bourbon would be good." She walked over to the window and looked out at the Hudson. It was still light out. "This is the first time I've actually seen your view, I think. We left in a rush that morning. I never noticed. It's gorgeous."

"Yeah. It's my favorite thing about the apartment. Or one of them, at least." He handed her a tumbler and sat down on the sofa.

She came over and sat down in the opposite corner. "I read in the paper that they found Mr. Chan floating in the East River. They thought it was suicide. Apparently he was depressed, or so they said. Do you think that was true?"

Hawk shook his head. "I think whoever he was afraid of caught up to him." He paused. "I think there's a lot going on in the society and it's going to be a bit difficult to go back to life as we knew it." That was a lie. He hated lying. *Fuck.* "I'm trying to pull my punches and not frighten you, but I don't want to lie to you. There's some serious shit going down. I totally get why your grandfather didn't tell you a thing about Lock and Key. But now you have no choice. Hell, you never had a choice.

"The thing is, Archer has said you will need protection." He got up, moved over, and sat down on the coffee table directly in front of her and held her gaze. "I promise you I will do everything in my power to keep you safe. I haven't been able to do it these last weeks, but I got the all-clear from my doctor this morning. From here, moving forward, I will make it my goal to keep you as safe as I can."

"Hawk, you don't have to do that. I'm sure Archer can provide someone. I don't want to impose on you anymore than necessary."

"Impose? What the hell are you talking about?"

Remy rubbed her face with her hand. "I forced you into an untenable situation. I ruined your life. You are now stuck with me forever. I don't want you to feel like you have to take care of me on top of that. I couldn't ask that of you. I can't ask anything else of you after what I did."

"You saved my life." Was she serious? "I wouldn't be here if it weren't for you. Remy—"

"Hawk, we don't know for sure if that's true. I did the selfish thing and asked Archer to help you because *I* couldn't stand it if you died because of me. The pain of seeing you lying there in a pool of your own blood. I just couldn't take the chance that they couldn't save you, so I gave in to Archer, and now you're tied to me for life. I'm so sorry."

Hawk sat there, almost too stunned to form a sentence. "Do you… You really think this is your doing? That I am angry at you for saving my life?"

She put her drink on the table next to him. "But what kind of life is it? Tied forever and a day to a woman you don't love? I've ruined your life."

The wrongness of her words ricocheted around his brain and his heart. "Remy, you're wrong."

She stood up and brushed past him. She walked over to the door. "If you'll just give me my coat, I'll go. Today is Friday, so we can go down to City Hall and get the marriage license next week. We'll just have to figure something out. Some way to live with this that sticks within the rules." She leaned back against the door.

Hawk stared at her. "No. Just no fucking way am I living like that." He got up and went to stand in front of her. He placed a hand on either side of her head. "You listen to me. I have no problem marrying you. I'm in love with you. I have been since the first moment I saw you. I stayed away from you for six weeks because my doctor told me I couldn't have sex and because I felt guilty for not doing a better job protecting you. I almost got you killed. Twice. Honey, we are partners. Whatever comes, we'll face it together." His stomach knotted. "Unless you would rather I kept my distance."

She blinked. "No... I... That is..." She paused and then she whacked him on his arm hard. "Six weeks because you felt guilty? Fucking seriously? I thought you hated me for what I'd done. I've been torturing myself for six fucking weeks! And you love me?" She whacked him again. "Don't ever do that again. Don't ever shut me out like that! You're my only family. I can't live with you being angry at me!"

He took a beat to let what she was saying fully sink in. Then he started to smile. It turned into a grin. "Do you love me, Remy?"

She glared at him. "Six weeks!"

"Do you love me?" The smile was gone. "Tell me, Remy," he growled.

"Fine." She crossed her arms over her chest. "I love you. But you have some serious making-up to do. Six long weeks' worth." Then she frowned. "Are you cleared for sex?"

The grin was back. "You bet your ass." He swooped down and captured her lips in a scorching kiss.

CHAPTER THIRTY

"I now pronounce you husband and wife. You may kiss the bride."

The words were music to her ears. She smiled up at Hawk. He bent down and kissed her hard on the mouth.

"Enough of that, you two. There's champagne to drink, and I like the look of the hors d'oeuvres downstairs," Mitch said with a smile.

Alex batted him on the arm. "Don't mind him."

Remy laughed. "It's okay. I'm kind of hungry, too."

They made their way back downstairs to the living area. She and Hawk had gotten married on the roof of the Callahan Security building with everyone there. Gus had flown back for the wedding and was currently chatting the ear off Lacy.

Alex came over to her. "I meant what I said before. You have talent. Swing by when you can, and I'll teach you some tricks of the trade."

Remy grinned. "I like the sound of that." She glanced around the room. This was her family. They might not be blood, but they were the people she could count on whenever she needed to. That's what family was. "I miss you, Gramps," she whispered.

Hawk wrapped his arms around her waist. "He's here with us. I just know it."

She nodded. "I'm sure he is." She stretched up and kissed her *husband*. She loved the sound of that. He broke off the kiss and gave her a hug. He whispered in her ear, "You're mine now. Always and forever."

Keep reading for a a quick note from the author, and a sneak peek at *Diverted*, Book 1 in the Coast Guard RECON Series

AUTHOR'S NOTE

I know. I know! You're wondering how could I have left a few loose ends? I *know*. But I tried. I really did. I swear. I started this book three times. I had a whole different story in mind for Hawk and Remy. It was a whole corporate thing. I was excited but apparently, they weren't. I just couldn't get it to work. They refused to tell me their story.

Then the whole Lock and Key Society thing happened. I've had that floating around my brain for *years*. I had no idea Hawk and Remy were involved. I swear it. But on my third try it just started pouring out.

The thing is, Archer Gray. He was insistent on being a part of it. More than that. He wants his own book. Actually, he wants his own series and, truth be told, he deserves it. Archer has been through a lot and there are a great many adventures to tell.

So, I apologize, but the Lock and Key Society will have its own series where all your questions will be answered. Archer demands it. You will see Hawk and Remy again. As a matter of fact, you'll see a lot of your favorite characters again.

Sorry for not having everything end in a neat bow this time. It goes against every fiber of my being, but Archer Gray has plans and no one wants to mess with Archer Gray...

A NOTE OF THANKS

YOU READ MY BOOK. You read the whole thing! I cannot thank you enough for sticking with me. If this is the first book of mine you've read, welcome aboard. I certainly hope it won't be the last! If you are already a fan then I can only say, thank you so much for your continued support! Either way, you have made my day, my week, my year! You have transported me from writer to *author*. I feel so special! You have made my dreams come true. Genuinely, truly, you are a fairy god-parent. So thank-you!

Now I'm hoping you love this new-found power of making dreams come true and, like a truly dedicated reader, you'll check out my other series, Coast Guard Recon and the Brotherhood Protectors World. You can find links to these books on my website, www.lorimatthewsbooks.com

If you would like to try your hand at being a superhero, you can always help make me a bestselling author by leaving a review for ***Cease and Desist*** on Amazon. Reviews sell books and they make authors super happy. Did I say thank you already? Just in case I forgot, thank you soooo much.

And now that you are reveling in your superhero status, I

would love it if you would stay in touch with me. I love my readers and I love doing giveaways and offering previews and extra content of my upcoming books. Come join the fun. You can follow me here:

Newsletter: Signup Form (constantcontactpages.com)
Website: www.lorimatthewsbooks.com
Facebook: https://www.facebook.com/LoriMatthewsBooks
Facebook: Romantic Thriller Readers (Author Lori Matthews) https://www.facebook.com/groups/killerromancereaders
Amazon Author Page: https://www.amazon.com/author/lorimatthews
Goodreads: https://www.goodreads.com/author/show/7733959.Lori_Matthews
Bookbub: https://www.bookbub.com/profile/lori-matthews
Instagram: https://www.instagram.com/lorimatthewsbooks/
Twitter: https://twitter.com/_LoriMatthews_

SNEAK PEEK: DIVERTED

About The Book

Nick Taggert was injured on his last assignment for the Coast Guard. Now, too hurt to go back to his former position and not wounded enough to be benched, he's assigned as the new Coast Guard team leader in...Panama. They're there as part of a drug interdiction unit, but really, they're Team RECON. Recon as in reconstructed. Each of the four men is like him; a Humpty Dumpty. Except they were trying to put themselves back together so they could do what they loved best, kicking ass and taking names.

Dr. Carolina Alvarez had moved on from research and was working for Doctors Without Borders. A chance meeting with her old boss set her on a dangerous mission to deliver much-needed medicine to South America. Her failure would mean the sure extinction of a tribe clinging to their ancient ways.

Nick should have realized from the instant Carolina walked back into his life things would not go according to plan. But harbored resentment still clouded his vision. Now they were on the trail of the missing vaccine, and the assignment just turned deadly.

DIVERTED: PROLOGUE

February 9th, 2021

Alejandro Garcia glanced at his watch and seethed. He abhorred tardiness, and the man was late. Stirring his coffee, he watched people stroll by the cafe window. He, unlike most of the world, hated Paris, especially in January. The cold invaded his bones, and gray skies hung heavy overhead. Even the Eiffel Tower looked dirty and dingy in the falling mist.

Garcia sighed. He found the French to be tedious. They thought too highly of themselves, and their lack of work ethic astounded him. The constant rioting about trivial things illustrated a society too pampered to be taken seriously. He had no idea why the French government tolerated such behavior.

He rechecked his timepiece and took a sip from his cup. However, they did serve excellent coffee, and for that, he was willing to forgive quite a bit.

A black car pulled up to the curb. The driver came around and opened the door. A tall distinguished-looking gentleman emerged. "Finally," Garcia mumbled as his ten o'clock appointment entered the café twenty minutes late.

Edward Langston approached the table, hand outstretched. "Sorry, I'm late. Ran into a traffic snarl. Protesters wouldn't let the car past."

Garcia stood and shook hands. "Of course. Please." He gestured toward the opposite chair. "May I get you something? Coffee perhaps?" It galled him to play host to this American, but it was a small price to pay for the benefits this man could provide to Garcia's country.

"I'm fine. Can't stay long." The men sat. "Look." Langston leaned forward. "Our agreement… I must say I have some misgivings."

Garcia ground his teeth. Langston couldn't back out now. Not when Garcia was so close to sealing his country's future on the world stage. "You don't want to run a live test of your experiment?"

"Of course, we want to run the test," Langston said. "Don't be stupid. I want to make sure you understand the risk you're taking. None of this can come out. Ever."

Garcia nodded. "Agreed. It would be bad for all of us and, yes, we understand the risk. Your mosquitoes will save millions of lives and change the world. We want to provide you with the opportunity to prove their efficacy. Many of our population are affected by mosquito-borne diseases; it is perfectly logical for you to test your theory in our country. As to the other part, that will remain a secret, I can assure you."

Langston hesitated before giving a curt nod. "We have a deal."

"When will the testing begin?"

Langston frowned. "Our people should be in place at the end of March, maybe slightly later. By the summer, we should know if it's working or not."

Garcia nodded again. "Good. The sooner, the better. No delays."

"Obviously," Langston snarled. "I'll be in touch when we're ready to go."

"Everything will be ready to proceed." Garcia forced a smile.

"Make sure it is. This is very important. To both sides."

Garcia's jaw ached. The American's attitude was insufferable. "It will be smooth on my end, I can assure you."

Langston studied him for a minute. "You're sure your boss is on board with this?"

"You need not worry, Mr. Langston. As I said, things will flow smoothly on my end." Garcia curled his hand around the coffee cup and squeezed. He would prefer if the cup were Langston's neck, but that was not in the cards. At least not yet. He reminded himself there must be sacrifice to achieve success. His day would come.

"Fine." Langston stood up, and Garcia rose with him. "I'll be in touch," Langston stated, then turned and exited the cafe. He got into his car and drove off.

Garcia returned to his seat and signaled the waiter, who brought another piping-hot coffee.

Americans. Another group Garcia hated. Not so different from the French. Always thinking they knew better and possessed the upper hand. Not this time. This time, Garcia had the advantage, and things were just as they should be.

DIVERTED: CHAPTER 1

"Bring him over here, Muhammed!" Dr Carolina Alvarez pointed to the now empty table along the wall of the tent in the makeshift hospital. Two local men half carried half dragged the unconscious man between them over to Carolina and put him face down in front of her. The sound of sporadic gunfire erupted, but everyone in the tent ignored it.

"We found him washed up on the beach," stated Muhammed, the taller of the two. "We didn't want to just leave him there. It would not be right."

Carolina gave him a brief smile as Gabe, a nurse, came over and helped her move the injured soldier onto the table. The man was dressed in military fatigues so helping him could be risky for Muhammed and his son, but they were good people. They put politics and religion aside to help someone in need. Carolina had seen that a lot in Yemen. What the world was told about the Yemenese, and the truth of the matter wasn't even close. Of course, she'd found that was the way of it in most of the countries she'd worked in. Doctors Without Borders only went to places in need, and most of those countries had political problems.

"Thanks for rescuing him, Muhammed. Do you know where he got shot?" Muhammed and his son Ahmed both shook their heads. The son was the spitting image of the father. It was like seeing double.

"He's not shot." Ahmed turned and mumbled something to his father in Arabic and then said, "Stabbed. In the back." It was hard to hear him over the din of voices in the tent.

Carolina helped Gabe turned the man onto his side. "Take his vitals," she said as she leaned over to see the injured man's back.

Muhammed cleared his throat. "We go now."

Carolina nodded. "*Shukran*, Muhammed," she said, trying to thank him in his own language but he was gone. Probably good he wasn't there to hear her butcher it.

There was a lot of blood soaking into the man's shirt. She peeled it back to reveal a long, deep gash that went right across the man's back from his right shoulder to his left hip. "Jesus. He was hacked, not stabbed." She peered closer at the wound. It was ugly and it was going to take a lot of work to fix. She cursed silently. A slash like this needed a plastic surgeon in a real hospital not a general surgeon in a make-shift hospital tent. She'd do what she could, but it wasn't going to be pretty. "Colin, I'm going to need your help!" Carolina didn't even look up as she yelled for the other doctor. "Gabe, how are his vitals?"

"They suck," he stated. "His pulse is weak and his pressure is low. His breathing is shallow."

"Hang a unit of blood and then grab the portable x-ray. I need to see if his ribs are broken."

Gabe quickly hooked the man up to the IV and then skirted the table and moved to the other end of the room.

"Colin?" Carolina called again as she noticed a birthmark on the man's right shoulder. It looked sort of like a four-leaf clover. Another flurry of gunfire sounded, drowning out

Colin's answer. Just then the flap of the tent was pushed open wider, and a new group of injured were brought in.

"You're on your own," Colin called. "I'll take the new ones."

"Shit," Carolina mumbled. "Let's hope your birthmark is a sign you're lucky." *You're going to need it.*

Gabe came back with the portable x-ray and set it up. He quickly took pictures of the man's torso. After a brief pause, he consulted the tablet on the machine's stand. "Look like four broken ribs."

"That's not good. Okay, let's get his wound cleaned and stitch it up. But first we need to see if any of his organs were damaged either by the hacking or from the broken ribs." She leaned closer. "It looks like it missed his spine completely. This guy is lucky as hell. Half an inch more, and his spine would have been severed."

She heard a grunt and straightened, looking down at her patient's face. The lines on the exposed side of his face were etched into his skin and his eyes were open. They were a very distinctive shade of blue. Like the sky on a cold day in winter. "Hey, can you tell me your name?"

He remained silent, staring at her.

"Do you know where you are?"

He watched her but said nothing.

"Okay, well then, whoever you are. We're going to take care of you. I'm going to give you something for the pain, and then I'm going to stitch you up. You were very lucky."

He raised an eyebrow. "Lucky. Sure." He closed his eyes again.

READ THESE OTHER EXCITING TITLES BY LORI MATTHEWS

Callahan Security

Break and Enter

Smash And Grab

Hit And Run

Evade and Capture

Catch and Release

Cease and Desist

Coast Guard Recon

Diverted

Incinerated

Conflicted

Subverted

Terminated

Brotherhood Protectors World

Justified Misfortune

Justified Burden

Justified Vengeance

Free with Newsletter Sign Up

Falling For The Witness

Risk Assessment

Visit <u>Https://www.lorimatthewsbooks.com</u> for details on how to purchase these novels or sign up for my newsletter.

ABOUT LORI MATTHEWS

I grew up in a house filled with books and readers. Some of my fondest memories are of reading in the same room with my mother and sisters, arguing about whose turn it was to make tea. No one wanted to put their book down!

I was introduced to romance because of my mom's habit of leaving books all over the house. One day I picked one up. I still remember the cover. It was a Harlequin by Janet Daily. Little did I know at the time that it would set the stage for my future. I went on to discover mystery novels. Agatha Christie was my favorite. And then suspense with Wilber Smith and Ian Fleming.

I loved the thought of combining my favorite genres, and during high school, I attempted to write my first romantic suspense novel. I wrote the first four chapters and then exams happened and that was the end of that. I desperately hope that book died a quiet death somewhere in a computer recycling facility.

A few years later, (okay, quite a few) after two degrees, a husband and two kids, I attended a workshop in Tuscany that lit that spark for writing again. I have been pounding the keyboard ever since here in New Jersey, where I live with my children—who are thrilled with my writing as it means they get to eat more pizza—and my very supportive husband.

Please visit my webpage at https://lorimatthewsbooks.com to keep up on my news.

Made in the USA
Las Vegas, NV
19 February 2024

85973976R00187